CLASH BY NIGHT

The wind blew colder, and clouds rolled in, were shrouding the stars. The sea gave no warmth. rmth. It was as black as...

There was one...

It came toward... direction of Thorolf Skjang's grave.

We all saw him. The warriors groaned. They wept. They yammered like dogs. Some shouted, "Thorolf! It's my Lord Thorolf come out to walk again."

He was a tall man, dressed full armor, with shield and spear and sword at his belt. He glowed all over with blue fire. He was coming to us.

"It's the battle-fetter!" someone cried. "Run! We've got to run!" But no one ran. No one stood on his feet. A few tried to crawl, but most stayed in their places, watching the walker-again come nearer and nearer.

Thorolf came ever nearer. I could see his eyes now. They were green-yellow, round and cold.

Then a hand fell on my shoulder. Erling said, "A psalm, Father! I don't ask you to fight, but sing me a psalm that I may fight—that one about the mountains falling into the sea and shaking!"

I found I still had the crucifix in my hand, gripped so tightly it was wet with my blood. I tried to moisten my lips. "Deus noster refugium . . ." I croaked. *God is our refuge and strength . . .*

I saw the demon cast his spear, and saw his mouth open in something like laughter. I saw him fend Erling's spear in return. I heard the whacking of blades on shields, and saw the dead man leap and whirl; and his leaps were head-high, and his whirls faster than birds' wings.

I spoke my psalm again and again, gripping the crucifix as a drowning man clings to driftwood. . . .

ERLING'S WORD

LARS WALKER

ERLING'S WORD

This is a work of fiction. All the characters and events portrayed in this book are fictional, and any resemblance to real people or incidents is purely coincidental.

A Baen Books Original

Baen Publishing Enterprises
P.O. Box 1403
Riverdale, NY 10471

ISBN: 0-671-87850-6

Cover art by Larry Elmore

First printing, November 1997

Distributed by Simon & Schuster
1230 Avenue of the Americas
New York, NY 10020

Printed in the United States of America

To my Aunt Jean . . .
Frequently mistaken for an angel.

Pronunciation Note

"Erling Skjalgsson" is pronounced "AIR-ling SHAHLG-son." "Ailill" is pronounced "Ay-LEEL" (Thanks to William Letmon for helping me out on that one). When pronouncing Norse names, remember that "j" is always pronounced as "y." The double "a," as in "Haakon," rhymes more or less with "go." For the rest, normal English pronunciation will be wrong, but not badly wrong.

CHAPTER I

Maeve screamed when they raped her. She screamed all the time they were raping her, and they raped her many times, for she was young and fair. I tried to run to my sister, straining the chain they'd bound me to, until some merciful soul laid the hammer of his axe against the base of my skull.

I was marching when I awoke, chained in a line with all the other Christian souls the Northmen had taken, men and women, the young and the strong and the hopeful. We hoped again the following day when a troop of bold young lads from Collooney came pounding over a hill and down upon us, swinging their axes and shouting their slogan, and they looked like the angels of God to me, beautiful as the love of children. But the Northerners met them with a tough shield wall and cast their spears and offered them axe and sword and thrusting spear, and those fair lads died, except for a few who were taken and bound with us. After that we saw no more resistance. The king was warring with the O'Neill that year, and much taken up with other things.

My head ached as if Satan had poked a toe in my eye, but I cared nothing for that. I had set my

1

heart to praying. The abbot would have wondered at the fervor of my prayers. I pleaded—I begged God—I promised Him that I would be a monk and a priest if only He would deliver me and my sister. I prayed without ceasing; I made vows to all the saints I could think of. I watched the heavens and the earth for an answer, refusing to doubt.

The Northerners had their camp in a river mouth in Sligo Bay, and they loaded us into one of their ships—a fat *knarr* with an open hold amidships, where we huddled with the beasts they'd stolen, and ate much the same fodder. I gazed back to shore, squinting for my miracle, refusing to know that I was leaving Ireland. I had no words for what was happening, but surely we weren't being taken across the sea. God was too good to let that happen.

But when we rounded Inishmurray and Sligo Bay fell from sight and only the waves to port and strange shores to starboard, I knew that my miracle would not come. And so I knew there was no God, and the only thing left was to die.

We were chained starboard of the mast, balanced by the livestock to port. The Northerners had strung a rope down the center and warned us not to approach it. When one of them was making his way from the stern to the foredeck, I gathered up my length of chain and threw myself at him. I caught him unguarded and we struggled a moment before the other Northmen pulled us apart and kicked me bloody. Then one of them, a squat bruiser who'd lost part of his nose and spoke barbarous Irish, put his face down near mine and said, "We're going to Visby on Gotland to sell you. If you make us mad we won't kill you, lad, no—we'll sell you to the Arabs, who'll take you far off to Eastland and geld you so you'll be quiet and good."

So I limped back and sat in bilgewater, and Maeve stretched to the end of her chain so that she could just touch my hand, and wept, and we sat like that until I slept.

Many are the years and uncounted the miles since the White Northerners took us from our home in Connaught. Where is Maeve now? With our ancestors, I suppose, long since, and glad of the rest. And I, against all hope, have stood before kings. I have seen a saint made and had for a friend the greatest hero since Cu Chulainn. I've seen high times and headlong deeds to outrun and leave in the dust all the dreams I dreamed, woolgathering in the monastery when I should have been construing my Latin.

But I call God's holy Mother to witness, I'd drown it all in the sea like a kitten if it would unmake one day of my youth and draw my sister's tears back into her sweet eyes again.

If ever a morning was gotten out of wedlock, that had surely been it. It had been raining the stones underground when I trudged into my father's yard to tell him that the abbot had driven me out of the cloister with a stick, shouting, "Son of six devils, you have the spleen of a tomcat and the brains of a chicken in the egg! You will never make a monk though Saint Columcille himself come down from heaven to box your ears!"

My father, of course, had no choice but to beat me about the head with curses, which I endured with Christian patience, and he was still at it when the Northmen swarmed down. They killed him, and my mother, for being too old to sell and my brother Diarmaid for no particular reason, but they took me and Maeve, and then she was screaming, "Ailill!" and the rest you know.

I dreamed I rode a snorting stallion over a pitched landscape.

High were the mountains, steep-sided, their peaks sharper than needles.

Deep were the canyons, cataract-cut, riven with yet deeper fissures and crevices that belched smoke, and sometimes I could glimpse the glow of Hell's fires at their bottoms.

But my steed spurned them all, leaping from peak to peak, clattering up and down rock faces, his hoofs striking sparks and making a noise like hammered steel. He was red as blood, my steed, with white ears and golden mane, tail and feet. On closer examination I discovered that he was attached to me where my privates should have been.

"Ailill, old son," I said to myself, "the abbot was right after all. He always said your organ would run away with you one day."

I tried to rein the horse in, but learned quickly I had no control over him.

"What do you want?" I cried, dizzy with fear.

Then I saw what he wanted.

There in the blue distance, poised on an outcrop like a goat, I caught a glimpse of a white hind. She was a glorious thing to look on, the fairest of God's creatures, whiter than ermine in January, with red antlers and black feet and eyes the color of a lake full of sapphires. The moment I saw her I wanted her, but as she bounded away I knew I could not have her.

"Such is not for us!" I cried. "That creature was not meant for farmers' sons! She's a proper quarry for Finn MacCumhail, or Bran son of Febal. Such as we can never catch her, and if we could what would we do with her?"

But my steed cared nothing for sense. On he plunged, and my heart rabbited back and forth between my collarbone and my belly as we leaped the heights and plunged headlong, but never came nearer our quarry.

And then we were across the mountains, and a broad, emerald plain, richly rivered and wooded, spread before us. To enter that land we must needs ford a raging river, broader than Shannon, and on its near side stood a man fifteen feet tall, with skin black as a Welshman's heart and long, straight black hair down to his waist, and a great axe in his hands. His face, strangely, looked a bit like the abbot's.

"Pay the toll if you would cross!" he roared.

"And what is the toll?" asked I.

"Your head, cut off neat at the neck!" he cried, and I tried to turn about but my steed would not be curbed. I heard the great axe whistle in the air and twisted to avoid it. . . .

The next evening, while we lay up in a harbor in the Hebrides, somebody whispered to me, "The Northerners are talking about you." I looked up at a cluster of them on the foredeck who whispered and pointed at me. I tried to dwindle from sight, but they hopped down into the hold, grabbed me and held my arms and legs.

I bellowed and cursed them for heathen horse-eaters, but they paid no mind as they brought out a razor and shaved my scalp forward of a line from ear to ear.

"We're barbering you like the priests in Ireland," said the boy with the bad nose. "We marked your robe, and sometimes there are churchmen in Visby who'll ransom priests at a good price."

It's a marvel the cuts I got didn't mortify.

We sat in bilge and vomit and waste all the way, in storm and fair weather, and the sun beat down on us, and the rain soaked our uncovered heads, and the ship bucked like a spring heifer and I was always sick. We were Irish when we boarded that ship. We were beasts when they unloaded us in Gotland.

They marched us up the jetty and into the walled town, and they kept us in sheds, the men apart from the women (I never saw Maeve again).

I saw no Arabs in Visby (it turned out the Arab trade had dried up long since), nor any churchmen with ransom-silver. But from time to time the slavemonger would bring in some prosperous Northman, perhaps a tattooed Swede with bloused eastern breeches or a Dane with his hair combed down in a fringe in front. He'd point out three or four of us and we'd be unlocked and led out, to be poked and pinched and examined for spots, and our teeth counted. I'm sure I was no beauty—filthy and bruised, my head sunburned and scarred and my robe ragged and the color of every kind of dirt.

I forget how many days we'd been there when I was led out for the approval of some fat old bastard in a fur cap (worn purely for show—the weather was mild), and the son of a carthorse let his hand linger longer on my backside than I thought strictly necessary. I'd believed I had no fight left, but the next thing I knew my fingers were about his neck, and everybody was grabbing at me, and then I was down in the dirt, being savaged with a whip, and I screamed a curse at God, who had the almighty temerity not to exist when an honest man needed Him.

And then the whipping stopped, and I looked up at what seemed the tallest man I'd ever seen. His hair, old-man white like that of many Norse, glowed in a sort of halo around his head, tied with a gold ribbon about the temples. His beard, in contrast to his pale hair and skin, was a reddish brown. He wore a red shirt edged in gold, and a sword hung at his waist. He smiled at me, and I thought it was surely the Archangel Michael.

"I took you for a priest, but you look a little young," he said, in passable Irish.

"Just ordained," I lied.

He spoke to the slave merchant and the fat man, and they argued for a few minutes, pointing at me, the fat man clutching at his throat, and at last the tall man said something to one of his followers (there were about thirty) who brought out a purse and gave some silver coins to the merchant. The merchant weighed them in a little balance and gave part of them to Fat-ass, and I was unchained and taken away by the tall man and his bullyboys.

They brought me to a certain building, and the tall man said, "My name is Erling Skjalgsson. You've that robe and tonsure to thank that you've just brought the highest price I've ever paid for a thrall, not to mention being spared the flaying of your skin off you alive. I bought you because I need a priest.

"I will not lie to you—I mean to take you to my home, Sola in Norway, and your welcome is unsure. I am a Christian; my father is not. My last priest he killed, and I could not avenge him under the circumstances. I make no promise that things will go better for you.

"But this I do promise. My priest cannot be a thrall. If you wish to come with me, you will come as a free man. If you refuse, I'll sell you—but not back to the merchant, or the fat man."

What could I say to him? What would you have said? He wouldn't make the offer if he knew I was only a failed monk. I knew enough of the offices to be priest for his purposes. God wouldn't care—how could He, not existing as He did?

"I accept your offer with thanks," I said, kneeling.

"Very well," said Erling. "This will be our first stop. It's a bathhouse."

chapter ii

I asked my Lord Erling, when they brought me before him in the clean priest's robe he'd gotten somewhere, if he would buy my sister as well. He didn't have to try, but he did. Maeve was gone. The merchant said he'd sold the girl, he forgot to whom.

We sailed out early the next morning. Erling walked beside me down to the harbor and pointed out his ship where she lay by the jetty.

"I know little of ships," I said, "but that looks to me a flying thing." Loath as I was to grant beauty to anything in these heathen lands, the vessel seemed to me graceful as a bird, slim and deadly.

"A flying thing indeed, Father Ailill," said Erling. "Her name is *Fishhawk*. She has twenty-eight rooms. That means it takes fifty-six men to row her. *Fishhawk*'s the fastest ship in Norway."

"Fifty-six oarsmen," said I. "You've a lot more than fifty-six men here." A great crowd of stout towheads were climbing the gangways, loading my lord's final purchases.

Erling laughed. "Over a hundred. They have to take it in shifts after all."

"But surely you could do with less than a hundred."

"The rest are for the sport."

"The sport?"

"Wait. You'll see soon enough."

I shed tears as we left Visby behind, casting off my last ties to Maeve.

Erling assigned one of the men, a freckled lad named Thorkel, not yet twenty, born in Dublin, to start me learning Norse. I found it easier than I might have thought, as it's similar to the damnable English tongue, of which I'd picked up a few scraps. My trouble was my stomach. Then and since I've been a bad sailor, and I spent the bulk of my time (and the bulk of my meals) at the rail. I lived for our nightly anchorages and encampments on the Swedish shore. I had just jettisoned my breakfast one morning when Thorkel clapped me on the shoulder and bade me look across the water, where a ship was lowering its sail and unshipping its oars.

"Now for the sport!" he cried.

"What's this sport?"

"This stretch around the point of Jutland is the thickest hunting ground in the world for pirates. They see us; they take us for a merchant ship and close in to fight, as these Vikings are doing now."

"Is that why you don't carry a dragon head?"

"The very reason."

"What if they come with more than one ship?"

"Two ships we'll fight. More than two—there's no shame in running. But wait—can you see? Up by the Viking's prow?"

"There's a man up there—he's shouting something down to his captain."

"They've spotted our armed men. They see we're

more than they can handle. They'll hoist sail in a moment and fly."

"But you can catch them, can't you?"

"We can catch anything."

Every man but I seemed to know his job. Some handled the rigging, following the mate's orders, letting out the lines and setting the stretcher boom to get the most of the wind. Others carried weapons up from stores, mostly bows and arrows and casting spears, for swords and axes and shields and thrusting spears the men had of their own. Others spread sand on the deck to soak up blood, and all looked to their own gear, whether helmet and chain-mail brynje or leather cap and padded jerkin.

Erling came back to me, wearing a bright brynje and a gilded helmet with a nosepiece. He carried a plain axe and a yellow shield—round and light, about a yard wide in the Viking fashion—and a leather cap with an iron frame.

"You'd best have these, in case of mischance," he said.

A big warrior named Steinulf objected. "I like not this arming of thralls," he said.

"Father Ailill is my freedman," said Erling. "More than that he is God's priest, and a mighty warrior in the household of the Lord. He'll pray a prayer to take the wind out of that Viking's sail and turn the hearts of his men to piss. You can do that, can you not, Father Ailill? A proper Irish prayer full of proper Irish curses?"

I laughed as I took up the arms. "I'll curse those devils for you, my lord, and with a good will. I'll make their heavens bronze and their sea blood. I'll call the souls of their victims up to tear out their livers."

What followed was sweet to my heart. I forgot my seasickness; I forgot that I no longer believed in God. I stood up in the stern before the steersman and watched as the Viking, with its diamond-patterned sail puffing, fell steadily nearer in spite of its crew's efforts. Soon we could make out the worried faces of the warriors above the thwarts.

"O God of hosts," I cried. "O God who gave might to Samson and victory to David, who smote the power of the Amorites with Thy strong hand and laid them in the dust, both them and their women and their little ones, do Thou stand with us Thy warriors in this holy battle. May the heathen see the power of Thy strong right arm and be unmanned. May their hair stand on end, and turn white, and fly out; may their ears buzz, and flap, and gush with blood; may their eyes see visions of the devils who will soon be their tormenters, and go blind, and fall out upon their cheeks, and be pecked at by seagulls; may their tongues break out in sores, and swell, and stuff their mouths and choke them. May their hearts hiccup in their chests, and batter their ribs, and lodge in their throats; may their stomachs be filled with squirming piglets, and swell, and burst, so that they trip on their guts. May their kidneys and rumps let loose together, and the waste fill the ship, so they drown in it; may their hands blister and blacken and shrink into claws like an eagle's and turn against their own faces and throats. May their knees hammer one on the other so they hear it in Jerusalem, and so break their legs and crush their stones; and may their feet tread on nails, and thorns, and venomous serpents, and swell to such size and weight as to bear them down to the bottom of the sea. May their fathers curse their names, and their mothers slice off the breasts that suckled them for shame, and may their uncles and cousins cry, 'Oh, that the day had never dawned when such a coward and woman and slinking dog was born to our blood!' "

With these and many other sweet coaxings I called wrath down on our enemies, and as we drew ever closer our men began to whistle and shout, and the bowmen on either side loosed their arrows, but we warded ourselves with our shields and they did us no harm. And at last the Vikings gave it up and lowered sail again, clearing their decks for defense and massing their shields on the near rail.

And Erling shouted for the men to lower our own sail, and even as it was done the oarsmen slipped their oars out through the holes, and the boatswain started them a song, and they sang as they rowed, keeping time, and I sang too, although I did not know the words, and then we closed with her on our starboard side, and the starboard rowers shipped their oars, and their comrades were already shielding them at the rail, and the ships bumped and scraped, and our men threw grappling irons, and then the dance began.

Oh, it was fair to hear the clang of steel, and the shouts of the warriors. I trotted about and found spears and stones that had been cast into our ship, and I took them up and cast them back where they came from, singing all I could remember of an imprecatory psalm. It wasn't long before our men had broken the shield wall, and then we were over the rails and on them—Erling Skjalgsson, his helmet shining, the first, and I, my robe kilted up in my belt, not last.

And oh, I was ready to believe in God again, for here at length was the thing I had dreamed of, to face the Northerners man to man with arms in my hands, and give them back twice and threefold for all they had done to my father, and my mother, and my brother and poor little Maeve. If these weren't the very Vikings who'd done those things, they were close enough and just as wicked. I knew no fear. I knew no weariness. I hewed and I shouted and I fended with my shield, and something like a red mist rose before my eyes, and when it was gone my own comrades were holding my arms, keeping me back from a few wounded wretches who had yielded themselves. And all the rest of that pirate crew lay dead or dying, and Erling's men were dumping them overboard. And I fell on Thorkel's neck, weary of a sudden, and I wept, or laughed.

They found a chest of silver in the Viking's hold, along with bales of woolen cloth, and the spoil was divided that afternoon, and I got my share.

And Erling ordered a cask of ale broached, and he said to his men, "What think you of my priest now?"

And the crew (and Steinulf was loud among them) cheered me three times over, and said that their lord had found a very proper man of God indeed.

CHAPTER iii

"Is my Lord Erling a king's son?" I asked Thorkel one afternoon when we'd rounded the Skaw and the oily North Sea was less vile than usual and I'd just been to the rail and so felt a little better. "I know there are many kings in Norway, as in Ireland."

"Best not to speak to Erling of kings," said Thorkel. "We've had a few high kings in Norway—Harald Finehair and Haakon the Good and Erik Bloodaxe, but they run to short lives. We've plenty of small kings, who rule whatever land they can stretch their swords over, and *jarls*, who are much the same as the small kings, except that a jarl's son can never be a king.

"Erling is a great-grandson of Horda-Kari, who laid all Hordaland under himself, but kept the title of *hersir*, not even bending to call himself jarl, although it's a higher title, for he and his race are proud that way.

"Horda-Kari had four sons—Thorleif the Wise was the first. Second was Ogmund, father of Thorolf Skjalg, Erling's father. Third was Thord, whose son Klypp the Hersir slew King Sigurd Sleva, son of Erik Bloodaxe, for raping his wife, and the fourth is Olmod the Old, who still lives.

15

"Skjalg's estate is Sola, in Jaeder, on the coast of Rogaland. Ogmund Karisson took it, and a piece of Jaeder, after its old lord picked the wrong side at the Battle of Hafrsfjord, where Harald Finehair became high king. Harald gave Sola to Ogmund and offered to make him a jarl, but he too turned the title down, for he saw how men kissed Harald's backside for it, and he said it made him want to puke. All this brought him great honor, for the Horders' power was now pushed into Rogaland, and Jaeder is some of the richest farmland in Norway. And our Jaederers are mostly pleased too, for Skjalg and Erling are the best of lords. Only this business of Christianity makes bother, and nowadays the old man hasn't a good word to say to Erling, though you can see he's pleased when men tell his son's deeds.

"We're following the coast of Agder now. Aft, to the east, is the Vik, where they pay tribute to the king of Denmark. Soon we'll pass Lindesness and the southmost point of the land. Then we swing north along Rogaland, and Jaeder. Sigurd, son of Erik Bjodaskalle, is hersir at Opprostad, south on the coast from us, and a worthy man, but his brothers Jostein, Thorkel and Aki are bitter towards Thorolf and Erling, thinking their inheritance whittled. They're descended from Viking-Kari, another Horder who got lands from Harald Finehair. Ogmund bested Kari in a boundary dispute, and they have long memories.

"Further north is Hordaland, then the Fjords and Sogn and More. Then comes the Trondelag, where Jarl Haakon lives, who is overlord of Norway. He's a strong heathen, and a great friend of Skjalg. Beyond that, the far north where only reindeer and bear and heathen Lapps dwell, but great profit can be made by hardy men."

"It must be hard to ward so long a coast."

"We have a means worked out by Haakon the Good years back. Haakon was the best king Norway ever had, and descended from Horda-Kari on his mother's side. There are balefires set up on hills along the entire coast, from the Vik to Halogaland. If an enemy fleet is spotted, they light a balefire, and the wardens at the next fire see it and light their own, and on up the coast. At the same time the wardens send word to their lords, who send out war arrows to cry up a levy of men and ships."

"Suppose the wardens saw a simple pirate fleet and took it for an invasion?"

"That's a problem. Haakon set grave penalties for any who gave a false alarm. Which was his bane, as it turned out. He was caught unwarned with a small force, took an arrow wound and died."

"And what do you do about such pirates?"

"We have small fires of our own, easily told from the great fires such as we keep at Tjora and Tunge. We have to buy the wood, as there's no forest on Jaeder, but it's worth it. And of course a simple horn signal will raise a local defense."

"There's comfort in knowing that your folk live in fear of Vikings the same as we."

Thorkel spat and said, "Yes, we're becoming good Christian sheep, more every day."

"Are you all Christians?" I asked. "I see some of you wear ornaments like crosses, but they're oddly made."

"Those are Thor's hammers. Erling compels no one to take his faith, though he favors Christians."

"Are you a Christian?"

"Oh aye. I was baptized in Dublin. It matters little to me one way or the other, but nowadays it's prudent to be a Christian in the wide world."

Then he wanted to drill me on my Norse, and soon I was sick again.

It was raining the day we passed the wide, surf-pounded Sola Bay, rounded the point at Jaasund, acclaimed by seagulls, and sailed down the broad Hafrsfjord (where Harald Finehair made himself high king). But it's usually raining in Jaeder. In the course of these recollections I may from time to time neglect to tell you what the weather was like. When that happens, you may assume it was raining.

The warden at the landing at Somme trotted down the jetty to greet us, spear and shield in hand. I followed Erling down the slippery gangplank and felt rocky on solid earth again. But I knelt and kissed the jetty's stones and swore I'd never get on a boat again (which God took as a challenge).

"Hail, my Lord Erling," said the warden. "I've sent word to the steading for your mother."

"And where's my father?"

"He rode up to Kolness to knock some fishermen's heads together. Some dispute over berths. Here come your mother and the household."

Fishermen looked up from their nets, and their families stared out the doors of their cottages at us as we trooped up the jetty and past the boathouse to meet the household. Erling's mother, who led a wet procession of housefolk and thralls, wore an overdress of embroidered wool wrapped around her body under the arms, over a long, pleated underdress of linen. The overdress hung by cords fastened with a turtle-shell brooch above each breast. A red shawl was draped over her shoulders, and a white linen cloth covered her hair. She was a tall, handsome woman, and her son favored her. The two fair-haired young women who stood on either side of her favored her too, and I took them for Erling's sisters. They giggled and pointed at me, but I pretended to be too high-minded to notice.

I was more interested in a fourth woman there. She was small, and her uncovered hair was the color of honey, smooth and shining. Her face was oval, her nose fine and her blue eyes bright under arched brows. She had a face you'd want to reach out and stroke, just to know if it was as smooth as it looked, like a pearl.

"Greetings, my son," said the older woman after Erling had drunk the horn of ale she'd brought and she and the lasses had embraced him. "You'll want a meal after your journey. Come to the hall; the thralls are cooking now, and we can drink until they've done."

"How's father?"

"He complains of his stomach and his bones; he chases the thrall girls but only out of custom. Nothing has changed. Who is this man in women's clothing?"

"You've seen a priest before, Mother."

"I'd hoped never to see another. But he must be fed, I suppose, like honest men."

The women turned back the way they'd come, and Erling gave orders to an overseer for the unloading. Then we set out for the steading.

The little I could see of the land did not impress. It was flattish, with sandy fields of tough grass facing the fjord. But the land rose somewhat beyond the waste, and our path led upward and to the southwest, past the fields of Somme farm to Sola itself. There was hardly a tree in sight. Moss and heather grew among the stones, which lay everywhere, singly and in heaps, in the meadows above. A large area atop the highest hill was hemmed by a low stone fence, and a walled lane led through it to the steading of Sola. The fields within the fence sloped south and looked well manured, but were nothing you'd remark on in Ireland. A hog watched us, rubbing its chin on a fence stone.

"Who's the girl with the lamplight eyes?" I asked Thorkel.

"She's Halla Asmundsdatter, Erling's leman."

"A strange name for someone so plainly Irish. I think she's the loveliest woman I've ever seen."

"It's said she's the fairest woman in Norway, save only Astrid Trygvesdatter, who is of course a king's child."

The steading was a loose rectangle of mostly turf or stone, turf-roofed buildings (some of them looking for all the world like little hillocks) around a central yard at the top of the hill. Largest of the buildings was the hall, wood-built, long and high, flanking the yard on the north. We entered through a side door near one end, then turned right through another door into the main hall. Two lines of wooden pillars marched down its length on either side of a long hearth. Low platforms ran along each wall outside the pillars, and on them benches and trestle tables had been set up. Helmets and shields and swords hung on the walls, and all the woodwork was carved with those squirmy beasts that writhe in pagans' brains, childish copies of the lovely Celtic knot with no art or balance to them. A peat fire burned in the hearth and the blue smoke hung about the rafters so that they could not be seen. Midway down either side a large chair with arms, big enough for two, was set on a dais between two pillars of great size, carved in the shapes of round-eyed, teeth-gnashing warriors.

"Sit in your places and the thralls will serve you," said Erling's mother. Erling went to a seat on the bench to the right of the north high seat and beckoned me to come up beside him.

Erling's mother stared at me a moment, then went out with her women, leaving us to take our places while thralls spread the tables. While we drank Erling gave me an eating knife and a spoon of silver, for all Norsemen carry their own. We ate the vile food when it came, flat as the landscape of Jaeder—boiled pork and barley bread and fish; but the ale was good. An older warrior named Hrorek stood up and recited a verse he claimed he'd composed on the spot in honor of the journey—absolute babble of course, even if you understood the Norse tongue better than I did. But Erling seemed pleased, and he took a silver ring from his arm and had it carried over the fire to him. All the men shouted and stamped their feet, so I suppose it meant something to them.

When our hunger was blunted and the ale was beginning to have its effect, Erling introduced me. There was no friendliness in his mother's eyes (I learned her name was Ragna) as she stared at me from her own high seat on the women's bench at the east end of the hall. I rose and gave them a benediction. There was a lot of grumbling, and I sat down. But Halla smiled at me, and that was worth seeing.

After the meal Erling and the lads sat drinking and comparing tattoos and telling lies and picking fights with each other. I had trouble following after awhile, so I excused myself, going out into the strange, light Norwegian summer night. A serving woman led me to the priest's house. It was built much like the hall, but small, and of turf. It needed no pillars. Benches had been made by the simple shift of digging a trench down the middle for the hearth fire, with flat stones set up to retain the sides. In one corner there was a box-bed, too short to stretch out in, in which I had no intention of lying in summertime.

I was ready to put out the soapstone lamp when I heard the door creak. Halla stood there, and the room brightened with her eyes.

"I want to be baptized by you," she said.

"Right now?" I asked.

"No—whenever it's proper. I've been instructed already, by Father Ethelbald, the old priest. But before he could pour the water on me, he was— he died."

"And you are keen to be joined to Mother Church?"

"I'm eager to do whatever Erling wishes." She sat on a bench and spoke easily, as if we were old friends. "I come of a good family, Father. My father is an honorable *bonder*, but we aren't rich or of the highest blood."

"Bonder?"

"A free farmer. Erling's mother wants him to make a high marriage, but I believe he cares for me, and if I'm a Christian he might marry me. I want him all for myself, Father."

So she would serve the Lord for a husband, as I served Him for my freedom. We were alike in our ill motives, except that she was not a hypocrite.

Still I asked, "Do you believe in the Father, the Son, and the Holy Spirit? Do you believe that Christ died for your sins, and rose again from the dead?"

She frowned. "I don't understand all that Father Ethelbald told me, but I think Jesus is a better god than Thor."

"Then you have more faith than some Christians I know," said I. "We'll see to the baptism when I'm settled in."

As she went out she turned back at the door and said, "May I ask about one of the things I don't understand?"

I said, "Of course."

"Father Ethelbald used a word—'evil.' It's not a word we have in our tongue. He tried to explain what it meant."

"Ah well, evil means there are . . . things about in the world, and in men too, and all they want is to do harm, just for hate's own sake."

She thought a moment.

"What a frightening world you Christians live in," she said.

I said, "And the one around us isn't?"

I thought about Halla that night, wrapped in my cloak on the bench, listening to the sea's muffled threats—poor lass, she had little hope of her heart's desire—and then I was thinking of Maeve, and home, and my parents and Diarmaid and time and miles and the wickedness of men, and I wept like a child wood-lost at night, until I slept, shivering.

I woke the next morning to the sound of shouting and dogs barking.

When I came out into the sunlight, I felt eyes on me from every side. They were all around the steading, their black and red and yellow hair cropped short, walking slumped in their shapeless, pale garments, barefoot or wearing wooden clogs. Thralls. Mostly Irish.

I stood and looked at them, and one by one they set down the bowls or spades or forks they carried and shuffled towards me, looking at the ground mostly, raising their eyes to meet mine for a second at a time, then letting them slide away. At last a cluster of them hemmed me in. And suddenly I was afraid of them; because I was free and they were slaves—for that they might kill me, Irish or not.

Then a woman sobbed and fell to her knees, clasping my legs, crying, "Father!" And then they were all kneeling—

"Father! Bless us!"

"Father! Pray for me!"

"Father, it's been eight years since my last confession—"

"Father, how are things in Ireland?"

"Father, do you know my family? They live in Connemara—"

And for a moment I forgot I was not a priest. I reached my hands to them and blessed them. I blessed them and promised them a mass soon. They wept as if truly comforted. Then they went off, smiling, to take up their labors again. I stood for a moment leaning against the wall with my eyes closed, winded as if with digging.

When I opened my eyes, there stood the biggest man I'd ever seen, not so tall as Erling, but broader, watching me. He grinned. There were interruptions in his teeth. He had wide shoulders, and arms like a strong man's legs. He was clean bald over the scalp, with a nasty scar that looked like a burn covering the left side of his forehead and stretching down to the ear, just missing one tufted eyebrow. His beard was short and brown. His eyes were small, and pale, and unfriendly as badgers.

"Will you bless me too, Father?" he asked.

"If you like," I said. "Come closer—I'll lay hands on you."

"It's you who mean to break the power of Thor at Sola? With your holiness and faith?" His hailstone eyes pierced the nooks of my skull, and I had to look at my feet.

He laughed. His laugh was stronger than my whole body. He walked away from me, laughing.

Thorkel came towards me from the hall. "That was Soti the smith," he said. "He was struck by lightning and lived." I crossed my fingers against the evil eye, for even smiths who've not had intercourse with heavenly fire know too many things.

"Erling wants you in the hall," said Thorkel. "There's trouble."

"What sort?"

"His father's dead. Aslak, his brother, too. Killed by Orkney Vikings at Kolness yesterday. Such raids are common—it was just ill luck that Skjalg and Aslak were there. They could have saved themselves by running away, but Skjalg was too proud."

The hall went silent for a moment as I raced in and took my seat. A thrall brought a bowl of water, in which I was expected to wash my face, and a towel. A woman set porridge and fish before me, and Erling passed me a horn. It was a strange horn, with studs set into it, running in a line from brim to tip.

"You drink to where the next stud is uncovered," said Erling. "That way nobody drinks too much in the daytime, when he needs a clear head." He spoke as usual, but there were red spots on his cheekbones that I'd seen before only in battle.

"I've heard about your father and I weep for your loss, my lord," I said when I'd had my measure. "What do you plan?"

"I'll hunt them down and kill them. If I knew where they were I'd be gone this minute. They have a strong force, so I'll need to take most of my armed men. Fortunately I still have the company I took with me to the Baltic. I've sent men out for news, and I expect I'll know more shortly. But I hate waiting."

"Shall I come with you? I'm always glad to fight Vikings."

"You'd best stay here. I didn't buy you for your

strong arm. Which reminds me, I haven't shown you my church yet. I want you to set it in order so we can have a mass for my father's soul, and for victory, when I return. I wish I had time for one this morning, but I hope to be gone soon. Pray for us when I am."

He took time to show me the church, and I left most of my breakfast behind. It was a stone building a little bigger than my house, with benches along the walls, but there was a crude stone altar at the east end, and a carved wooden crucifix hung above it.

"I want to build a better one someday, but this will have to do for now," said Erling. "One day I'll raze the holy place of Thor and build you a church on that spot."

"Has she been properly hallowed?" I asked, waving some cobwebs aside.

"We haven't had the chance to get a bishop here for that," said Erling. "But I have some surprises for you." He called in a thrall who bore a small chest, which he laid on a bench. Erling opened the chest with a key and handed me a bundle of cloth. "Father Ethelbald's vestments," he said. Then he drew out an object swathed in linen. He unwrapped it for me.

"A chalice!" I said. "A lovely chalice, in silver!"

"There's this too," said Erling, and brought out a paten.

"Wherever did you get such things? No—don't say it. Prizes from your Viking days?"

"Not as bad as that. The king of Agder had them for his high table. I paid a pretty price for them."

"God will reward you," I said.

"One more thing." From the bottom of the chest he brought a book. "I don't know properly what it is, but the pictures inside look holy."

" 'Tis a psalter," said I, "and a lovely one, though some impious hand has pried the gems from the cover ornaments. But no matter. The true treasure's inside. Many a church in Ireland is less well furnished than yours, my lord. I am grateful for this. I can read—a little."

"What's this—a housewarming?" said a booming voice. Soti the smith strode over the threshold. "A fitting time for a gift. Priest of the White Christ, I give you a thrall for your service."

I stared at the man.

"No, not one of your Irish stoneheads—I'd not insult you with shoddy goods. My gift is a Norse thrall, one you'll enjoy beating."

"You try my patience, Soti!" said Erling. He turned to me. "The thrall he means is a man called Lemming. We call him that after a mad beast of this land, which goes off its head sometimes and runs into the sea to drown. Lemming has said often he means to die. He says he means to be hanged for the murder of his master. Soti is the only one strong enough to control him; partly with his arm and partly through his spells."

"The priest is a big, strong fellow," said Soti. "And surely he has magic of his own, being a servant of your Christ. Such a man need have no fear of Lemming."

"I'll hear no more of this!" cried Erling. "Get out, Soti."

"Hold, my lord," said I. "I accept the smith's gift."

Erling spoke softly. "You don't know what you say. Lemming is half bull."

I whispered back, "I can't let this man call me coward."

"Lemming will kill you."

"I take a bit of killing, my lord."

"I can't afford to lose another priest. You cost me much in Visby."

"And I can't afford to lose . . . we call it losing face in Ireland. It's Christ's honor at stake."

Erling scowled. "May He protect you then."

Soti said, "A word with you, my lord. I've a thing to tell you, but not in this place." They went outside and I locked the chest and went out to join them. It was a wonder how easily I slipped into the priest's role. I didn't know what trouble I'd bought, but I could smell that, Christ's honor or no, I dared not give place to the smith in anything.

"You bear me no love, Soti," Erling was saying.

"But I loved your father, and I'll not see him lie unavenged. I've looked into my forge at white heat and seen the Orkneymen where they beached one of their ships, damaged on the rocks. They lie in Soknasund, not far at all."

"You swear this is true?"

"When have I ever read falsely? And if I'm wrong, what have you lost? As good one way as another when you track your quarry over water."

I may no longer have believed in God, but I was not such a fool as to doubt that there are devils. No Irishman was ever that much a blockhead, nor ever will be.

"My lord, may I speak?" I asked.

"I'd be grateful," said Erling.

"What I say tastes ill in my mouth, for I lost my own father and brother not long since, and I know as well as any man the cry of blood. But this Soti is as great a devil as you'll find even in this devil's land."

"And you think he lies?"

Soti was glaring at me.

"I fear he tells the truth. I'd not have you in his debt. A Christian, my lord, is not strictly required to take vengeance—even, God help us, for a father. Not when it sets his soul in peril."

"Thank you for your counsel, Father Ailill," said Erling with a pale smile. "Pray for me, then come back when you've advice I can follow."

Erling went off with Soti and the ship was gone with most of the warriors in what seemed a few minutes. It was a fine morning for Jaeder, cloudy and blue but not actually raining yet, and the fog was dwindling. Thorkel, who had been left behind with a small guard commanded by Hrorek, met me and we watched them sail away. Then he took me to a place where we could see most of the neighborhood. Sola lies to the northeast of Sola Bay on the sea, above its sand dunes, at the north end of a great crescent of farmland and bogs, ringed by hills inland. He pointed out the various farms nearby, some owned by Erling and rented to tenants, others held in freehold by bonders. To the north, west of the Hafrsfjord, we could see Kolness, and on a hill beyond it Tjora farm, where the jarl's balefire was, and he showed me one or two nearer hills where

Erling had his own fires. He explained how the
peninsula stretched north into the Boknafjord, and
how Erling would round its point at Tunge and sail
east to Soknasund. The day being clear, we could
see mountains over the hills to the southeast, beyond
Gandalsfjord. To the south was the commanding
view of Jaeder and Rogaland and the sea lane which
made Sola so valuable in the land's defense. . . .

Then I heard a great roar, like that of a beast,
behind me, and I knew without looking that the
thrall Lemming had found me. I whirled to meet
him and ducked under a great swinging arm,
spinning aside as something the size of a church
went flying by to land rolling in the mud and sit
for a second staring at me before heaving itself up
to attack again.

I had only a heartbeat to take my enemy's measure
and (as my father used to say) he was a man you
needed an hour or so just to look at. I saw a shaggy,
straw-colored beard, and a badly broken nose, and
shoulders that it must have been weary work to carry
around.

He roared again and came at me, and I leaped
out of his way. I'm no little man, and I'm no weakling,
and I like a good brawl as well as any Irishman,
but I thought all the biggest bruisers in Norway
must be smelling my scent and swarming at me at
once.

I had more skill than Lemming, thank God. He
counted on his strength, and if I'd let him catch
me it would have been over. But I danced about
outside his grip, teasing him, tripping him up, even
landing a punch in his gut (with no effect I could

see) as he went by. My only hope was to tire him. After several minutes I was breathing like a wind-broken horse, and he still came on like a gale out of the north.

Thorkel watched all this standing hipshot with a hand on his swordbelt, a smile on his face. He was too wellborn to meddle in a fight with a thrall of course. A crowd of folk gathered to watch us. Some of them even cheered me.

Then Lemming caught me a punch on the side of the head, and I saw stars, as they say—and they say it because that's what you see—and then he had me about the chest in a bear hug, and I couldn't breathe. And the world began to dwindle and travel rapidly away from me, and I heard a horn and a cry, as if from a great distance—

"Ships are coming! We're under attack!"

ChAPTER IV

I stood in the abbot's cell. I felt muddled because, though being called in for a beating was hardly strange to me, I couldn't recall what I'd done this time. He sat slumped on his hard bed, and he sighed and looked up at me with an old horse's eyes.

"Unlike some people, I know how to do what I'm told," he said, getting to his feet. "I don't like it, but I do it, because without obedience the world falls in. Is that not so?"

"Very true, Father," I said.

"Don't lie to me. A lying tongue like yours should be torn out at the roots and fed to dogs, and the dogs stoned, that our calling be not disgraced. And to think they want you—you don't even believe in God, do you?"

"I suppose not, Father."

" 'I suppose not, Father.' You're worse than the rest. You live in this prison, this shambles, this slave pen of earth and you watch the evils that fall on the innocent, and as long as it touches you not it bothers you no more than the death of a bedbug in Babylon; but let the blow fall on you or someone you care about and you shout, 'There is no God.' And the joke of it is that you don't disbelieve in

Him at all. You're just trying to hurt His feelings to get His attention. As if God suffered by your disapproval."

"He acts as if He's not there. What am I to think?"

"Think anything you like. It matters naught to me. I only called you here to give you the message entrusted to me."

"Entrusted? By whom?"

"By Authority at the highest level, of course. I act only in the orthodox fashion: I come in a dream, which is not, strictly speaking, me coming to you at all, but only a fantasy of your sleeping mind. The fathers of the church condemned with one voice all attempts to communicate with the dead, although Origen . . ."

I knew he'd go on like this for hours if I let him. "You're saying you're dead?" I put in.

He looked at me as if he'd forgotten my existence. "Of course I'm dead," he said. "You mean you didn't know? The last thing I ever saw on earth was the welcome spectacle of your back heading down the road and away from the abbey, before I fell into the apopleptic fit that killed me. You may add to your catalogue of sins the occasion of a good man's death."

I thought of apologizing, but decided there would be no point. "What's this choice you speak of?" I asked.

He looked disappointed then, denied the chance to throw my "sorry" back in my teeth. "You have a choice," he said. "You may take your martyr's crown now . . . martyr's crown, by God!—you who wouldn't even pay the toll!—or you may go back and continue your mission."

"Martyr's crown. You mean—"

"Yes, the blessings of Paradise. Manna for breakfast. Water sweeter than wine to wash it down. Music by David and Asaph and all the greatest bards. Games on the grass with the Holy Innocents. Hunting with St. Sebastian, and your evening dinner cooked by St. Laurence. Then a friendly wrestling match between St. Augustine and Job, and dancing led by Mary and Martha. And with all this to do, you let it all slide just for the pleasure of gazing on the face of the Beloved."

"Or I can go back to Jaeder and live among people who hate me, going always in fear of my life?"

"And get rained on. You mustn't forget the rain. And wait till you spend a winter in Jaeder. You'll long for your old cell then, I promise you."

"Is this a test of some kind?"

"Everything's a test. Look, why should we waste time? I know your nature—you'll never choose a life of suffering, however good the cause, when you can have a martyr's crown at a bargain price. So I'll just go and tell them your decision. . . ." He moved toward the door.

"Hold on!" I cried. "You think I'm soft, don't you? You think I've no guts! Well roast you! Send me back to Jaeder. I'll earn my crown—what do you know of martyrdom, anyway—"

And a man came up from behind the abbot—an old, bald man with white hair and keys at his belt, and he reached his hands out to me . . .

I woke with a dull feeling that I'd been had.

Horns were blowing and people were running about, shouting and toting things, but I lay on my back in the mud, looking up at the clouds, trying to decide whether it would be wise to get up. My head ached, and I had an idea that if I tried to move my arms and legs I'd regret it.

At last a thrall running with an empty barrel tripped over my legs and sprawled on his face. I groaned and rolled half over, then sat up slowly. I felt as if my body'd been used as a roller for a ship's portage. The thrall frowned at me and got up and ran after his barrel, which was tumbling toward the low side of the steading.

Very slowly I got to my knees and, bracing myself against a wall, achieved my feet. Then I turned my head carefully to see what was happening.

The thralls and the women were carrying things— barrels, chests, bales of wool, hams—out the gate and down the lane. At its end they headed east, in an ant line toward the higher hills. The fifty or so warriors Erling had left behind were forming up near the gate, and a few bonders who must have been in the neighborhood when the call went out were being outfitted from the armory. Looking down toward the bay I could see the last of three ships beaching itself boldly on the sand, while men disembarked from the other two. There looked to be three or four hundred of them.

I found Thorkel among the warriors and said, "We don't stand a chance."

Thorkel's face was pale behind the nosepiece of his helmet. "All we need to do is slow them down. We're moving the people and treasure to the stronghold on the hill there—" he pointed east. I spotted it then—a tooth jutting up from one of the hills. Clusters of people were running there from every direction. "Hrorek has sent men to light the balefires, and we'll have the more distant bonders joining us with their spears soon after. The thing now is for you who aren't warriors to get to the stronghold fast, so we don't have to die in the open warding you."

"Ward yourself," said I. "I'm getting arms." I ran to the armory and took a leather shirt with iron plates, an axe, a shield, a spear and a helmet. I poked my head inside the church and noted thankfully that the priest's chest had been taken.

The steading was empty now, and we warriors felt it no shame to sprint for the stronghold, given the odds. It was no easy run uphill carrying iron, but our enemies had the same handicap. Those already inside closed the gates the moment the last of us got in.

We posted our little force around the walls. The stronghold was a very plain, circular pen with six-foot banked turf walls and a wooden parapet. One turf-roofed house stood in its center. I stood beside Thorkel on the south side, my spear ready for thrusting.

"A little time, that's all we need," he said between his teeth. "Time for the balefires to be lit and the farther-off bonders to come in. Do you see smoke anywhere? I'd think they'd have the fires going by now."

"Nothing," I said. "No sign of smoke."

"At least we can be grateful Aki won't burn the steading. If it took fire, Erling would see its smoke and come back."

"Is this Aki? The Opprostad hersir's brother?"

"Aye. I know his ships. The plan's plain enough. He sent those Orkneymen to attack Kolness and run away, expecting to draw Erling off and leave Sola to him. You've got to admire his courage, beaching his ships in the surf at Sola Bay. He came from the north, so he must have had his ships behind some island or in some inlet, waiting for Erling to pass."

"But how could he know Skjalg would be at Kolness?"

"That would be luck, from his point of view. Watch yourself."

An arrow flew past my ear with a little *whup* sound and a puff of air. Aki's men were taking their places behind their shields, or behind rocks and boulders, on all sides, their bowmen beginning their work from the cover.

We warded ourselves with our shields for the next few minutes. Someone began to scream from near the gate.

At last a man came around to us and said, "Eystein says that if they get over the wall, we're all to gather around the house to defend the women and children."

"Eystein?" said Thorkel. "What happened to Hrorek?"

"He didn't make it inside."

"God rest him," I said.

"God rest us all if those balefires aren't lit," said Thorkel. "Has anyone seen any sign?"

"They won't be lit," said the man. "One of the boys we sent to light them got back before they hemmed us in. He said the wood had been wet clean through to the ground. Aki has friends hereabouts."

"That's it then," said Thorkel. "It comes to us all in time. I'd thought to kiss a few more girls, but the Norns decide."

"That's not Christian talk," said I.

"I suppose when it comes to the point, a man finds out what he is. Sorry, Father."

I didn't know what to say to that. The other man went away.

We made them fight for it. Our cover was good, and we had plenty of arrows of our own, if not so many bowmen.

With true Norse perversity, the weather stayed clear. The clouds drifted off, the sun beat on us and dried us, and the women who came around with water moved slowly for fear of the arrows. When they got to us, they never had enough.

"Why doesn't Aki burn the steading?" I asked Thorkel.

"I told you. The fire would bring Erling back."

"Why should he care whether Erling comes back? He could sack the place, burn it to the ground, and be gone before Erling could get here."

"And have Erling come after him? He doesn't want Erling's goods—he wants Erling dead. Otherwise he could have done all this while we were voyaging. I suppose he plans to wait in the steading and surprise him when he comes home. He'd have the high ground then. He knows he can't beat Erling in a fair fight. That would be why he's sparing his men too. They could take us with a rush from all sides, but it would cost them."

"Perhaps. But if I were he I'd be wondering now whether to settle for what I could get."

"To be honest, so would I."

"In that case, there's a chance he might decide to leave us alone up here."

"Too late. The tide's ebbed since he beached his ships. And there's one more thing. He's sworn to take Halla Asmundsdatter to his bed, and we have her."

"So the abbot was right. He always said the lust of the flesh would be the death of me. I'd thought he meant my own flesh."

The shadows were lengthening when we heard someone cry, "The fire! The fire!"

I wondered if they'd decided to burn the steading at last, but someone shouted, "They've lit the Tjora balefire!"

"The jarl's balefire!" said Thorkel. I craned my neck and caught sight of the black smoke to the north.

"Thank God," I said.

"The man who talked the wardens into lighting it will hang."

"Well if I knew his name, I'd not betray it. We should get help now."

"And Aki knows it. So we can expect—here it comes!"

Then was a time. The arrows rained on us until our shields were hedgehogs' backs. One man after another screamed and lay screaming until the arrows finished him, for we were too busy to help. Aki's men attacked on all sides, and we thrust at them with spears, and when one went down another took his place, and if he warded well with his shield he got in close to the parapet and we had to discourage him with axes and swords. I had thought my shield light at first. Now it weighed like an anvil, and my axe like the earth.

The attack ended at last. We knew there'd be another soon, and we were weary and fewer than before. I wondered how long we'd been at it. The light night gave little clue.

"I need to talk to Eystein," I told Thorkel. "Where will I find him?"

"Probably near the gate. Don't go away long—I need you here."

"Maybe I can make it easier for us all," I said, and ran off, keeping to the cover of the wall.

I found Eystein huddled with some of his men, tying a bandage on his arm. He was dark for a Norseman. He scowled at me and said, "I'm busy, god-man."

I said, "Let me arm the thralls."

He said, "You're mad. We've never armed thralls in Jaeder."

"We'll all die if we do nothing."

"Thralls are no use with weapons. Besides, it's wrong. I won't save my life by wrong dealing."

"For God's sake—think of the shame to Aki! Think what men will say if he's beaten in part by thralls!"

Eystein scratched his beard. "I never looked at it that way," he said.

"Well think quickly."

"Oh, Hel," he said. "Do it. I'll probably be sorry, but right now I'd like to live long enough to be."

So I ran to the house and inside. The free women were huddled on the benches, watching a kneeling red-haired woman chant over a pile of sticks near the hearth. The thralls crouched near the entryway. They knelt when they saw me.

"Which of you want to be Aki's thralls?" I cried to them.

They exchanged dull looks.

"Who is willing to fight to keep a better master?" I said.

One man asked, "Do you mean, take arms?"

"Yes! Will you take them if they're offered?"

"You mean they'll let us fight?"

"Yes! But we've got to hurry!"

"What is this?" came a woman's voice from the other end. Ragna, Erling's mother, strode towards us.

"Eystein's agreed to it. We need every man we can get."

"You upturn the world, god-man!"

"Perhaps. But we'll never know if Aki wins through."

She stared at me. "If thralls can fight, so can women," she said. "There were shield-mays in olden times. None of us has the thews for such work, but we can cast a spear or draw a bow."

A cry of "Yes, yes!" came from the hearth. It was the woman with the sticks.

Now I was shocked, but I said, "All right, let's all do what we can," and led the lot of them out. I let them loose in the weapons pile and ran back to my place beside Thorkel.

"I've armed the thralls and some of the women. They'll be with us soon."

"Thor help us," said Thorkel.

When they made their next attack they got a

surprise. The women and thralls had gotten bows, and a wealth of arrows lay on the ground. The shooting wasn't of the best, but there was plenty of it, and once again the attackers fell back, leaving a good number dead and wounded.

A wounded man lay near us outside the wall. He cried, "Thor! I'm belly-shot! I have the porridge sickness! Someone help me!"

A woman—somebody's wife judging from her headcloth, shouted back, "Good! I hope you suffer! I hope you linger days! I hope the ants find you and nibble away your eyes and your nose while you yet live! I hope Vikings come and rape your wife and take your children as thralls, and I hope you hear of it in Hell!"

Thorkel looked at me and said, "There are tales of women warriors in old times. Fortunately we're more civilized than that now. Or we were until you came."

When the light faded our bows were of less use. We were all up on the walls then, those who were left, and it was thrust and hack work, and Aki's men came on and on, and we were weary. The woman who had taunted the wounded man fell beside me with an axe-cloven skull, and I wanted to be sick. A man goes to war precisely not to watch his own women die.

Someone shouted, "The hall—it burns!" and we craned our necks a moment to see the smoke go up from Sola, and we knew we were down to the apple core.

Then Aki brought fire and broke the gate, and we fell back to make a shield wall before the house, and the women fled inside but most of the thrall men stayed with us. We stood shoulder to shoulder, arms aching, barely upholding our shields, and Aki's men's eyes glowed in the torchlight, and then falling sparks told us that the house was burning behind us, and the women and children ran out screaming to huddle behind our backs. And somebody began to sing a death-song, and all the men took it up, and I tried to follow it too. Consider it when your day comes. It helps a little.

And then there was a shout from somewhere, and Aki's men looked around, startled, and I saw a spearpoint stick out the belly of one of them.

And they fled before Erling Skjalgsson's warriors. And I saw Erling himself in the firelight, sword in hand, shouting, "Aki, you son of a troll, I'll have your liver for breakfast!"

CHAPTER V

We ran back to the steading to save the hall, but only made it in time to see the last rafters fall. Once the ruin was complete the windows of heaven opened and soaked us all with rain. Not much was saved there, but most of the stone and turf buildings suffered little damage. My church was fine. I trudged around with some women and thralls getting our wounded under a roof, while other women went with knives and cut the throats of Aki's fallen. I bound limbs and fed leek porridge to those with stomach wounds, so we could tell by smell if the gut was pierced. Erling organized the household to march over to Somme, which, like many farms in the neighborhood, was his property. Aki and his men who still walked were locked in a storehouse there.

I got a bed on a bench among the warriors. I was wearier than I'd ever been in my life, but I couldn't sleep. It was the same all around me. The warriors, especially those who'd defended the stronghold, were whispering to each other in the dark, telling what they'd done and what they'd seen done, speculating on what would have happened *if*. They'd been through something they'd tell their grandchildren of, and they wanted to know how it would sound.

They'd been given a little horrible beast to carry about with them, and they wanted to build it a cage so they could scare the girls without anyone getting bitten.

An older man named Bergthor, lying next to me, was composing a poem. I couldn't tell you what it said—the usual nonsense about "the flame of the wound" and "Atli's devourer," but I listened to him anyway, and in time I must have slept.

Somebody kicked me awake no more than two minutes later, saying, "Get up or we'll sling you out. The jarl's come to breakfast."

I shook my head, stiff everywhere and feeling five hundred years old. "The jarl?" I asked.

"Jarl Haakon, lord of Norway. He was sailing south, saw the balefire, and now he wants an explanation. So you'd better think of one."

"Me? I didn't start any fires."

"No, but your thrall did. The man they call Lemming. He's under close guard now. By our law the master answers for his thrall's deeds."

Thrall women were setting up the tables, and I pushed by them as I limped out in the yard to find Erling.

Erling was busy, in counsel with a short, broad, brown-haired older man in a rich green cloak whom I took to be Jarl Haakon. They were headed for the hall, followed by the jarl's bodyguard, and when Erling saw me he put a finger to his lips, which advice I heeded. I watched them go inside, then followed, taking a new seat like the rest of the household across the hall from where we usually sat (or would have if this had been our own hall), since Haakon had been given the high seat. The men we'd displaced moved to a new bench across the table from us. A fat old thrall in a fine blue shirt hovered at the jarl's elbow, running errands for him and shouting commands to other thralls. I did not join the toasts to Thor, Odin and Frey which began the meal, but I drank when Erling and Haakon *skoaled* each other, and ate some breakfast in spite of my nerves and the pain I got when I tried to raise my arms. I hadn't eaten since the morning before. Erling whispered, "You'll be all right, Father. Just let me talk."

I looked around and missed a face I wanted. "Where's Thorkel?" I asked.

"Didn't you know? He died at the stronghold last night."

"Poor lad. I lost sight of him after we fell back from the wall. I'll bury you as a Christian, Thorkel, and let God judge."

"What's that?"

"Just a thing between us two. By the way, I was wondering—did you actually find the Vikings at Soknasund?"

"Oh aye. We were almost on them when someone saw the fire and we headed home instead. I don't care about them—they were only tools."

"Then Soti is a true seer."

"Yes, though his wife has the real sight. The women usually do."

"But he didn't see the greatest danger."

"No. And he had no good explanation."

"That's the trouble with seers, my lord. They see only what the Devil wants known."

The women of the household mingled with the guests, as was custom, but I missed Halla and Erling's sisters. I asked Erling whether they had come to harm.

"None at all," he said, "and I mean to keep it that way."

Jarl Haakon called across the fire, "Well then, Erling, what's to be done about my balefire? This thrall of yours attacked the wardens when they demanded proper tokens, and they've both got broken bones. I've had to send ships back up the coast to call off the levies, and it's me they'll blame for lost field time."

"In my view," said Erling, "the lighting was justified. This was not a simple *strandhogg*, with a few Vikings slaughtering cattle and stealing thralls. This was a cold stab at my authority, and so the authority of every lawful lord in the land."

"Fine words," said Haakon, "but the kings and landed men of Norway have been stealing each other's rule since Freya was a virgin. That's how your grandfather got Sola. Aki wants satisfaction for the lands your father took. You'd do the same."

"I'd not do it by stealth."

"There's nothing wrong with stealth. There is something wrong with using my balefire for private warfare. That must be paid for. Who owns the thrall?"

"My priest, Father Ailill."

"A Christian priest? That bull-calf there? It gets worse and worse. All right, god-man—what do you have to say for yourself?"

"My lord," I said, "I've seen the thrall but once

in my life, and at the time he was trying to break my neck. He was given me as a gift only yesterday, and he's never even slept under my roof. I might add that I never asked for him. I'd as soon ask for a boil."

"Aye, I've never yet heard a Christian priest own the blame for anything."

"I can swear that he tells the truth, my lord," said Erling.

I said, "There's one thing I'd like to say though." Erling shot me a cautioning glance. "The thrall did his best to protect his master's home and person. For that he should be rewarded, not punished. But if you must punish him, you should know that it's his wish to hang."

"What?"

"That's why they call him Lemming, my lord. He's been trying for years, they tell me, to get himself hanged. In a way, to hang him would be to reward him."

Haakon said, "Hmm, I suppose we could flay him . . ."

Erling said, "My lord, this trouble over a thrall is beneath your notice. If you leave him to me, I promise he'll get a rope around his neck."

"Yes, all right, as long as it's done."

"Good, then may I say that I rejoice the fire was lit?"

"What do you mean?"

"So that you might be here for my father's and brother's grave-ale. You and father were always friends. And you can pass judgment on Aki, a matter suitable to your rank."

Jarl Haakon leaned back in his seat. "I wonder if I wouldn't be better served were it Aki hosting me now."

I buried the Christian dead the next day, doing the service as best I could from memory and filling the rest out, I'm afraid, with plain mumbo jumbo. At the same time Erling was sending messengers with invitations to his father's and brother's funeral, a week hence. While they waited he spent handsomely on hospitality for the jarl. I don't think the man was once without a full ale-horn the whole week. We must have all been a nuisance to Odvin, the man who lived at Somme with his family and had to let the great folk use all his best beds, but he was a tenant after all and had no say. Every morning Erling and I and a few others trooped up to the church before breakfast, and I gave them mass, and I said vespers each night.

One of those first evenings I stepped out to take the air. I recognized one of Erling's thralls, a lad named Enda, who came to me and said, "Father, there's trouble among the slaves."

"What trouble, son?"

"It's Kark, the jarl's slave." He meant the fat fellow who followed Haakon like a dog. "He's making hell for the girls. He bullies them and handles them, and makes them lie with him, and then brags about it afterward. The men he beats for the least thing, and no one dares cross him, because the jarl holds him so dear."

"It's often the way, I'm afraid, with us who sit at the world's bottom. When we find someone to spit on, we make the most of it. But I don't know what I can do. This Kark is no Christian; he won't heed me."

"That's just it, Father. He fears you. Everyone's marked it. He makes the sign against the evil eye whenever he sees you. You're magic to him. He thinks you're not a man and not a woman, begging your pardon, and you speak with men long dead through books, and commune with spirits in a strange tongue. We thought you might put the fear of God in him."

The idea had charm. I went with Enda to one of the thrall houses.

"They say he was born on the same day as the jarl, and he's been with him all his life. The jarl treats him like a pet. It's a bitter thing, Father, to be bullied by one who's no better than you."

"Lad," I said, "don't tell anyone I said so, but I've been a slave and I've been free, and the only things I've seen to make one man better than another are how he thinks of himself, and how he treats others."

"I don't follow. You can't mean I'm as good as my lord Erling?"

"Well no, hardly anyone is that . . ."

We found Kark lying in a corner of the house with one hand under the dress of a sobbing girl. I held my lamp near my face and said, *"Morituri te salutamus!"* in my most sepulchral voice.

Kark looked up at me with round eyes. I've heard many tales told of Kark in the years since, and with each telling he grows more stunted and twisted and dark and ugly, the picture of a thrall as the Norse see them. I will do him justice. He was one of the fairest men for his age I'd seen in Norway, with snow-white hair and great blue eyes, pretty as a woman almost.

"*Arma virumque cano!*" I intoned.

He let go the girl now, and cowered in the corner. "*Vox clamantis in deserto!*"

The wretch went into a fit. He groveled at my feet, and I had to put a hand on him to stop him screeching. This only made it worse, and he scrambled away, cringing back in the corner with his arms over his face.

It had been too easy. I said, "Now leave the other thralls alone, my lad. And if you tattle to your master, I'll turn you into a herring."

I'd been right, I thought as I went back to the hall. There was real pleasure in finding somebody to spit on.

A few days later the guests began to arrive. Chief among them was the head of the family, Olmod Karisson, an actual son of the famous Horda-Kari. He was, I think, the oldest man I had ever seen, with a hairless head as fragile-looking as an eggshell, and a long white beard. They had to carry him on a litter. But, unlike his late kinsman Thorolf Skjalg (whose name had meant "squinter"), his pale blue eyes saw everything. He sat in his place next to Erling, eating little, drinking less, but marking each man and all his actions. It seemed to me he spent no little time watching Erling.

With him came his son Askel, a big, laughing, easygoing fellow whom all liked but no one minded much. And Askel's son Aslak, a pimply, red-haired boy at the teetery age of about fifteen summers.

He had the kind of meager mouth you often see on red-haired men for some reason, and he watched Erling with a dog's worship.

There were other relations too, all great men at home, but I have less cause to remember them.

The first day of the feast, after they had laid Thorolf Skjalg and Aslak Skjalgsson in their graves with proper heathen rigmarole and the sacrifice of two horses and three dogs, Olmod crooked a finger to me and I went up and sat by him.

"God-man, I have a question about your religion."

"I'll answer as best I can, my lord."

"I'm told that Christians are expected to love their enemies. Doesn't that make them unfit to be lords and wage war?"

"Not at all, my lord. Think of Charlemagne, and Alfred of England, and Brian Boru. A Christian is commanded to do as he would be done by. Would any lord wish other lords to stop making war? Of course not. It would take half the fun out of life. Besides, our scriptures say that the king bears the sword, for the punishment of evildoers."

"Good. That's useful information."

"Are you thinking of becoming a Christian, my lord?"

"Don't talk hog slop."

On that first day Erling was expected to sit on the pedestal of the high seat (in this case the guest seat) until he had drunk a toast to his father's memory and made a vow. The vow he made surprised everyone.

"I have a debt to repay," he said. "I am told that my thralls helped save Sola for me. Therefore I vow that every thrall I own will be given the chance to earn his freedom."

A buzzing went around the hall. Most people liked this vow little, but the thralls serving us looked suddenly glad. Olmod stared, but from where I sat (further down the bench than usual, out of deference to the great folk) I could not see his expression.

At one point I overheard Olmod saying to Erling, who sat now in his father's seat, "You know how to host great men, my kinsman. It seems to me Jarl Haakon's ale is stronger than lesser men's, and your servants keep his horn ever filled."

Erling smiled and said, "Yes, great lords must be treated as fits their dignity."

I think that by the third day of the feast Jarl Haakon had forgotten all about the balefire.

That was the day one of Erling's men came in and stepped up by his seat to whisper in his ear. Without a word, Erling rose and went out. The messenger went to each of his fellow bullyboys in turn, and they all went out the same way.

They were gone some time.

When Erling returned it was with three tall, well-dressed men. They stood together before Jarl Haakon.

"My lord Haakon," said Erling, "may I present Sigurd, Jostein and Thorkel, the sons of Erik Bjodaskalle of Opprostad?"

"I know them well," said the jarl, looking over the rim of his horn. "You are the brothers of Aki."

"They came under the shield of peace," said Erling. "But they came with three ships."

"I care nothing for their ships. Where I guest there is peace by law."

"We cannot promise future peace, though, unless our brother is returned to us," said Sigurd, the oldest, a very handsome man approaching middle age who wore wide Russian breeches. His only defect was a head too large for his body, but it was a fine-looking head. "He was mad to go out as he did, but he's our brother, and we'll not leave him to the mercy of the son of Thorolf Skjalg. We wish to see him now, and make some kind of peace settlement."

"See him you shall," said Haakon. "It's time I judged this business of arson and murder."

Erling motioned to one of his bullyboys, who went out and came back in a few minutes with Aki, his red tunic dirty and torn, but well cared-for and more sober than we. He was a thick-bodied man with a dark blond beard and eyes full of hate for Erling.

"Aki is my brother, and I am a hersir," said Sigurd. "I demand to know why he is held like a thrall. The law says that a man can be killed when caught in the act of arson, but not held for killing later."

Jarl Haakon stood up, swayed and sat down again. "The matter here is not arson, or not arson only. It is murder. The murder of a hersir. For common men we have *Things* where free men can judge cases. But in these matters of war, between landed men, it falls to the lord of the land to mediate. I am the lord of the land."

The brothers bowed. "We gladly submit to the wisdom of such a man as you, Lord Haakon."

"You sodding well had better. What have you to say for yourself, Aki? By what right did you kill my friend Thorolf Skjalg and his son, and burn the hall at Sola, and try to take Erling's inheritance?"

"By the same right whereby Ogmund Karisson and Thorolf Skjalg took our farms of Oksnevad and Figgjo, to name but two," said Aki.

"My lord," said Erling, "the difference lies in this—that we won the fights, thus proving our rights before heaven. He who loses the fight loses his rights. So it has always been. So it is with Aki."

"Don't listen to this *Christian!*" shouted Aki. "How long do you think you can trust him, when there are those in the land who wish to turn you out and put a cross-man in your place? Whose side do you think he'd take, sitting there with his magic-man on the same bench?"

The jarl's eyes narrowed as he looked at Erling, and at me, and at the brothers. "I've heard that you're a Christian too now, Sigurd," he said, "and that you have famous friends."

"I claim the right to judgment by duel!" cried Aki. "I will meet Erling Skjalgsson in *holmganga!*"

"So let it be," said Jarl Haakon.

"What's this *holmganga?*" I asked Erling as we left the hall. The skies were cloudy, but it hadn't started raining yet.

"A formal duel. We fight in a marked space, and we each get three shields. The man who first draws blood can claim victory, but I think neither of us will settle for that."

"Can you take him?"

"On my worst day. I only wish I hadn't had so much to drink."

He went to put his armor on, and Aki was taken to the armory to get his own back. We trooped out to a nearby meadow, well grazed, where Erling's men cleared all the stones and dung out of a space about ten feet through, laid a large cloak on it and set stones to hold down the corners, then dug three furrows around the edges to make boundaries. Jarl Haakon examined the field and pronounced it acceptable. Erling and Aki took their places on opposite sides, each with a man to keep his extra shields. They had to wait a bit while Olmod was borne up on his litter.

Haakon called for a horn and held it up before us all.

"I hallow this horn to the honor of Thor, guardian of justice. May he watch over this ground, and make the right victorious. Skoal!"

The men cried, "Skoal!" and Haakon drank, then passed the horn to Erling and to Aki. Erling made the sign of the cross over it before drinking.

"Aki," he said, "I offer you peace before this goes further. Admit my rights and swear to let me and mine alone, and you may go home with your men and ships."

"Hear how the coward scrabbles for a bolthole, now that he faces the avenger! Don't think to talk your way out today, Erling Skjalgsson! I've sworn to drink your blood and bed Halla Asmundsdatter. Prepare to meet your southland god!"

They stepped onto the cloak. They took each other's measure, feinting and circling, testing reach and quickness.

"Strike then!" said Aki. "The first blow is yours as the challenged! Don't keep me waiting!"

The next thing I knew, Aki's head was flying

through the air, and his body, spouting blood, was collapsed on the cloak with his shattered shield on top of it. The head rolled a bit and came to rest not far from my feet. It had been the fastest thing I'd ever seen.

The men cheered, and Erling took his helmet off.

"We have seen the judgment of Thor!" shouted Jarl Haakon. "I declare before all men that the death of Thorolf shall cancel the death of Aki, and no *mansbot* may be demanded for this day's business. Furthermore, two of Aki's ships will be forfeit— the first to Erling, for his losses, the second to me for the troubling of the peace. Aki's men may go home in the third. Last of all, the sons of Erik will pay a fine of thirty-six *aurar* for the death of Aslak Skjalgsson. Let this be the end of the matter!"

Erling's men mobbed him and lifted him to their shoulders while Aki's brothers wrapped the body in the cloak and the Horder chiefs gathered around Olmod's litter, speaking in low voices.

CHAPTER VI

In the course of the feasting the free men held a *Thing*, or assembly, and acclaimed Erling hersir in his father's place by banging their weapons on their shields and making an ungodly racket.

The men half carried Jarl Haakon to his ship when the feasting was done, and he said he couldn't remember having such a good time in years. Only two men had been killed during the drinking, one of them by accident in a wrestling bout, so the peace had held.

"Thank God he's gone," said Halla as we watched his ships sail off. "Erling kept me and his sisters hidden away all the time he was here." We could hear the sisters' voices, shouting and laughing, as they skipped about like calves turned out of the byres in the spring.

"That was wise. Haakon kept himself to thralls this visit, but I'm told there are a lot of angry husbands up in the Trondelag."

"Why can't all men be like Erling?"

"Who'd sit in the lower seats?"

When the guests were gone, Erling set about making repairs at Sola. He had arranged to buy timber from a cousin, to rebuild the hall.

We were having supper at Somme one of the first evenings thereafter when Erling had Lemming brought in. Lemming had been locked up since the night of the fires, and they brought him in chains. He stood before the high seat and eyed us like a penned boar.

"Thorvald Thorirsson, known as Lemming," said Erling. "You have been accused of lighting the jarl's balefire in breach of the law of the land. What say you to this charge?"

"Hang me," croaked Lemming.

"Not until I understand better. You did not love your old master, Soti the smith, did you?"

"Bugger him."

"And you do not love your new master, Father Ailill, either?"

Lemming spat.

"And you do not love me, the lord of Sola?"

Lemming only growled.

"Then explain to me, Lemming—why did you take such risks to save the lives and wealth of so many whom you do not love?"

Lemming hung his head like a scolded child and said nothing.

"No answer?" said Erling. "Are you going to leave us with a mystery?"

Lemming still said nothing.

"Then there's nothing for it but to pass sentence. As you may have heard, I promised Jarl Haakon I'd put a rope around your neck."

Lemming raised his head and looked Erling straight in the face. His eyes were cold as caves in a glacier.

"Bring the rope I chose," said Erling. One of the men went out to the entry room and came quickly back in.

Lemming tensed his entire body, never taking his eyes off Erling, as the man laid around his neck a braided torque of pure silver, then loosed his bonds.

When Lemming reached a hand up and felt what was there, he gasped, and we all did the same.

"No man who saves my home and title, and the lives of my people, will be hanged for it, jarl or no jarl. This is the rope I give to you, Lemming, and with it your freedom. You may go or stay, as you like."

Like an oak felled after a hundred years, Lemming toppled to the floor and lay as a dead man.

Later that night, when most of the men had rolled up in their cloaks on the benches and Erling and I still sat and talked, his mother came in with a sheathed sword. She held it out in both hands and said, "This should be yours now, Erling."

"My father's sword?"

"*Smith's-Bane* was his, and his father's before him. It comes to you."

"I thought you laid it with Father in his grave. Surely he would have wished it."

"It is right that the heir should carry the sword."

"Mother, I am grateful, and I will keep it as a treasure." He took his father's sword.

"And you will bear it in battle?"

"No, that I will not. I have a better sword." He drew Smith's-Bane from its sheath. "Do you see how the steel is patterned along the inside, like wheat sheaves and writhing snakes, and bright on the edges? That's how they made swords in old times—with steel and iron pattern-welded together, and pure steel at the edge, because steel was dear. But my new Frankish sword is steel all through. It's lighter and stronger, and it won't be bent as easily."

His mother snatched the sword. "I'll take it back then, and bury it with your father! I thought you'd be glad to carry the weapon your ancestors bore with honor since the day it was found in its maker's dead hand. But I see that you care only for what is new. The old you throw off like worn clothing, whether your father's sword or your father's faith! You think this Christ too is greater because he's new!"

"No," I broke in. "Not because He's new. Because He's true. No other reason, ever."

I don't know why I said that. I didn't believe Christ was true at all. I suppose I was getting accustomed to my role.

She turned on me, her face white. "I didn't ask your counsel, god-man! Never speak to me unbidden." She spat on the floor and went out.

"Far be it from me to tell you your business, Father Ailill," said Erling, "but I gave up long ago trying to convert my mother."

I slumped on the bench. "A man must work at his trade," I said.

Erling was silent for a time, watching the flames on the hearth. "How did you feel when your father was killed?" he asked at last.

I pulled my cloak tighter around me. "It was as if—as if someone had taken a cleaver to the world, and chopped it off sheer before my feet, leaving me teetering on the edge."

"That's it," said Erling. "I felt it, but I couldn't find the words. You must stay with me always, to say these things for me."

I baptized Halla, along with a bonder and his wife and some of the thralls' children, the following Sunday. Erling gave her a brooch as a memento, and she looked happy as a bride in her white gown.

The smiles of pretty women are gall and poison oak to priests. Worst of all is to be an unbelieving priest, who cannot profit by prayer and fasting for the mortification of the flesh. And in fact a true priest can get away with some backsliding, and often does, especially in the outposts of Christendom. As a false priest I dared not.

Besides, she was Erling's woman. I would not touch Erling's woman though she implored me with tears (which was unlikely), and not only out of fear.

But that did not exorcise the memory of her eyes, and the echo of her laughter. I went out that evening and walked about the farmstead in the long dusk (I'd moved back into my own house at Sola now), hoping to lose my itch in weariness of the body. The sky was clear for a change, and the breeze carried a rumor of winter.

"You can't fight it, you know."

"Who's that?" The voice startled me. It was a soft voice, but clear.

"When have you ever curbed your lust? You'll watch her, and watch her, and someday it will be too much for you, and you'll try to take her, and

Erling will kill you, or sell you. Do you think you're really a free man?"

"I don't know what you're talking about," I said. It was an uncanny voice. It seemed to come from no direction, almost like my own thoughts, as if someone had wormed into my head and spoke from behind my eyes. I looked around in the red and silver light and saw no one. The only shapes nearby were two hillocks of earth, overgrown with heather.

"You may fool Erling, and you may fool the yokels in the church, but there are those who cannot be fooled."

"Are you God?"

"You may call me 'god' if you like. That would please me. You would do well to please me. The time is coming when you will be much in need of friends."

Yes indeed, there are devils. I ran back to my house as swiftly as I could, stumbling and ignoring it. In my haste I blundered into a large, hard body. I landed on my rump and looked up at Soti the smith, who had come up the path from the other direction.

"Out so late, god-man?" he asked. "Calling to your spirits? You come from the direction of the Melhaugs. I'd stay away from Big Melhaug were I you, especially at night. There's a dragon under that mound. It's said it was a human once, long ago, and the *haug* is its grave, but it's a dragon now, and it eats men's souls."

I said nothing, but bolted for my house. Behind me I could hear the smith laughing.

❖　　❖　　❖

I took my meals with the household at Somme, and one evening after the drinking was done, Erling called me to him and said he wanted my help.

"I've vowed to give my thralls the means to their freedom," he said. "I owe them for the night of the fires, and it seems to me a fitting task for a Christian lord. Do you agree?"

"With all my heart."

"Good. Now my problem is that I can't just turn them loose and bid them godspeed. For one thing, they're not prepared. Have you seen Lemming in the last few days?"

"From time to time. He seems to do a lot of dicing with the bodyguard. By the way, you paid me too much for him. I got him for nothing, after all."

"Say no more of it. I like to do things properly. I thought Lemming might have somewhere he wanted to go, and the silver I gave him would pay for it. But he says one place is like another. He bought a fishing boat, but lost it at dice. Now he just drinks from a cask of ale he bought, and hacks pieces off the torque and gambles them away, and when the silver's gone God knows what he'll do."

"And you're afraid the others would do the same."

"I can't afford it. By our law a master answers for the living of any thrall he frees. I need to see that my freedmen have livelihoods."

"Have you something in mind?"

"I have a plan. I want to give each thrall a set amount of work to do each day. When that is done, each should have a piece of land or a task or craft they can ply, to earn silver. When they earn the price of their freedom I'll sell it to them, and set them up with some land and a cow. That way I can get people on land that's fallow now, and they'll pay rents and my lordship will prosper. And there's something else . . ."

"Yes?"

"You've been to Visby. There's a class of people there, and in other market towns, who are neither farmers nor priests nor bodyguards nor landholders. They're more like Soti. They live by working at crafts, and selling what they make for their own profit. The lords of the towns tax them. I think it would be profitable to have such people of my own."

"But you have no town."

"I've thought of founding a market, perhaps just in the winter. Risa Bay, north of Kolness, might be a good place."

"You want to train your thralls as craftsmen?"

"Do you think they're too stupid?"

"My lord, I was a thrall too not long since."

"Indeed. I apologize."

"There's something else you could do, my lord."

"What's that?"

"The silver they pay you. You could use it to buy more thralls."

"I'll have to. I can't run my farms without thralls."

"And you could offer them the same bargain. You'd have the hardest-working thralls in Norway!"

Erling frowned. "I don't know. It might make me a laughingstock among the landholders."

"It would make you great in the eyes of the Lord. And it would pay you well! How much would the landholders laugh when they saw your fields wide and rich, and your storehouses full of grain and silver?"

Erling smiled. "You could be right. If my vow works as we hope, it might be worth considering. It might well be. And it would be fitting for a Christian lord. We've never had Christian lords in Norway. Someone will have to show the way."

"Very true."

"I need a man to be in charge. Someone with brains and a heart. You said that you read a little. Can you write?"

"A bit. Not much."

"More than anyone else here. I'd like you to keep records so that there'll be no question about accounts."

"I can work out some kind of system of marks and ciphers, I suppose. I'd need parchment and pens and ink."

"You'll get them."

"I'll see what I can do then, my lord."

"Then God bless us both!" said Erling Skjalgsson.

ChAPTER VII

I called Erling's thralls together in the church the next Sunday after mass and laid out his plan. The scheme, I said, would begin in the spring, with the spading.

"But how long will it take?" asked Turlough, a big, black Irishman who talked, as they all did, haltingly, careful not to misspeak.

"That's up to you. If you work hard in the evenings, perhaps two years—perhaps less. If you don't work so hard it may take three or four years. Or more. And of course the weather will make a difference."

"Can we go home then?" asked a woman named Bridget, no longer young, with a wind-dried, seamed face. How old had she been when they took her from Ireland?

"That's up to you. You'll be free to work and save, and go where you like. Erling hopes that most of you will choose to stay here."

"What about our children?" asked a Norse thrall woman named Thorbjorg.

"Children under three go with their mothers. Those over twelve may earn their own freedom."

"How do we know we won't be cheated?" asked Turlough.

"That hangs on whether you trust me. I'll keep the records. I'll make a sign like this on a sheet of parchment—this will be your sign, Turlough—and when your grain or handiwork is brought in to the stores and weighed or valued, you'll be credited with its worth in silver ounces, and I'll make a mark for each ounce beside your sign. When the ounces reach half your value, I'll take the sheet to my lord Erling, and he will declare you a freedman. You won't be fully free, of course, until the other half is paid or you hold your freedom-feast according to law."

"Why not just pay us and let us hold the money?"

"Two reasons. The first is that we don't trust you. I'll not lie about that. Look at Lemming if you wonder why. The second is that it's too easy to rob a thrall, and I'm afraid you'd have the devil's own time getting justice against the thief if he's a free man. But what you earn is yours, and if you have trouble that requires ready money, come to me, and I'll speak to Erling, and we'll give you the silver if we agree it's needed."

"It's an insult, that's what it is," said Turlough.

"No," said Bridget. "It's a better chance than we ever hoped to get in this land, and I thank God for it. Count me in, Father Ailill, and see how fast I can buy myself."

A knarr sailed in with the timber from Hordaland, and Erling announced that work on the hall would begin the next day. He asked me to be there at the start to bless the building.

As I walked in the mist with a bowl full of what I called holy water the next morning, I found a small crowd gathered about the site, both men and women, with Soti at their head. He led a goat on a rope, and was trading hard words with Erling.

"It has been thus since men first lived at Sola, and so must it be!" he shouted. "The people expect you to uphold the custom, and the gods and spirits will not brook change! You do not know what you dare!"

"I know what I dare," said Erling. He spoke low, but there were red spots on his cheekbones. "I know that my God is greater than all your gods and spirits together, and all men together, and this hall will be hallowed in His name, and His alone! I bear with you, Soti, because of my mother, but on this I stand firm. Now go away, and take your goat with you."

Ragna pushed through the crowd. "If your father were alive, he'd flay the skin off your back!"

"If my father were alive he'd be lord of Sola and could do what he liked. I am lord of Sola now, and I must do what I think best."

"Do not think yourself beyond your father's power!"

The voice was a woman's, and it belonged to Soti's red-haired wife. She was much younger than her husband, a thin woman with a longish nose, but not unlovely. I'd seen her the night of the fires, kneeling and chanting in the house at the stronghold. Her name was Ulvig. She held by the hand a fair, blue-eyed girl, about twelve, their daughter.

"Your father is nearby, sleeping in his howe," said Ulvig. "Do you think he forgets his home and its affairs? Do you think he cares not whether his gods are welcome in their accustomed places? Do you think he will not act?"

Ragna said, "When the gods see the hall built without sacrifice, they will want their gifts with interest. Are you willing to pay the price they will ask, my son?"

"I owe nothing to the gods. Let them howl for their blood."

"They will do more than howl," said Ulvig.

"I fear them not," said Erling. "I have Christ's messenger with me, whose merest word will put all spirits to flight." He reached a hand out and clapped me on the shoulder.

I felt very cold of a sudden.

They all watched me as I went about the site, sprinkling water and reciting scraps of Latin. Inside I prayed, because I could do nothing else, to the God who had sat and watched while Maeve was raped and my parents and brother killed. To the God who did nothing to protect us from capture and slavery. Who did nothing while wars raged over honest people's farms and wrecked their harvests to starve them, who did nothing while children died of pestilence, who watched the strong and the selfish put their boots on the faces of the weak. I knew what to expect from that God, but where else could I turn?

"*Gungnir.*"

It was Soti speaking. He repeated, "*Gungnir.*" I knew the word. It was the name of Odin's spear.

The people took it up. "*Gungnir.*"

"*Gungnir.*

"*Gungnir.*

"Gungnir."

The chant grew louder and louder, and drowned my baby Latin altogether.

They chanted until I finished, then went silent. The wind came up strong of a sudden, out of the north.

"Odin has heard," said Soti. "Watch yourself at night, Christ-thrall."

The workmen (mostly farmers working out obligations to Erling) had only begun setting the wallposts and pillars into the earth when the rain began. It rained harder and harder, until each man's clothing weighed heavy as a sheep and no one could see, and they had to stop. The rain continued, and the men went home to their farms at last, saying this did not bode well.

It did us no good that lightning struck one of the pillars that night and left it in two pieces.

The next day it threatened rain again, and the farmers told Erling they would do their service in some other way. They would not labor on a cursed building. The red spots appeared on his cheeks, but he let them go.

"Why not let the thralls work on it?" I asked Erling. "They can start earning their freedom now. They're none of them skilled carpenters, but they know how to work, and you must have some Christian workman who can guide them and won't be afraid of the old gods."

"I have Christian workmen," said Erling. "But I'm not sure they don't fear the old gods."

"You're not going to give up?"

"No. Not if I have to raise my hall with my own hands. Say a mass for my hall, Father Ailill."

I almost sobbed. "My lord," I said, "I would God that He had sent you a worthier priest."

"Father Ailill, I've never stopped thanking God for you. I would not trade you for the Archbishop of Cantaraborg."

I said his mass, just as if it would do some good.

I was sleeping badly, and as I lay waking that particular night I heard a tapping at my door.

I lay in my robe for warmth, although I hadn't yet moved into the box-bed, so I sat up on the bench and poked the hearth fire and then went to the door.

It was a young woman who entered, a plump thrall girl of Soti's. I didn't know her name, as she did not come to church. She was pretty in the porridge-faced way you often see in Norway, and her short hair was yellow.

"My master sent me, Father Ailill."

"What does he want?"

"He says I am to lie with you tonight."

I was surprised. I would have expected a better plan from Soti. "Run home and tell him I said no," I answered, heading back to my bed.

"Please, Father, he'll beat me if you refuse."

That was more like Soti. "Wait a moment," I said, while I pulled on my shoes. Then I took her by the wrist and led her back to Soti's house.

I banged on the door until a thrall woman opened it.

"I want to see your master," I told her.

"He's in bed."

"Then wake him."

"I dare not!"

"Then I'll do it." I pushed past her and strode down the hearthway to the box-beds. "Which one does he sleep in?" I asked.

The woman pointed with a trembling hand, then ran out.

I banged on the box. "Soti, you bastard, wake up!" The thrall girl tugged on my hand, trying to get away. I held her fast.

The door opened and Soti's head appeared. "What do you want, god-man?" he growled.

"Keep your thrall girls at home. I don't want them."

"What are you babbling about?"

"You sent this girl to me with a threat to beat her if I didn't lie with her. I'm telling you to leave off, and if I hear that you've laid a hand on her, Lord Erling will be told of it!"

Soti crawled out and sat with his feet on the step, a blanket around him. "I don't know what you're talking about, god-man. You know you can't believe what these thralls tell you. Half of them don't even believe in the gods, so how can you trust their word? This girl has been telling you tales. I'm sorry she disturbed your sleep. She'll be punished."

"Leave her alone, I said!"

"Fine, fine, whatever you want," said Soti, and crawled back into his bed and shut the door.

The girl fell on the floor, sobbing. I patted her head and told her it would be all right, then trudged home and lay down. I could not sleep.

Again, the tapping at my door. "Father Ailill! Father Ailill!"

It was the same girl. I opened to her, and she slumped against my chest.

I led her inside and lit a lamp. She'd gotten the kind of skillful beating that leaves no lasting marks and breaks no bones, but her eyes were blackened, and she bled from a corner of her mouth.

"My master says . . . you must lie with me or he'll beat me again, and say again that it was all my idea. If you go to Lord Erling, he'll say the same, and beat me worse. Please, Father, is it so terrible to lie with me?"

I stroked her hair. "No, child," I said, "you don't understand. A priest isn't allowed to lie with a woman. He may not even marry, not in law."

She wept then, and I told her she might lie the night on the other bench.

She curled up there with thanks, and I listened to her breathing a long time. When I woke in the morning I found her warm against my back, and my male parts were aware. I jumped up and went out to walk it off.

That day the weather was better, and I spoke to the thralls and got several men willing to work for their freedom-silver. Erling had a man to train them, and they began the labor. It went slowly, and the foreman cursed them loudly and often as they fumbled the staves in the rocky ground.

"At this rate the work won't be finished before snow comes," said Erling.

"They'll learn. Once they get the feel of the work, and know what it's like to do a job well, for their own good, they'll be fine."

"I wonder. We've always believed that there is

no chance in life. If you become a king, it's because you were fated to be a king, because you are kingly. If you become a slave, it's because you are slavish, and you run into your right place as water into a hole. Can these things be changed?"

"My lord, we were all born thralls of sin, fated for Hell because we were ourselves hellish. But Christ had mercy on us, and paid a great price to make us sons of God. It seems He believed that people change."

Erling granted that was true, and I walked off wondering if Christ had been too hopeful.

I waited for her knock that night, and it came at last.

"Father," she said, "my master says you must lie with me truly, as a man lies with a woman. Otherwise he'll kill me." She fell on her knees at my feet. "A master may kill a thrall, Father, and there is no punishment. None may interfere. Don't let him kill me, Father!"

She was soft and warm, and she tried very hard to please me. And oh, she did please me. It was sweet as laughter to lie in her arms, and touch her, and do all that was forbidden a priest. It was as if I eased a cramp in my soul, and when I slept at last, I slept better than any night since I'd left Ireland.

I was awakened by another knocking, this time very loud. I opened the door to find a man standing in the morning light. "Lord Erling sent me," he said. "He wants you at the new hall, right away."

I ran there and found a crowd of people gathered

around one of the pillars. They were looking up to where a spear had been driven into it, about two men high. A walrus-hide rope was tied to the spear, near its head, and from the rope a man hung. He hung close against the pillar, a dark shape against the pale sky, for the spear had been dragged to a downward angle by his weight.

It was Turlough the thrall.

Soti the smith was there, and he said, "See—Odin has taken his first sacrifice! And it is far from over."

Erling said, "Get a ladder and cut him down."

A raven flapped down, black as blindness, and perched atop the pillar.

CHAPTER VIII

Erling, Steinulf and I walked about the building site after the body had been taken away. The spear still stood in the wood.

"Who could drive a spear deep enough at that height to bear a man's weight?" asked Steinulf. "I couldn't do it. You couldn't do it. Soti or Lemming couldn't do it. Sigurd the Volsung could have done it maybe, or Svipdag, but such men are rare nowadays."

"It happened. There must be a way," said Erling.

"Oh, there's a way. It's on everybody's lips. One of the gods, or one of the underground folk, or a walker-again."

Erling turned and looked at him. "You speak of the newly dead."

I said, "No, my lord, not your father or brother. Their souls have gone to a place far from Sola. If their bodies or anyone's walk again—I'm not saying they do, I'm only supposing—then the spirits that use them are not theirs. Your father and brother were human sinners, no worse. This is demon's work."

Erling said, "Couldn't someone have hammered the spear in—climbed a ladder somehow and—?"

"Can't have done," said Steinulf. "The higher you climbed the ladder, the further you'd get from the butt of the spear. That's a six-foot shaft. No man has that kind of reach. And someone would have heard."

"I'd thought your blessing would frighten the spirits off, Father Ailill," said Erling.

"My lord, the holy apostles themselves found some spirits unmasterable except by prayer and fasting. I'm a weak reed to lean on when you face demons of this power."

"Can you fight them with prayer and fasting then?"

"I can try, my lord, but I'm no apostle. I fear the Lord hearkens not much to my prayers."

"You must do what you can. I ask no more of any of my warriors. You eat at my table, you must stand in my shield wall."

I bowed my head. "As you command, my lord. I've had no breakfast. I will live on water until this business is ended."

"I will have my hall," said Erling. "It will not be hallowed to Odin. Not while I am above ground. Father, I think it would be good for me to join you in this battle. I will fast also. Now let's see Turlough's family."

They shared a low turf house with three other families. There were no box-beds, but there were low stone partitions dividing households. The place stank of sweat and fish and unwashed wool. Turlough's wife, a shapeless, brown woman named Copar, sat leaning against a partition and scrambled to her feet when we entered. Her three dirty, snuffling children clung to her skirts. She bowed, unsteadily. Someone had given her beer.

"I am sorry for your loss, woman," said Erling.

"It's very kind of you I'm sure," said Copar. "It's hard to understand the ways of the Lord."

"Your man fought for me the night of the fires. By his death he has earned your freedom—yours and your children's."

The woman gasped and fell at Erling's feet. "No, my lord! Don't send us out by ourselves—not now when we've none to protect us! It's a cold land in a cold world, and things walk at night that should not walk—"

Erling put his hand on her head. "No one will send you out. We'll find you a living first. Only I want you to know that your man didn't die for nothing. He would have wanted you free, I think."

"Aye, my lord," she hiccupped. "He was a hard man, and he beat me when he was drunk, but it was because he was shamed to be a thrall, you see, and mad at the world. We're in your hands, my lord. Do what you will."

Erling spoke to each of the children, and asked their names, and gave Copar some bread from the hall. Then we went out and breathed fresh air again.

"It's best to believe in fate, Father Ailill," he said. "I must think those people different from me. If they're not, it's almost beyond bearing."

"What now, my lord?"

"I'll see about getting the thralls out to build today. You will go to the church and say masses. Then get some sleep. Tonight you and I will watch together at the hall."

❖   ❖   ❖

I sleep badly when I'm hungry, and worse when I'm frightened. When the voice began to speak, I wondered who had come in without my hearing; then I knew it for the voice from Big Melhaug.

"It all comes from the sin you call superbia, overweening pride."

"I am many kinds of sinner," I muttered, "but I don't think I'm especially proud of myself."

"No? You talk of your god as if he were your father; as if he felt and pitied."

"God help us if He does not."

"Why should he? On what grounds do you assume his love? On the word of a Jew a thousand years dead? Who could believe such things?" Did I see eyes—unblinking, yellow snakeish eyes? *"Does the hawk pity the rabbit? Does the wolf pity the sheep? Where in all the world is there mercy for weakness except in the ravings of your religion? When has this mercy ever been shown? And what use is mercy unshown?"*

"Then what is there but despair and death?"

"There is courage! Face the darkness! Be strong enough to make the sacrifices. Harden your heart. Life can be a wonderful thing, but you must seize it by force!"

"My Lord Erling believes. I can at least believe in his faith a while yet."

"Don't think that you will thereby prevent the sacrifices. The sacrifices will be made. . . ."

"There's a saga of a hero named Bjovulf," said Erling as we sat under the stars and purple heavens that night amid the ribs of the hall. He was in full armor and had two casting spears at hand. I was armed with the crucifix from the church. "He came to Hroar, King of Denmark, to rid him of a troll who broke into his hall each night and killed men."

"What happened to him?"

"Oh, he killed the troll. Ripped his arm out of the socket and let him run away to bleed to death. There were great men in those days. Are you my Bjovulf, Father Ailill?"

"You need no heroes, my lord. This Bjovulf can have been little ahead of the man I saw fight Aki."

"Even Bjovulf couldn't fight all the heathens in Jaeder and all the gods of Asgard together."

"How did you become a Christian, my lord? What keeps you firm? I've heard of your king Haakon the Good. He tried to live as a Christian, but the lords made him sacrifice and he was buried as a heathen, they say."

"We went a-viking in Ireland," said Erling, "my father and I. I saw a man—a priest—die for Christ. We were holding him and others for ransom, and some of the lads were having a lark and thought it would be sport to make him eat horsemeat. He refused, and the lads took offense at his manner. They tied him to a tree and shot him full of arrows. He died singing a hymn. I thought he was as brave as Hogni, who laughed while Atli cut his heart out. My father said not to talk rot, that a man who dies over what food he'll eat dies for less than nothing."

"I've never seen a true martyrdom," I said. "I'll wager it wasn't like the pictures."

"No," said Erling. "It looked nothing like the pictures in the churches. Martyrs die like other men, bloody and sweaty and pale, and loosening their bowels at the end."

"So I'd feared."

"What of it? The pictures are no cheat. Just because I saw no angels, why should I think there were no angels there? Because I didn't see Christ opening Heaven to receive the priest, how can I say Christ was not there? If someone painted a picture of that priest's death, and left out the angels and Christ and Heaven opening, he'd not have painted truly. The priest sang as he died. Only he knows what he saw in that hour, but what he saw made him strong.

"I saw a human sacrifice once too, in Sweden. When it was done, and my father had explained how the gods need to see our pain, so they'll know we aren't getting above ourselves, I decided I was on the Irish priest's side."

"And you're sure our God doesn't need to see our pain?"

"Not in the same way. I serve a God who will not have human sacrifice. You've never believed in human sacrifice, but I did once, so I can tell you it makes no little difference."

I said nothing for awhile. A cloud bank was moving in from the northwest. I hoped we wouldn't get rained on.

"They tell me you've taken a leman," said Erling.

I jerked my head up. I'd almost fallen asleep. I said, "It's often done."

"Father Ethelbald said the Irish church was strong in forbidding such for priests."

"We are, we are. But the nights are long, and the

flesh is weak, and many think it's better to cleave to one woman than to lust after the whole race of them."

"It's one of Soti's thralls, isn't it?"

I didn't want to talk about this. "Yes, as it happens," I said.

"Is there some trouble, Father Ailill? Does Soti hold anything over you? I'll help if you ask."

"It's . . . it's between Soti and me, and nothing you need trouble over."

"Be that as may be, remember I'm ready to help. As you yourself said, Soti is as great a devil as you'll find in this land. He does nothing in sport."

"I'll remember, my lord," I said.

Why didn't I tell him? Did I think he couldn't protect the girl? Was I ashamed of my weakness?

The true reason, I think, was that if Erling helped I'd have no further excuse for bedding her. I didn't want to stop, and a small surrender to Soti seemed worth it. A mere sin of the flesh, after all, and all in the open, would put me under no great obligation to the smith.

Someone screamed in the night.

It was a loud scream, and a long scream. A man with a belly wound, or a woman in fouled childbirth, screams like that sometimes.

"Down by the byres," said Erling, and set off running.

I followed, all the hairs on my back lifting.

People came tumbling out of houses to gape at us, the men carrying axes. We reached the byres and ran around them, then poked in the grass and among the stones, finding nothing.

Half-dressed men came to join us, and no one found anything.

"Oh God," said Erling at last. "My hall."

He raced back as fast as he had come, with me at his heels.

It was a different pillar this time, but the same kind of burden. Erling seized the man's legs and lifted him, but he was already dead.

CHAPTER IX

Erling spent the night praying in the church, knees on cold stone. I tried to keep vigil with him, but fell asleep.

"This has gone far enough!"

The voice of Ragna woke me. She swept in followed by a serving woman.

"What kind of troll's cavern is this place? Give us light!" The serving woman had come prepared with a soapstone lamp, and she went, very irreverently, up to the altar and lit my tallow candles.

"Mother, this is a church," said Erling, rising stiffly.

"That means nothing to me. I have words for you, and they will be said. And you will listen!"

"Of course, Mother." Erling sat on the bench.

"Do you know what they say out there?"

"I suppose they're saying that the gods are against me and my luck is gone."

"They say that. They also say that the ancient kings of Rogaland have heirs in Ireland, and perhaps it's time to call them back."

Erling stretched his neck. "I thought it was something like that."

"And what do you intend to do about it?"

"I will catch whatever's doing this, and kill it."

"Even if it's your father?"

"Not my father. His walker-again. Just a devil in his body."

"Slowly, one bit at a time, you cast aside everything that ever you believed, everything your father and I believed."

"I must do what is right."

"People are dying, Erling! *Your* people are dying. First it was a thrall. Last night it was a free man. Tomorrow night it will be a warrior, or perhaps one of us. When you are dead, who will look to my welfare?"

"We have many kin, Mother, if it comes to that, but it won't come to that. I will stop this thing."

"Bait not the gods, my son! You are strong and brave, but you are not stronger and braver than fate! You are proud—like your father and his father, and Horda-Kari and all the rest of that blood. And my blood too—I come of proud stock also. But there is such a thing as too much pride. Ask your priest— is there not a sin of pride?"

Erling said, "Please go now, Mother. I want to speak to my priest."

"I'll go and sew your shroud. If you are set on making me weep, I must be prepared."

She gusted out, and Erling remained sitting and ran his hands over his face. "I've prayed most of the night, Father. I thought there'd be a sign from God."

"And?"

"Nothing. Not a word. Am I too proud? Was my father right? Is it folly to hazard your life over a footling matter like food, or a goat buried under a doorway?"

The man fed me to be his priest, so I answered him as a priest.

"My lord, when the early Christians were martyred in Romaborg, all that was asked of them was to sprinkle a little incense on an altar. They didn't have to pray to or believe in the false god, just go through a ceremony that even their enemies didn't believe in. But they would not. They let themselves be burned alive, and torn by wild beasts; they let their flesh be ripped by pincers. They accepted it not only for themselves, but for their wives and children, and they shouted encouragement to them as they watched them die. It was a stubborn thing they did, and wrongheaded from any sensible point of view. But it was not pride. And in the end they won, although they never lived to see it."

"Yes," said Erling. "That's what I learned from the sagas when I was a boy. That it matters not when you die, or by what means, but only how you face it. A young man in a tight place, facing deadly odds. Such was Christ himself, at the battle of Calvary."

What would he have done had I counseled him to be sensible? Why didn't I counsel him to be sensible? I truly do not know.

Erling said, "I must find a place to sleep or I won't last the night."

I said mass for the two of us, and he went out. I snuffed the candles and went to my own house to sleep. My stomach whimpered like a dog at the door, and sleep, along with a draught of well water, was the only relief I could offer it.

Halla called to me as I was going inside, and I stayed to greet her.

"You've got to stop him," she said.

"I cannot. I wouldn't if I could."

"He'll be killed!"

"If you wanted a man unlikely to be killed, you should have chosen a herdsman or a farmer." Or a priest, I might have added, except that in this land priesthood was risky.

"If it were only men, I wouldn't be afraid! Erling can defeat any man!"

"Well you should be afraid of men. There are such things as arrows."

"Fighting the gods is different!"

"We fight the gods every day, my daughter. Odin with his deceit, Thor with his anger, Frey with his lust—they all live within us, and they threaten terrible things if we deny them their sacrifices. A Christian must learn not to believe their lies, even when they seem truth of all truth. Even when it means death . . ."

"I'll be glad when you're dead!" she shouted. "If you have to be a martyr, good for you. But my Erling!" She ran off, weeping.

Cold eyes, yellow-green and round. *Why do you say such things? Why are you so cruel? You are no martyr. If you had lived in those early days, you'd have sprinkled all the incense they asked for, and thanked them. Whom do you look to impress by this self-slaughter?*

"No!" I said through clenched teeth, and covered my ears to keep out the voice of the dragon.

"It's time."

Erling, standing in my doorway, woke me. I shook myself and got up to join him.

"Are you hungry?" he asked.

"I could eat that old cheese you Norwegians like."

"Then let's be done with this, and we'll eat till we burst."

"It'll be Friday in the morning."

"Then we'll eat all the fish in the sea."

We set out together for the hall site. No work had been done there that day. There was a sliver of moon. The sun balanced on the horizon, ready to tip off for the short night.

We sat facing each other, our backs against two of the pillars.

"What are those birds you have painted on your shield?" I asked him.

"Eagles."

"Why did you choose that emblem?"

"I watched two eagles battle once. I thought it the grandest thing I'd ever seen. Soaring and spinning, talons and beaks, far above the earth. If men could fight that way, would they have the courage?"

"I think you would, my lord. That's not flattery. I've seen you fight."

Erling laughed. "Everyone talks about my duel with Aki Eriksson, the easiest of my life. He fought like a sheep. My mother could have killed him. But folk tell the story as if I did something great. I think some day I may regret killing that half-wit."

"Why so?"

"Sigurd Eriksson, his brother, is a good man, and a Christian. They tell a tale about him. They say that when he was serving King Valdemar in Russia he visited a marketplace in Estonia. There he saw a handsome thrall lad. He thought the lad looked wonderfully like his own sister Astrid, widow of King Trygvi Olafsson of the Vik. Astrid had disappeared years before, fleeing Norway by ship. When he spoke to the boy, he learned he was indeed Astrid's son Olaf, and that they'd been caught by Vikings and sold into thralldom.

"He bought the lad and set him free, and they say he's a man grown now, a great warrior and a Christian. I'd like to meet this Olaf Trygvesson. I think Jarl Haakon may have come to the end of his thread—

"What's that sound?"

I listened. "Footsteps. A lot of them. Coming towards us."

"Do you think all the gods are coming?"

I began the Pater Noster as we stood and faced the noise, trampings up the walled path. Erling held his shield before him, spear ready, and I held the crucifix high.

It was dark now, and they were shapes in the dimness as they approached, twenty, fifty of them. Starlight glinted on helmets, spear points and shield bosses.

"Lord Erling!"

"Steinulf!" shouted Erling. "I told you men to stay at Somme!"

Steinulf stepped forward. "We talked about it, my lord. We decided that you had no right to demand it. If you die alone, we are shamed for life. You have the right to command us to die. You have no right to command us to live."

"Not all of you are Christians. Did you all come?"

"Every man."

"Then it seems there's nothing I can do. Watch with us. We mean to end it tonight."

The wind blew colder, and clouds rode in on it, shrouding the stars. The men sat back to back, sharing warmth. It was black as Judas' grave.

> *"Three knots bind the heart;*
> *Three links chain the mind;*
> *Three words make a man a craven.*
> *These are the knots that bind the heart:*
> *Never to touch the fair girls again.*
> *Never to drink the brown ale again.*
> *Never to do the deeds that men remember."*

I thought I'd heard the voice before. It sang on the wind, and it sang against the wind, and it sang under the wind.

> *"Three knots bind the heart;*
> *Three links chain the mind;*
> *Three words make a man a craven.*
> *These are the links that chain the mind:*
> *Never to hold your son in your arms.*
> *Never to see your son raise a beard.*
> *Never to sit by his side in the hall with the*
> *warriors."*

The wind came up stronger, and raindrops fell, cold as a river under ice, and I began shivering to rattle the flesh off my bones.

"Three knots bind the heart;
Three links chain the mind;
Three words make a man a craven.
These are the words that cravens make:
'Sometimes the arrow leaves you blind.
Sometimes the spear will leave you lame.
Sometimes the sword will geld you and not
kill you.' "

"A hymn, Father Ailill! Sing us a psalm!" It was Erling's voice, but it seemed very far away. I tried to sing, but my teeth were chattering. I bit my tongue.

The world was very black.

There was one light in all the world.

It came towards us, over the meadow, from the direction of Thorolf Skjalg's grave.

We all saw him. The men groaned. They wept. They yammered like dogs. Some shouted, "Thorolf! It's my Lord Thorolf come out to walk again!"

He was a tall man, dressed in full armor, with shield and spear and sword at his belt. He glowed all over with blue fire. He was coming to us.

The men began to beat at the earth, and at the pillars, and at each other. "He walks again!" they cried. "He comes to make the sacrifice!"

"Run!" someone shouted. "We've got to run!" But no one ran. No one stood on his feet. A few tried to crawl, but most stayed in their places, kneeling or sitting, watching the walker-again come nearer and nearer.

"It's the battle-fetter!" someone cried. "Odin has set the battle-fetter on us!"

All the men groaned and rolled on the ground, and I rolled with them.

Thorolf came ever nearer. I could see his eyes now. They were green-yellow, round and cold.

"Death!" cried a man. "It is our death, each and all of us!"

The wailing rose like steam from a bog in winter.

Then a hand fell on my shoulder. I could not see the face of the man, but I knew his voice. Erling said, "A psalm, Father! I don't ask you to fight, but sing me a psalm that I may fight—that one about the mountains falling into the sea, and shaking!"

I set my forehead to the stones and tried to gather my wits. I found I still had the crucifix in my hands, gripped so tightly it was wet with my blood. I tried to moisten my lips. I licked the blood from my hands.

"Deus noster refugium . . ." I croaked.

"God is our refuge and strength, a very present help in trouble.

Therefore we will not fear, though the earth be removed, and though the mountains be carried into the midst of the sea.

Though the waters thereof roar and be troubled, though the mountains shake with the swelling thereof.

There is a river, the streams whereof shall make glad the city of God, the holy place of the tabernacles of the most High.

God is in the midst of her; she shall not be moved: God shall help her and that right early."

I could not see the fight that Erling fought. Only now and then the witchlight of the walker-again flickered, and I knew that flicker for Erling's shadow.

I saw the demon cast his spear, and saw his mouth open in something like laughter. I saw him fend what must have been Erling's spears in return. I heard the whacking of blades on shields, and saw the dead man leap and whirl; and his leaps were head-high, and his whirls faster than birds' wings. I spoke my psalm again and again, gripping the crucifix as a drowning man clings to driftwood, and I wept for my lord, and all the men wept for him, and they cried, "My Lord Erling! My Lord Erling! I'd come to you if I could, but I am only a man, and not a hero, and I weep to see you die alone, as heroes always must."

And I found I was saying the same.

Faces blossomed before my inner eye.

My father saying, "Sparrow-heart! Stop wiggling or I'll leave the splinter in your flesh, and you'll carry it to your grave. Crying too? Such a baby! Are you my son or a heifer-calf?"

The abbot saying, "Hold still. You weren't afraid to transgress, now take your licks like a man!"

And a boy named Aoife who put his red face close to mine so I could smell his breath and said, "Now admit you're a liar or I'll break your finger. I'll do it too—you know I did it to Dathi and I'll do it to you. I like the sound when the bone snaps. So say it. Say, 'I'm a filthy liar.' Say it now. . . ."

I do not know how long it took. We watched—we could not do otherwise—and it went on and on. Parry and thrust and leap and slash. Strike with the sword and strike with the shield boss. Circle and watch, then in with a flurry of blows.

But at last we knew that the morning was coming.

And as the sun edged the eastern mountains, the battle-fetter was loosed. And we looked at one another, crouched and kneeling and wet and filthy, useless weapons flung about in the stones and dirt, and we were filled with shame, and groaned aloud. And we scrambled to our feet and rushed into the meadow.

Two bodies lay on their backs in the stubble.

One had once been Thorolf Skjalg. It was ugly and putrid but no longer a danger. Steinulf struck its head off with his sword so that it might not walk again.

The other was Erling, bloody and pale. We knelt about him, weeping. "Bjovulf can have died no better," I said.

"Sigurd died not so well," said another.

Someone else said, "He breathes!"

CHAPTER X

We bore Erling to my house on a shield (not his own—that was smashed) while some of the other men reburied Thorolf with his head at his hip.

Two men had to hold Erling still as we carried him. He thrashed about and cried, "Father!" or "Jesus!" or "No, no!"

Ragna arrived from Somme about the time we got him into my box-bed. No one had told her her son was hurt; no one needed to. She sent everyone out but me.

She leaned into the bed and began pulling off his brynje. "Lie still, my son, your mother's here. All is well. It is good that courage is passed along in the blood," she sighed. "I think few women could bear what we heroes' mothers must."

Erling had another fit then, and she held his shoulders and spoke soothing words, and he grew calmer at last, but he did not know us. He babbled to himself, and his eyes rolled.

"I should not have buried Smith's-Bane with Thorolf," she said as she continued stripping him. "A blade turned against kin is unlucky, and borne by a walker-again it can be venomous."

"He's very strong," I said. "And there's no serious bleeding."

"There is a wound though. Here—do you see? Near the heart. That it bleeds not is the unhealthiest thing of all. When did you ever see a wound this size—three fingers wide—that did not bleed? Don't say it; I will. Only on a corpse. This is a deadly hurt, a fey sore. Hardly or never is a wound like this healed."

"There must be some medicine—"

"Oh aye. Battlefield herb. Little Hero. A paste of stinging nettle. We can get them and try them, but they won't be enough for this. We need help from the gods, and will the gods help my Erling?"

I had no reply to that.

"What of your god, priest? Does he heal the sick?"

"It's said He does. For great saints. I'm not a great saint."

"What good are you, god-man?"

I slumped on the bench. "God knows," I said.

I could not forget my terror in the night. It had been like a long fall; it had been like slow smothering. There was a wound near my heart too—having been mastered so utterly by fear, would I ever master myself again? Something had broken inside me. Would it heal?

Someone came in the door. I looked up to see Ulvig, the red-haired wife of Soti. She carried a goatskin bag. "I have herbs and runes of healing," she said.

Ragna flew at her. "Out! Out! Get away from my son, you witch!" She bore the woman out the door and told the bullyboys, "Don't let her near the house!

Take her bag and burn it unopened! Do it now!"

"Don't stare at me," she said when she came back. "I'd be glad of Ulvig's skill were it honest. She's been a help to me often. But in this we are not allies. She would kill my Erling for the gods' sake. Her herbs would be nearly right, but only nearly. Her runes would be cut just on the edge of wrong. Only a master would know the difference. But they would sicken my son. I know Ulvig too well.

"I have none to lean on but you, god-man. My gods and spirits are of no help here. So do your magic. Go hungry, and pray, and sing over your holy meal. Light candles. Do you want to ward your only protector? Do you want to show all Jaeder the power of your god? Then save my son. Because I promise you, if he dies there will be none to avenge you when you die, and you will surely die."

I had not broken my fast. I did not break it in the days that followed, days of impassioned, craven pleading to a God I had denied, broken only by spells when I lost my senses and fell on the stones of the church floor for hours at a time.

Later that first day I woke to find Halla giving me water, holding my head in her lap like a child's. I crawled to the altar and prayed when I was refreshed, and she knelt beside me and kept me company, nor left me except to fetch more water.

I prayed all the prayers I knew. I opened the psalter and went through it from beginning to end, then began again at the first page. The colors of the illuminations shimmered before my eyes, and the misshapen people who dwelt in them seemed to walk about and speak like living men.

I forgot how to count the days.

I don't know when it was Halla said to me, "You must eat, Father, or you die."

I took a sip of water and went back to my prayers without answering. To look on her beauty would be a kind of food, and I refused it.

God, all-knowing and craftier than any man, had found the hook to draw me back to Him. The hook was fear, cold as a January night. No, more than fear. Cowardice. The whining cowardice of a dog too much beaten.

God did not care for my love. All He asked was that I bow my neck like a defeated soldier, that He might put His foot on it.

"*Salvum me fac, Deus. . . .*"

"*Save me, O God; for the waters are come in unto my soul.*

I sink in deep mire, where there is no standing; I am come into deep waters, where the floods overflow me.

I am weary of my crying; my throat is dried; mine eyes fail while I wait for my God. . . ."

I thought one of the patriarchs in the illuminations in my psalter looked wonderfully like my old abbot. He had the same face, and the same stooped back, and when he walked about in his painted rectangle, he had the same stiff shamble.

He said to me, "It must be true that the mercy of the Almighty is boundless, for here you are, still above ground, while better men and women are in Hell. I know not why they send me to you a second time, except that such menial errands are salutary for a soul in Purgatory. But what good it can do a child of perdition like you I cannot guess.

"Nevertheless, I bear you a message, which you will doubtless misconstrue, making your last state worse than your first, and filling your cup of iniquity to the brim.

"Here is the message I bring—if you wish your foreign lord to live, do as I tell you. . . ."

When I came to my senses I found that I'd fallen asleep on my knees, the psalter on the stones in front of me. It was dark in the church.

I tried to stand, but could not raise myself. A hand took my arm and helped me up. I looked into Halla's eyes, hollow with hunger and sorrow. My leg bones felt as if they'd been sharpened at the ends.

Turning to go out, I was amazed to see the church full of people. There were thralls, and free men and women, and several men of the bodyguard. They all looked at me as at some monster.

I tottered out between them, supported by Halla, scattering blessings out of habit. The night air felt like a cold bath when we got outside. We went slowly toward my house.

A tall man approached us as we went. He wore a dark cloak and a dark hat.

"There are other ways," he said.

"You come late with them," I mumbled.

"Not to save the Squinter's son. You don't need him. I can make you great in this land. You will do wonders, and speak oracles. Men will fear you. Women will not refuse you. Remember, you're a fraud. How long do you think he'll defend you when he learns the truth?"

"He's the best man I've ever known. I'll not betray him."

"Suppose I offered you this girl at your arm? Would you do me a favor for her? I don't ask you to raise your hand to him; only let him be a little longer."

"You talk like a madman. They deserve each other. It's good to see them side by side, the brave and the fair. It makes me feel there's justice in the world."

"What if I offered you another girl? A girl called Maeve? I could find her for you, and bring her to you—nothing easier. Your friend has had a good life. He's done great deeds. Men will sing of him for generations. Could you not trade a little time of his—how long do warriors live after all—for some good years for your sister? To loose her bonds and lift the yoke from her shoulders? Soon she'll look like an old woman, bent and gray, living as she is now."

I groaned. "You speak to the wrong man," I said. "If I were free, or brave, I might strike hands with you on that bargain, but I'm a slave and a coward, and I fear the God of Abraham."

Then we were at the door of my house, and the man was gone.

"How is he?" I croaked to Erling's mother, who sat by the bed.

"He moves not at all. He doesn't even struggle. Little is left."

"One thing remains," I said. Lightheaded, leaning, I bent and poked my thumb in a soapstone lamp that hung from a spiked sconce in one of the bed pillars. With the oil I marked a cross on Erling's brow and on his breast.

"In the Name of the Father, and of the Son, and of the Holy Ghost, come out of him," I said. "You know who I mean."

Erling went into a gagging fit, and a great black beetle scuttled out of his mouth and tried to run away across his shoulder. I reached my hand out and grasped it before I knew what I'd done. It made high, screeching sounds and waved its many legs.

"Enough of you," I said. I held the thing over the lamp flame. It screamed high and loud enough to hurt my ears, and it bit at me, but I held it there until it was a taper of blue flame. The pain seared my nerves from fingertip to heart, but I heeded it not. In a few moments all that was left was a smudge of black on my fingers and a smell something like burnt hoof.

"He sleeps the healing sleep. It is well," said Erling's mother.

I sank onto my bench. "Halla," I said, "that man who met us as we came—do you think he could have been—"

"Man? I saw no man. You spoke as if answering someone, but there was no one there, and I couldn't understand your words."

"That's right," I said, wrapping my cloak about me and lying down. "I hadn't even marked it. Odd that he should speak Irish. . . ."

CHAPTER XI

We took it in turns to watch through the nights with Erling the first week, his mother and Halla and I. Sometimes he wrestled hell-things in his sleep, and then he'd wake, staring and sweating, and we'd have to hush him like a child ridden by the nightmare.

Once when this had happened, and he knew at last that the voice with comforting words was mine, he said, "Father Ailill—your father was killed."

"Aye, my lord."

"If someone had asked you to dig up your father's corpse, and look on his face, would you have done that?"

"Never."

"No. No man would, willingly. A rotting corpse is not your father. If an enemy had cut him up after he died, it would anger you, but you'd not feel his honor had been touched. Decay is the same, a foul desecration of a corpse, but no harm to him.

"I saw my father walk again though, Father. The eyes that watched when my first arrow hit its mark, the mouth that smiled when I wrestled my cousin Thorgeir to the ground and made him yield, the tongue that called me a fool and a woman when I was baptized—they were all there, in that hellish blue light. They mocked me. They shamed my father. They told me that everything I believe—and everything he believed—is a lie. They said that life itself is a lie, because it promises goodness and hope and love, and all that awaits is death and rot. They said that the real rulers of the world do not think and do not feel and care nothing for good or evil— they merely are. And someday even they will not be. They said that those who build high and those who dig deep are the same, because all will end in a level ruin."

"This was the wickedest of devils, my lord."

"Aye. But I did not let it defeat me."

"No, my lord."

"That's all you can do with a walker-again, you know. Not let it defeat you. You can't kill it. You can drive it from its corpse, but it will find another. Then someone must fight it again. The fight goes on all our lives. We shall not see the end of the battle before Judgment Day."

"We need not be fighting all the time," I said. "God gives His beloved sleep."

"You mistake me. I'm not weary—not in my soul. In my father's walker-again I saw that thing you priests call evil—a twisting, a decay of what was noble. I hate evil now. I hate it with a pure hate. I will be strong for the Lord, and I will plant His church here, and woe to any man who stands in my way!"

The Norse call the time between mid-August and mid-September "Corn-cutting Month." It brought the finest weather I'd seen in Jaeder (it only rained half the time). The haying was done; all the grass on the farm had been cut and ricked for the winter, along with heather from the hills. Now the free men and thralls worked together to cut the oats, rye and barley with their sickles. The air was dusty and sweet, the skies occasionally blue, and nobody expected me to join in the work. People said I had mastered the gods, and they bowed when I passed. My little church was full every Sunday. Even Ragna asked for baptism. Perhaps God was pleased with me after all.

Erling had dragged himself out of bed, over our protests, the second week. He had walked three steps and fallen, but each day he went a little further, and before two more weeks were done he was swinging a sword in the yard and wrestling short bouts with Eystein. He laughed and drank in the now-completed hall with his men as before, except that he was short with Soti, who took to eating in his own house.

Erling's new hall stood bright and handsome, carved and painted in red and gold, a landmark from anywhere in the neighborhood. He had replaced the old box-bed-in-the-corner sleeping arrangement for the master with a loft room above the entry room, reached by an outside stairway. When Halla was not standing in the steading, spindle at work, eyes on Erling, you could generally find her in the weaving house, working on a tapestry of David and Goliath for the wall.

There was a stranger who lived in my clothes, who heard confessions and said masses and preached little homilies and comforted the sick. He seemed a decent fellow, sincere and faithful and compassionate, though oddly unlifted by his success. But at night, when he closed up the church and went to his house to lie in the arms of his leman, he vanished quite, and a carnal Irishman named Ailill took his place. Only, when he lay in the darkness with her warm in his arms, he imagined she was Halla.

I'd best give my leman her name, since by now she was becoming a human to me, and not just "that woman." Her name was Steinbjorg. She came from a long line of thralls, she loved honey and being tickled, and she was terrified of thunder.

I was paring the tallow out of the candlesticks in the church one morning when Soti walked in. He stood by the doorway, arms folded.

"I've seen your holy place," he said. "It's only right you should see mine. Or would that frighten you?"

"Those that are with me are more than those that are with you," I said, setting the sticks aside and getting up. I followed him out.

"True enough, true enough," he said, as he led me down the lane. We walked in a light drizzle. We could not see the sea, although we could hear it. "It seems everyone wants to be a Christian now."

"I was speaking of the unseen world. One of our holy men said those words to his servant, then opened his eyes so he could see the armies of God camped around them."

"If your god has these great armies, then why did he let men kill him?"

"For the same reason a father would die for his children—to save them."

Soti shook his head. "No. It goes against decency. We must not think of the gods as our parents. It sets us too high. Your god humbled himself, let himself be shamed, and you glory in his shame. Do you not see that it eats all law? If the great are to be low, and the base are to be high, then someday thralls will bear swords, and lords will carry dung. This cannot be."

"Christ came to satisfy the law, and fulfill it."

"No. This thing of yours is the end of law. My gods uphold the law. When they are gone wolves will swallow the sun and moon, and winter will last a hundred years."

"Law is good," I said. "It keeps us from tearing each other to bits. But there is a better thing than law."

"Yes there is, but it's not a thing for men. Look there—there you see my holy place!"

It was outside the walls, at the west end of the hill, overlooking the sand above Sola Bay, a stone house with a turf roof.

Soti opened the door and led me inside. It was much like any other house in Jaeder, except that there was a sort of dais built at the far end, topped by a number of carved and painted wooden posts— three large ones at the center and a number of smaller ones grouped around them. The light from the hearth fire was poor, but that only made the images more threatening, full of imminence.

"Sticks of wood," I said. "When the swallows soil them they cannot clean themselves, and when the rats chew them they cannot shoo them off. Your gods are rotting, Soti."

"And does your god float in the air if you drop him during your magic meal?"

"The Eucharist is a mystery. You wouldn't understand."

"These images are mysteries also. Do you think I believe these posts are all there is to my gods? My gods are far greater than these posts! But in the images I meet them, and they speak to me. They speak truly."

"They speak half truly, perhaps. Enough to get men killed, and damned."

"If the gods wish a man dead, is that not their right? Does your god ask leave when he takes a life? You call your god trusty, but in your heart you know him ruthless and forsworn as my gods. Look— Here is Odin—" he pointed to the tall post furthest to our left, a figure with a hole for one eye, and a long beard and a spear in one hand. "—Odin is the wisest of the gods. He knows all that happens in all the worlds, and he knows all that happened in the past, and all that will happen to the end. He works magic by unspeakable rites. He gives victory to his favorites, but he betrays them all in the end. I say it openly, for it is true. Are any people so wise as the Norse, who trust not even their gods?"

"You are to be pitied," said I. "Your chief god is a liar."

"Odin is not chief god. Oh, some will say so. Kings and jarls and hersirs and poets. They think they see one of their own in Odin. But the bonders know better. They know that when you choose a god, it's plain power you want. Have you ever seen plain power, god-man?"

I thought of my scrap with Lemming.

"Whatever you're thinking of, it's not even close. I have felt power. I was struck by Thor's hammer. He left his mark on me to carry to my grave. If they dig up my bones a thousand years hence they'll trace its black stain on my skull.

"Look on Thor!" He pointed to the image at the center, built wider than the other two, with a spiky red beard and great round eyes and a hammer in one hand.

"It was when he struck me down that I saw how little I was, and how great is the sky. I saw myself less than a gnat, less than a grain of dust that the breeze carries off. It was in kindness that Thor showed me this. I, who have felt his power, can never fear a man again—even you, god-man—and I know that when Thor takes time to notice you and your insults to him, he will crush you as a man crushes a louse between his fingernails, and with less concern.

"But even if you should somehow evade the hammer, you are not safe. Look on the last of the great three—his name is Frey."

Frey was the worst. In Odin's and Thor's images there had at least been some hint of majesty—the kind of glory you found in the ancient gods whom worthies like Virgil and Alexander had worshipped. But the round little eyes of Frey were the eyes of a swine, and he grinned an idiot grin on top of the long beard he stroked, and with the other hand he grasped an enormous phallus, fully the size of one of his legs. Most idiots I've known have been decent fellows, but if you can imagine an evil idiot, he would look like Frey.

"Any man who could worship that would be happy in Hell," I said, looking away.

"Yet I think if you are likely to bow to one of these three, it will be Frey," said Soti.

"You lie."

"And how is Steinbjorg these nights? I always found her most warming when the weather grew cold. There was a thing she used to do with her toes—"

I wanted to flee that place of abomination. Instead I said, "All right, how much?"

"How much for what?"

"For Steinbjorg. She serves you days but sleeps in my bed. It's unhandy for both of us. Name a price and I'll buy her."

Soti smiled. "No, I think not," he said. "You just go on enjoying her, god-man—or turn her out, it's all the same to me. I'll name my price when the time is right."

"You're trying to put a hook in my mouth."

"I have a hook in your mouth. You've taken it and run with it. I'll pull you in in my own time. Enjoy the bait, but remember who holds the line."

"Lines can be broken."

"By big, strong fish. Are you a strong fish, god-man?" Soti stepped nearer. "I know your secret wound, man of Ireland. I can't say who it was— someone close to you—a woman or a girl, I think. You wonder why there was a miracle for Lord Erling, and none for her. And you fear the answer your heart knows, that she was lost because she was nothing to your god. Like mine, he cares for the great ones, not for the little ones. They fall and he marks it not, for his eyes are on great dooms and high deeds. But he has said it is not so, and that makes him a liar, and you cannot bear that."

I said, "If I understood all I would be God, and I am not. He who would believe must endure to have a few questions unanswered." And I turned and left the shrine before he could reply, as if my answer had been a strong one.

Coming out into the pale light, I saw Soti's daughter Freydis racing towards me along the path. Whatever the smith's and his wife's sins, they must have been good parents, for their daughter was as smiling and sweet as she was fair. She wore a green frock this morning, and she beamed at me.

"Father Ailill!" she cried. "See the pretty stone I found!"

She held it out for inspection, and I pronounced it a pretty stone indeed.

"Is my papa in the shrine? I want to show him my stone."

I said, "Do you go to the shrine often?"

"Oh yes. Is papa there?"

"Do you like the shrine?"

She laughed at me. "It's just the shrine. It's where the gods live. You don't believe in the gods, do you? They'll kill you some day."

I sighed. "Yes, your papa is in the shrine," I said, and walked back to the steading. I spent an hour in prayer.

CHAPTER XII

Mid-September in Norway brings what they call Autumn-month. With it comes a Thing. Erling summoned Soti for manslaughter and arson by witchcraft.

"I care nothing for Soti," I said to Steinbjorg in bed one night, "but it seems a weak case to me. The laws against witchcraft in Norway can't be very strict. Of course I know nothing of heathen law."

Steinbjorg laughed. "That's not the point." Her arm lay across my chest and her hair tickled my face. The nights were colder now, and we lay curled in the box-bed, her warmth a comfort. "The law is in how you use it, like any other weapon. Lord Erling has friends and kinsmen, and he's hersir of the district. No one will deny his suit. Soti isn't even a Jaederer by birth—he comes from Halogaland. Some say he's part Lapp."

"Why doesn't he flee?"

"Soti has never fled anything."

I believed her.

I said, "I can't see Soti as a folded-hand martyr. He's planning something."

"Of course he's planning something. He's always planning something. But you have the great god,

113

so what is there to fear? Now pay attention to me. I don't want to think about Soti. I have something to tell you."

"What?"

"I'm going to have a baby."

I wept then, as if a baby myself. All I could say was, "If it's a girl, her name is Maeve."

Soon folk began to come in, by ship or boat or riding, and set up tents in the Thing-meadow, near Soti's shrine. Erling set up tables loaded with food for everyone twice a day. When I said mass I was surprised at the number of strangers who partook. I hadn't known there were so many Christians in Jaeder, if any Norseman could be truly called a Christian (saving my Lord Erling, of course).

On the other hand there were men, especially the older ones, who looked quickly away when I came near, and did something with their hands behind their backs. Often Soti could be found deep in talk with such men.

On the first morning of the Thing some men went to the meadow with hazel poles and set them in the earth in a large ring around several rows of benches near the shrine. To these they knotted a rope, called the "Peace Rope," and made a barrier within which the twelve judges took their seats.

After saying mass I followed Lord Erling, carrying the crucifix as I'd been instructed, from the church out to the Thing-stead.

Erling stood near the Peace Rope and cried, "In the Name of the Father, and the Son, and the Holy Spirit, I declare the Peace of the Thing. Any man who breaks this holy peace, let him be outlawed, turned away from God and good men; outcast as far as wolves run, or fire burns, or earth gives grain, or children call to mothers, or ships sail, or shields shine, or the sun rises, or snow falls, or Lapps skate, or fir trees grow, or hawks fly—"

A voice cried, "Unlawful! The Thing is unlawful and the Peace is unlawful! I appeal to the judges— is this the law of Sola-district?"

And there was Soti, dressed all in black, coming from the shrine, and in his hand he waved a great gold ring of twisted strands.

The oldest of the judges cried, "What business is this, smith?"

"Since the law first stood, the Thing has begun when the hersir sets the ring of Thor on his arm and proclaims the Thing-peace! Never has the peace been declared under the sign of the White Christ!"

The old man scratched his beard and said, "What say you, Lord Erling?"

"The gods of the lord are the gods of the land," said Erling. "One lord holds by Thor, and cries peace in his name. Another holds by Odin, another by Frey. I worship the White Christ. I've told no man whom his god should be. No man will force me to take up Thor's ring."

"So spoke King Haakon the Good, when the times for sacrifice came," said Soti. "He would not honor custom, for he'd picked up the Christ-worship in England. But the bonders and lords, who loved him, would not be satisfied, and in the end he sacrificed, and there were good harvests and good fishing all the years of his reign. And after him came the sons

of Erik Bloodaxe, and they too called on the White
Christ, but they would not be persuaded, and
stiffened their necks, and all the time of their rule
there was foul weather and bad harvests, and
unpeace in the land. And I say to you that the same
will follow here if Lord Erling calls not on Thor!"

"The true God rules earth and sky and sea, and
gives or takes their bounty at his pleasure," said
Erling. "You all know what has occurred here at
Sola these last months. In all my dangers, I have
had beside me the priest of the White Christ, Father
Ailill" —here he pointed to me and my crucifix—
"and neither man nor devil has overcome me. At
the same time the priest of Thor here has given
twisted counsels and caused much death and loss,
of which I shall say more later."

"I am no priest," cried Soti, "only a poor smith,
who must care for the holy fires since the proper
ward, our hersir, will not do so. But even in my
weakness, I dare risk the iron-ordeal. Does the Irish
priest, who came here as a thrall, dare so much? I
challenge him!"

Erling looked at me then, and everyone looked
at me, and what could I say? I said, "I accept!"

The crowd broke into excited shouting, and I
whispered to Erling, "What's this iron-ordeal?"

The abbot had often told me that rashness would
be my downfall.

This is the iron-ordeal:

Everyone goes to the forge, where the smith takes
an old iron kettle or whatever lies to hand, and heats
it red-hot. Then he takes an axe and chops the iron

into bits, which are dumped in another kettle (in our case, as we were having a sort of competition, there was a kettle with scraps for each of us). Then the one being judged washes his hand and plunges it into the kettle, takes up a handful of the scraps, and carries them twelve paces to a trough, where he must toss them in. A mitten is bound on the hand, and four days later the judges examine the burns and judge his truthfulness.

We stood there, Soti and me, side by side before the judges, arms outstretched, and waited for the word to start.

Erling said, "Wait! The smith has hands like a turtle's back from years with hammer and tongs. My priest has hands like a child's. This is not an equal test."

"We will bear that in mind when we view the burns," said the chief judge. "Prepare yourselves."

"I am ready," said Soti.

"Any time," said I (I should have stuck my tongue in the kettle).

"Proceed," he said.

I looked into the kettle, where the air swam like water, and thought, No man can do this, and then I was reaching down and taking up the iron.

There is no pain like burning. I wanted to watch Soti and hold the iron at least as long as he, though my fingers be singed away, but I couldn't see him. I couldn't think of him. There was room in the world for nothing but burning, blistering, biting, boiling, melting pain, and the need to walk my twelve steps as quickly as ever I could. The one thing I remember seeing in the crowd is a very fair, pale-haired woman with great, wide-set green eyes, a stranger. I don't know how long I held the iron. It can't have been long. I made it to the trough after a journey of a thousand miles and dropped my torment, and I was surprised to see that my hand still had its shape, though the skin was not whole. I heard the shouting of the crowd as if through three inches of wool, and there was a not unpleasant smell of roasted meat in the air. Someone grabbed my arm and jammed the mitten on, tying it tight.

I swayed, and Erling caught me. I whispered, "Get me away from here. I'm going to faint."

When I came to myself I lay in my bed, and my hand was singing to me, and an unfriendly song it was. I looked at the mitten. Its ties had been sealed with wax. Ragna sat on the edge of the bed, looking at me. Halla and Steinbjorg peered in over her shoulder.

"You're quite mad, you know," Ragna said.

"That is very clear to me just now," I answered, "Give me something to drink."

She put an arm around my shoulders and lifted a cup of something foul-smelling to my lips. "Get it past your nose and all will be well. You'll sleep a long time. And have no fear for your hand. God wouldn't let an honest man's burns mortify."

What a cruel thought to sleep on. . . .

I dreamed of the fair woman in the crowd. I can't have seen her more than a few seconds, but I remembered each pore of her skin, and where each lock of hair hung, framing her face and tumbling to her shoulders. I also dreamed of things I had not seen—breasts and thighs and long, shining length of leg, and I dreamed of doing with her everything a man can do with a woman, and everything beasts do with one another, and sometimes she enjoyed it, and sometimes she cried out in fear or pain, but I didn't care, because all I did only filled me with a starved-wolf hunger to do yet more and more to her.

Do you understand me when I say that that dream filled me with fear when I woke to find its memory in bed with me? Or that I laid penance on myself for it greater than ever I had for lying with Steinbjorg?

The wait for a decision on the iron-ordeal didn't delay the regular business of the Thing. There were cases to try, and fines to be decided, and taxes to be paid, and wares to be bought and sold, and wrestling matches and horse fights to watch and wager on.

I had a pastime of my own—sitting alone and staring at my mitten, imagining the foulness inside. The pain was such when I tried to flex my fingers that I wondered whether I'd lost their use for good.

I didn't stay in bed after the first night. The pain was just as bad in bed or out, except when I bumped the hand against things, which I seemed to do every minute or so. And gradually the pain got better, at least while I kept my fingers still, and I took more interest in the goings-on around me.

I couldn't help looking for the woman I'd seen. She would have been hard to miss, but I did miss her. Since she wasn't from the Sola neighborhood, she must have come with some party or other, which made it unlikely she'd just gone home. I even asked Lord Erling whom she was, but he said he'd never seen such a woman, and would have remembered if he had.

"Perhaps she has a jealous husband," he said, "and he's keeping her shut up in the tent."

I said, "She wore her hair loose."

"A protective father then. What concern is she to you?"

"Just curiosity."

"I don't like to criticize, Father Ailill, but I've noticed in you an interest in the women I hadn't looked for in a priest."

I sighed and said, "Well, I'm Irish after all."

The day came for the examination, and Soti and I stood before the Peace Rope, bare-handed at last, while the judges paraded past us and studied our hands. I sneaked a glance at Soti's, and it looked as if he'd handled nothing less gentle than a baby. My own looked like something the ravens would be interested in.

"Have either of you anything to say before we pass judgment?" the chief judge asked.

Soti said, "I am Thor's man. Anyone can see how he has guarded me from harm for his own honor."

I opened my mouth to say something, but heard Erling's voice break in.

He stepped up beside me and said, "It is customary for men to bring witnesses to attest to their truthfulness. I challenge Soti to bring forward any free man who will call him true. Father Ailill, though, has many to vouch for his word—look! Here are men of Sola to speak for him!"

And we looked behind us, and there were something like two hundred men in a circle around the meadow, fully armed.

Soti cried, "Unjust! He tries to sway the court by force! Thor has force too, my neighbors—don't think he'll forget what you do today!"

Erling said, "My men have done no violence here, nor will they if good order is kept. As hersir, it falls to me to keep a guard. Carry on, judges, and don't even think about these men."

The judges mumbled among themselves, but it didn't take them long to judge in my favor. "It is doubtful," said the chief judge, "that any man could hold the iron as long as Soti did, unburned, except by black witchcraft."

Soti bellowed and threw himself upon me, but many hands pulled him off, and I was only a little bruised.

"Now," said Erling, "I wish to bring my suit against Soti for the deaths of my father and brother by witchcraft. I have witnesses to bring in this case."

And Erling told his tale, and many men vouched for his honesty, and Soti got his turn, and spoke bitterly.

"Well I see that I'll get no fair hearing today," he said. "Therefore I beg Lord Erling to accept self-judgment in this matter. I will pay whatever fine or penalty he lays on me, even up to outlawry."

"This is the penalty I demand," said Erling. "I wish Soti to be given into my hands for torture, until he shall receive the true Faith."

"THOR!" Soti shouted, face to the sky.

CHAPTER XIII

Torture wasn't a usual penalty among the Norse in those days. Erling told me he'd heard of it from Father Ethelbald. It hadn't appealed to him at first, but his mother favored it, and for Soti it seemed just the thing.

I said I could appreciate the thought, but what use would a forced conversion be? You can't twist a man's arm to believe.

Erling said, "I don't care a fishbone for Soti's soul. If he burns in Hell, so much the better. I just want him to stand before the people and deny Thor. We'll find our work much easier when that happens."

"Take care you don't kill him then."

"That's where you must help. You must be there to watch when we torment him, so we don't overstep."

I could think of ways I'd rather spend an evening.

The Thing broke up. We'd chained Soti in his forge, and kept men watching him, and each day after supper we'd forgo the drinking bout and go down to see to his education. One of the men of the bodyguard did the actual work. Erling didn't want to leave obvious marks, so we tried this and that and settled on applying the flat of a red-hot axeblade to the soles of his feet.

"You haven't the calluses there that you have on your hands," said Erling.

Soti said, "Thor is great."

I said, "Only God is great, and He waits with a father's love to welcome you into His family. This burning can become cool ease, and your thirst delightful freshness, if only you will accept the mercy He offers."

I'd often been disgusted with myself. Not until now had I been disgusted by my office.

Ulvig, Soti's wife, stopped me one night as I trudged back to my bed, weary as never in my life, my hand itching.

"Do you think you will break my husband?" she demanded.

I said I didn't know.

"My husband has defeated you already."

"How so?"

She smiled. "You'll see soon enough," and she was gone.

As the nights wore on, and Soti remained obstinate, Erling took to going to him later and later; sharing a few skoals with the lads before beginning his work. Before long he would not start before he was well drunk, and I thought it a good plan and followed his example.

My right hand will never be fair to look on again, but I'd not trade it for Soti's feet. There's no pleasure in sitting in red forgelight, seeing hot iron pressed to flesh until it smokes, smelling the burning, hearing a man's screams, and hardening your heart to pity.

At length people complained that the howls in

the night troubled their sleep, and we moved the business to the daytime. This forced Erling to get drunk before supper, which had never been his habit.

I stayed in the forge one afternoon when Erling had stumbled out, and I crouched in the dirt near the stinking man and said, "For God's sake, be baptized and make an end of it! You can't bear this forever. Your heart will burst. I'm not sure I can take much more myself."

Soti croaked, "Give me water," and I dipped some from a bucket and held the dipper to his mouth.

"I am—almost—finished with my work," he said when he had drunk. He licked his cracked lips and smiled. "Soon I will have you where I want you."

"You're mad," I said, getting up. "You're a prisoner on the point of death. Be sensible. Freedom is there for the taking if you only will."

"Would you have so counseled—one of your holy men of old?"

That hit home. "It's not the same thing," I said.

"No it isn't. Not nearly. Your holy men—so far as I can tell—suffered to be like your weak, tree-hung god. I suffer to defeat you!"

"How can you defeat us?" I asked. "You're powerless."

"I can make you—I am making you—what I am."

I went out into rain, suddenly sober and loaded with truth heavy as lead. There was a crash of thunder and blue lightning close by.

Erling and I were late waking the next morning, and I found him in the hall eating a solitary breakfast, in which I joined him. Ragna sat nearby on the bench.

"It has to end, my lord," I said to him. He looked at me with hollow eyes.

"It will end. When Soti receives baptism," said Ragna.

"No, my lady," said I. "This has been his plan from the first. He knew he couldn't defeat us in law. He accepted this ordeal as his service to Thor."

"Then let him die screaming."

"Then he wins most surely. He'll fling it in our faces as he dies. When you try to do Christ's work by force and cruelty, you deny all that Christ taught. You speak Christ's name, but it's Thor you serve, for it's Thor who rules by the strong arm."

"I am a hersir!" cried Erling, standing and turning his back to me. "Do your Christian lords at home spare their enemies when they have them in their hands?"

"Such matters are too great for me," I said. "But I know this. You cannot build Christ's church with the hammer of Thor. Soti is counting on that."

Erling turned to me and his eyes shone. "I have one more arrow in my quiver. It came to me before I slept last night. Wait for me at the forge, and see if I don't win this game."

I went, and sat on a block of wood, and stared at Soti.

"What's on today?" he asked. He looked like a devil, a thing from underground.

"Erling is coming. He has something new to try on you."

"Good," said Soti. "This foot burning was growing wearisome."

Erling came in. "I have a new tormenter for you, Soti," he said.

"Einar lost his stomach, did he?"

"All work is best done by men who love it. There is one man who dreams of torturing you. . . . Come in, Lemming."

The giant walked in, stooping through the door. Soti's face went white. We left the forge.

Then the screaming began. Everyone on the farm—the thralls digging peat, the fishermen tarring their boats, the bullyboys whacking each other with blunted swords for practice—all stopped and shuddered at the sound.

I've known despair. I've stood in the place where hope is seen for fraud, and all that remains is death— the sooner the better. So I recognized the screams of Soti.

I went to the hall and found Erling slouched in the high seat, an empty horn in his hand, calling for more ale. His eyes were puffy; his mouth hung open; he stared as if he didn't know me.

"It must end," I said.

"I struck Halla last night," he said. "Why would I do that? I don't even remember how she angered me. She looked at me like a hurt child. I've become . . . some man I don't know."

"Let Soti go, my lord," I said. "Or kill him. But while this wrong continues you are not lord of Sola. You're not even lord of yourself. Thor rules here."

Erling groaned. "What does Christ want? If you serve him weakly, he's angry. If you serve him too strongly, he's angry again."

"It isn't easy, my lord. The right thing is never easy. When you shoot with a bow, there's only one bull's-eye, and six hundred hundreds of ways to miss."

"So I'm beaten this time."

"You've not often been beaten."

"Almost never."

"No man wins always. If you learn something, you've made a profit. Be satisfied."

He smiled and pulled himself up. "I suppose it's like this when you die," he said. "At the very end, it's a relief."

Inside the forge we found Lemming standing over Soti, a glowing poker in his hand. One of Soti's eyes was out, and there were burn marks all over his naked body, especially in the male parts.

"*Mercy!*" he screamed. "*Get him away from me! I'll be baptized! I'll do anything!*" He twisted in his chains and tried to draw his knees up. His grimed, marred face ran with tear channels.

We stood and stared at him.

"Blessed be Jesus!" cried Soti. "Blessed be Jesus and his father, and his mother, and their ghost, and the holy bread, and that fellow in Romaborg, and that other fellow in Cantaraborg, and—"

Erling placed a hand on Lemming's shoulder, and the giant turned. I thought for a moment he would strike Erling, but he lowered his hands.

"Set him free," said Erling. "Let him serve Thor in peace. I never looked for this. I am shamed before God."

CHAPTER XIV

Soti was awhile in bed, but he came to me in the yard one bright October morning, halting and leaning on a stick, grinning and peering at me with one unbandaged eye.

"Good morning, god-man," he said.

"Good morning," said I.

"Have you heard the news? Erling offered me a mark of silver to move away from Sola."

"I heard. When do you go?"

"Oh, I wouldn't leave here. After all I've been through to serve my gods here, how could I? No, I'll stay close at hand, and be ever in your sight. You've made me—what is your word?—a martyr."

"You denied your gods."

"That's your story. I don't recall it that way at all. As I remember it, when the pain grew fiercest and I was all but on the point of death, Thor himself appeared in the smithy and commanded Erling to set me free, and Erling fell on his knees in fear and did as he bade. At least that's the story people tell in the countryside."

"You'd serve your gods with lies?"

"Why not? Do you actually believe the stories you

tell? Virgin births, and rising from the dead, and walking on water?"

I tried to think of an answer that wouldn't be a lie.

"Come," he said, "I'm not a man who bears a grudge. We've scored off one another, back and return, since you came. Why be enemies? I'll make you an offer—we'll set up an image of your Christ in my shrine, and we'll worship all together. We've seen that we believe in the same things—why should we be fenced by the names we call the great powers? We'll join forces!"

"When pigs play pipes," I said, turning away. Whatever I thought of Christ, I knew He didn't belong in the same shrine with Frey.

"You couldn't have killed me, you know!" he shouted to my back. "I'll tell you a secret! I am not as other men! I have no heart in my body! If you put your ear to my chest you'd hear never a beat! I keep my heart in a locked casket, and the casket is in a secret cave, and the cave is in a magic mountain, high up in Lappland, and no man may come to it but by the death of his firstborn!"

Soti laughed then, and he laughed a long time. Ulvig came at last and led him home.

I went into the weaving house and watched Halla standing at the loom, working with the beater and colored yarn, building her tapestry of David and Goliath.

"Tell me of this David," she said. "Did he have a wife?"

"He had many wives, for he was a great king," I said.

"Did he have a leman?"

"Quite a few, truth to tell."

"The Jews must have been much like us."

"I suppose they were, in many ways."

"Did King David have one wife he loved best?"

"Well, there was one named Bathsheba—"

"That's a funny name."

"I fancy they'd have laughed at our names too."

"What about this Bath—this woman? Why did he love her more than the others? Did he pay a high bride-price for her? Was she more beautiful than any other woman? Did he have to fight her father and brothers to take her?"

"Ah, the price he paid was high indeed. And I have to think he must have loved her more than the others, because he chose her son to succeed him, though he wasn't the oldest. And if he loved her most, it must have been because they suffered most together.

"It was like this. The king stayed home while his armies went to war, and one night he stood in a high place and saw this Bathsheba, a warrior's wife, in her bath. He sent for her and lay with her. We aren't told what she thought about it. Then, when she told him she was with child, he tried to get her husband to come home and lie with her; and failing that he made shift to have him killed in battle. Then he wed the widow.

"The child was born, but the Lord slew it, although David wept for mercy. And the Lord laid a curse on David's house, so that there was rape and murder among the children. But another of Bathsheba's sons inherited."

Halla's hands were swift with the beater. "The

Lord is very hard on those who sin, is He not?"

"I—I suppose. But then David was pretty hard on Bathsheba's husband."

"And this thing David did—this is what you priests call 'evil'?"

"One kind of evil, yes."

"Are there not stories of God closing a woman's womb because he was displeased? I think Father Ethelbald said something such."

"Well, yes, but it's not always because—"

"I think I'm barren, Father." Her hands did not pause.

"Have you talked to the older women about it?"

"Yes. They think I'm barren too. I've been with Erling two years. There have been times when I thought there was a baby, but it came to nothing. Is God angry at me because I'm with Erling and not his wife? Am I evil?"

Of all questions she could have asked, that was the one I was worst fitted to answer. I opened and shut my mouth a few times and tried to think.

"Why don't you speak? Is the answer so terrible?"

"I just don't know what to say," I said. "The Church teaches that men and women should be married or celibate, one or the other. But as it works out, we don't usually make much fuss if a man—especially a great man like Lord Erling—takes a leman. And here in Norway it's thought highly honorable. I haven't noticed that lemans are more often barren than other women—"

She stopped her work then, and covered her face with her hands. "He'll never marry me. Not if I can't give him sons."

I put a helpless hand on her shoulder, and she turned and wept against my chest.

"When are you going to marry Halla?" I asked Lord Erling a few minutes later. It was an impertinent question, but I felt impertinent. I had found him standing amid the stubble in the home-field, exercising his best falcon. He squinted as he stared into the blue, watching its trackless path, living in faith. A gaggle of bullyboys stood around to lend moral support. Everyone wore heavy cloaks, and the sun was no match for the breeze.

He answered in a voice that told me Halla was not foremost on his mind just then. "Marry her?" he asked, still staring upward. "When did I ever say I'd marry her?"

"Well, why don't you? What better wife could you find?"

"Excuse me a moment, Father. Whitefoot's stooping."

The bird fell like a hailstone and strangled a hare.

All the men whooped and cheered, and we ran together, leaping a fence, to the kill. Erling retrieved the bird, and one of the men set to dressing the hare, making sure that Whitefoot got his share.

"Now what was this about Halla?" Erling asked as he hooded the bird.

"You ought to marry her. She wants to be married, and God would be pleased."

"Pardon me, Father, but did I promise to marry her? I don't recall that I did."

"I haven't heard of any promise."

"And have I treated her in any way shamefully,

or failed to give her the respect due a lawful leman?"

"Of course not."

"And did she bid you come to me and ask for marriage?"

"No. She knows nothing of this."

"Then I fail to see why I should marry her."

"My God, she's the fairest woman in Norway! She loves you more than her life! What else do you want?"

"She's not the fairest woman in Norway," said Erling with a smile. "The fairest is Astrid Trygvesdatter, whom I saw once and can never forget. I fear she'll never have me though, since I slew her fish-wit cousin Aki. But even so, fairness has little to do with it. Walk with me, Father, and I'll tell you how I mean to marry." He strode away from the bullyboys, bearing the falcon on his arm as if it were no heavier than a poor man's lunch.

"The sons of Horda-Kari have been hersirs for generations," he said. "We take pride in the title. We like to say that a hersir out of Kari is worth any jarl and most kings. You've heard of Klypp who slew King Sigurd Sleva?"

"Oh, aye."

"It's a fine story. But I think the time for our kind of pride is over. Norway isn't what it was. Like it or not, we'll be one land under one king in the end, like the southern lands and Denmark. Then there'll be a long tug-of-war between the lords and the king. And we lords will have to gather all the power we can under his rule. That will be a time for jarls, and I fear no hersir will be left with enough turves to roof his house.

"I need to get the name of jarl, Father. The best

way I can figure to do that is to make a high marriage. Maybe I'll never have Astrid Trygvesdatter, and maybe the woman I get will have a walleye and a humpback, but be a jarl I will, and I cannot look lower, even to comfort Halla.

"I know she dreams of marrying me, Father. I'm not blind. And it pains me to disappoint her. But it cannot be. More than her happiness, or mine, is at stake."

It was mightily sensible, and I hated the sound of it. I muttered, "I see," and shambled off.

"By the way, Father," Erling called after me. "When are you going to marry Steinbjorg?"

I wondered how much mansbot would be laid on a priest who strangled his lord.

I stomped around the steading and thought, and the more I thought the angrier I grew. Soti was sure he had a hook in my mouth. Erling judged me of little account, it seemed, and comical to boot. Halla looked to me for help, but I could do nothing for her.

I needed to put my hands to something, something I could break, or I might kill somebody. Then I thought of one thing I could do, a thing that would give me joy and remind people who was priest around here.

I got an axe from the toolshed and laid it on my shoulder, then ambled down the path to the shrine of the old gods.

Inside, it looked as I remembered it. I marched to the dais, laid the axe on it, spit on my hands and took the axe up again.

Frey first, I thought. I swung the axe back over my shoulder . . .

"*Stop!*"

I knew that voice. Where had I heard it? I turned around—

And there was the fair woman I'd seen at the Thing, of whom I'd dreamt shameful things. Have you ever seen a beauty that is almost deformity— the eyes too great and wide-set, the mouth too large and soft, the figure too lush? Almost a kind of jest? And yet desirable—a thing—"thing" seems the right word—to lust after?

She walked toward me, the sway of her hips rousing me in a moment, as if I were a stallion with the mares in heat. Did I smell something? I seem to remember that I did.

"*There are pleasanter things to do, Ailill,*" she said.

Then I knew the voice.

It was the same voice I'd heard speaking from Big Melhaug—the voice of the dragon.

I fled, leaving the axe behind.

It's a fearful thing to meet the gods on their own ground.

ChAPTER XV

Winter in Norway starts in mid-October. In late October you can pick bearberries in Jaeder if it isn't raining. Rich men can go hunting if it isn't raining. Poor men thresh grain if it isn't raining. And the swallows fly south, proving that God gave more sense to them than to us.

It's a cold rain, the rain of Jaeder in October. It blows in from the sea with the ocean's lungs behind it, and it soaks through your cloak and your shirt, and works in around your ankles and down your collar, and drives an icy spike next to your heart, so you're a long time by the fire getting warm again.

"This country isn't fit for men," I said one evening in the hall. "It's fit for rats and gulls and toads, but not for Adam's sons."

"Well, it's no worse than Ireland," said Erling.

"Slander," I said. "Ireland is fair and green, with gentle breezes and warm sweet rains, and the children go barefoot even in February."

"Only because they're too poor to get shoes. I spent a year in Ireland, remember, and some of the lads thought it colder and wetter than Jaeder, and others said not, but we all agreed it was no better."

He had passed me the horn while he spoke, so I

was swallowing when he finished and didn't get a chance to reply right off.

"Has anybody gotten a look at the Milky Way?" asked old Bergthor. "You can tell how the winter weather will be by studying the different parts of the Milky Way. I used to know how to do it when I was younger."

"You have to get a look at the Milky Way first," said I. "I'm not sure I'd know it if I tripped over it, it's been so long."

"God is good to us," said Erling. "He gives us winter that we may better enjoy the summer's warmth, and hunger that we may relish our food, and thirst that we may get drunk with a good heart."

"If you put it that way," said I, "that could be what the Lord meant when He said that the poor are blessed, although I doubt it."

That was when one of the men came in and said, "There's a balefire lit, my lord."

Erling sat up, aquiver like a hound. "One of the jarl's, or one of ours?"

"One of ours. To the north, at Randaberg."

"Then it must be Vikings. Sound the horns for a levy. Send runners to question the watchmen, so we'll know whether to expect company by land or sea." He called to the men, "Get some rest! It'll be an early morning, whether we march or sail. The wind's northerly, so if it's ship business we'll have to pull for it."

The men scrambled up and those who slept in the hall began rolling out their beds, while the thralls dismantled the tables.

I went to my own bed then, and it was still dark

when Erling's shoeboy shook me awake. Erling stood in the doorway.

"We're sailing; you might as well come too," he said to me. "You've been owley lately—I think you need the excitement."

Out into the black rain we went, down to the fjord where *Fishhawk* was being launched from her house. The moment I stepped up the gangplank I knew I'd be sick, and I was hard tempted to beg off; I wasn't much practical use after all. But pride prevented. I kept trying, without success, to find a place to stand where I wouldn't be in somebody's way. It's a fine thing to be part of a well-drilled team, where every man knows his job. It's less fine to be a stumbling stone.

At last the weapons were stowed, and the lines secured and the first shift of rowers seated on their sea chests, and as the western mountains lightened the lead man started the rower's song, and we pulled away from Somme. I did not row. I puked.

Imagine a world made entirely of water—all of it black, all of it moving against you. The water in the air flies in your face and blinds you and soaks you; the water below you lifts your ship the height of its masthead and then slides suddenly from under, letting you drop. And this goes on over and over, through a pale morning that does not end. Is this Hell, O Lord? If so, I repent all my hard words and thoughts. Anyone who could create such a sweet thing as dry, solid land must be good beyond imagining, and if You'll only bring me back to it safe I'll never blaspheme again, I swear it.

My clothing weighed like the turf roof on the hall, and it was woven of ice. A man who has only a suit of ice to warm him is miserable indeed. And yet it might not have been so bad if only my stomach had kept still. . . .

I sat in the stern near the steersman, and I had to tug my robe loose where it had frozen to the deck. I'd had the sense to wear boots, but the wind wormed in underneath and painted my shins blue. I got to my feet and stomped, blowing on my fingers. Our ship looked like an angel craft, rimed all over with ice. The wind had calmed somewhat overnight and fog walled us in; we sat quietly in the water, the men dipping their oars from time to time to keep us in place. I thought I'd be all right for the time being if I didn't eat anything.

"Ready for breakfast?" asked Erling, coming up behind me and slapping me on the shoulder.

"Today's a fast day," I said.

"Really? What's it in honor of?"

"I'll think of something."

"Well I'll explain where we are, since you're a stranger hereabouts. We're facing northeast as we sit. Aft is Tungeness. It's the northern tip of Jaeder, where the jarl's balefire is. East and south, though you can't see them for the fog, are the Boknafjord and Sokn and Bru islands, and between them runs Soknasund, where I chased the Orkneymen. Our watchmen tell me our visitors were headed in here, so they'll probably have overnighted somewhere in the Boknafjord, and if they're headed south along the seaway they'll tumble into our arms like a newborn into a midwife's. We'll see their sails before they see us."

"And until then we wait?"

"Until then we wait."

"They could have gone past in the night."

"Unlikely. It's bad enough sailing in the daytime this time of year."

"Is it indeed?"

Erling said, "The wind's picking up again. It's almost due north. That's good." Then he called to the steersman to keep us headed into it.

He settled his elbows on the rail. "It's odd about Soknasund," he said. "I keep coming back to it somehow. Like a dog who's always underfoot, no matter where you walk. I killed my first man there— an outlaw who'd raped a 15-year-old girl. We ran him down like a mad dog, but it was I who put the first spear in him. They made much of me for that, and a good thing too. You need a lot of assuring the day of your first kill."

I found no reply to that. My first kill had been during the sea fight rounding Jutland, and I'd never been troubled an eyeblink by it.

I said, "It's a kind of mercy to kill a man that sunk in evil."

"A hard mercy, Father. Life has too many hard mercies, I think."

He roused himself. "Well, come on! Somebody do something! This waiting makes a man heavy-hearted."

Someone shouted, "I see something!"

"What do you see?" yelled Erling.

"Two ships—coming our way!"

We all stared to starboard through the wall of mist. At first I saw nothing, but then there was the glint of silver or steel through a rent the wind tore in the fog, and soon we could make out a pair of sails—one striped in red, the other a solid yellow.

"They're coming to us," said Erling. "Hold steady, lads."

It seemed to take forever for the strangers to approach, close to the wind as they sailed. As they drew nearer we could see that these were warrior ships, nothing else, white with ice like us. They sailed heavily under men and steel. I went to the arms store and got me an axe, shield and helmet.

Erling was about to hail them when the call came from their side.

"Who are you?" came a ringing voice. "Where are you from and what do you want?"

Erling told the steersman to cut them off and shouted, "That's for me to ask," as our oars dipped and rose. "I am Erling Skjalgsson, hersir of Sola and north Jaeder. If you come in peace, you're welcome to guest at my home. If you come for a fight, we're ready for that too. Who are you?"

"No one for so great a man as you to fret over. I'd hoped to come and go unmarked, and no man the worse. My name is Ole, I am an honest Viking out of Russia and England, and I only wish to go home."

"And where is home?"

"The Vik."

"You're off course if you come from England."

"We sailed directly oversea, and made land at Moster inside Boml Island. Yesterday we got this far south and thought it best to overnight in the fjord. We put ashore on an island and had morning mass."

"Are you a Christian?" Erling called. "Have you a priest with you?"

"I have six priests from England. Are you a Christian?"

"I am that. I have a priest too. I know he'd be glad to meet yours."

Don't be so sure of that, thought I.

"Perhaps another time, Erling Skjalgsson. As it is, we're late in the season, and we must make sailing time. Let us part as friends, and I warrant we'll meet again."

"But surely you can take a meal with me!"

"Nothing would please me more, for I know your name and reputation. But today it cannot be. Will you be so good as to give us seaway?"

Erling ordered the men to row us out of Ole's course, and we sat and watched as the two long ships sailed by. They were a tough-looking crew, and well outfitted. I waved at the English priests, who looked sour when they saw my Irish tonsure. And we all stared at this man Ole, who wore a red shirt and a fur hat and cloak, and stood very tall and handsome.

"What is your farm?" cried Erling. "Who is your father?"

"I have no farm now," said Ole, and his blue eyes sparkled even at that distance. "My father is dead. But I'll have my inheritance one day, and you'll hear from me."

We watched them disappear in mist, and somebody said, "That's a lot of priests for two ships."

CHAPTER XVI

A day came when the herds and flocks were brought in from the outpastures and Erling and his foreman looked over the cattle and the pigs. The foreman marked with tar the ears of those least worth feeding through the cold months, and the next day thralls took axes and knives and did the winter slaughtering.

It was my job to gather all the children, free and thrall, and lead them down to Somme, where the slaughtering was done another day, and keep them occupied. Halla came with me. For luck, it did not rain while we walked, and we got a dry place in a guest house.

We played games until I was tired, and then I told stories with good success, for of course Irish stories are better than Norse, and they were new to the children. I was getting well along when Halla, who had disappeared a moment, came inside dragging two screaming children by the ears.

One was a bullyboy's son, and the other was Soti's daughter, Freydis.

"Guess what I found these doing?" Halla cried. "They were in the hay, with their clothes off, playing with each other."

"Take your hands off me or my papa will skin you alive!" shouted Freydis. She looked less pretty than usual, with a red face and stalks in her hair.

"No such talk," said I. "What will your father think when he learns what game you were playing?"

She shook herself loose and crossed her little arms. "He knows I play the game. He says I may do anything I like, because I am the gods' gift. You play the game with Steinbjorg, and you'd like to play it with Halla. That's what my papa says."

My face felt hot and I could not look at Halla, and all I could think of to do was to swat the boy.

"What's happening to the sun?" I asked Erling one evening in the hall.

"Don't tell me you never noticed winter nights are longer?" Erling replied.

"Within reason, yes. But as late as the dawn is coming now, there'll be no day at all left by Christmas."

"Be comforted. We never lose our day altogether. They do lose it farther north, up in Soti's country. The night lasts months on end up there."

"Christ have mercy," I sighed. "I've come to the gate of Hell. No wonder there are so many devils in Norway."

Erling said, "I've seen good men from Lappland, and wicked men from Arabia. And the other way around. Tell me, are North Irishmen wickeder than South Irishmen?"

"Ireland is a blessed land, hallowed by the bones of ten thousand saints," I said. "Devils fear to approach Ireland."

"Then we Norse are mighty indeed," said Erling,

"for we fear not to attack where devils quail."

"Only a Norseman would be proud of out-deviling the devil," said I.

I haven't said much about Erling's sisters. It's not that they weren't charming and lively lasses, darting in and out and chattering at the tables, but their lives turned on things that mattered little to me, and I rarely spoke with them except in confessions, and of course I couldn't tell you about those even if they'd been memorable.

The older one was called Thorliv, the younger Sigrid. They were both fair and tallish, as I've said, and almost like enough to be twins. Thorliv had a rounder, merrier face, though she was dreamy and quiet by nature. Sigrid had a longer, graver face, masking a devilish humor.

Sigrid came to me one day while I was shooing out some chickens that had got into the church through a door left open. She sat on the bench fidgeting, with the face of Cleopatra forced to wait for her dinner while the slaves cleaned up a spilled kettle.

"How long is this going to take?" she sighed.

"It'll be quicker if you help me," I said, waving my arms and trying to herd the squawking birds toward the door.

"No, I'll watch you."

"Very wise. Good for your education."

"Maybe it would help if you made noises like a dog."

I ignored her advice and finished the exorcism. "All right, darling, what's on your mind?" I asked, sitting down.

"First you have to promise me you'll never, never tell anyone we talked about this."

"I think I can do that."

"Do you think Erling will become a jarl?"

"I think he can be most anything he wants to be, and a jarldom is what he's after."

"How long do you think it'll take?"

"That's hard to say. From what I hear, there are big changes coming, and soon."

"Would you marry a man and woman without the blessing of the bride's family?"

"Never, unless she'd lost her family, like the thralls."

She scowled. "Even if they'd die if they were kept apart?"

I said, "What's this all about? Do you want to get married?"

She sighed. "You won't tell anyone?"

"Not a soul. Unless you run off with him. Then I promise I'll tell the world, and lead the hue and cry after you."

"I want to marry Halvard Thorfinsson."

I paused. "He's a good lad, one of the best in the bodyguard, but he's only a bonder's son."

"But he could marry a hersir's daughter! That's not impossible. What I'm afraid of is that Erling will become a jarl, and then I can never marry Halvard."

"Have you talked this over with your mother?"

"How could I talk to her about it? She'd promise me to a king's son if she could." She made a face as if that were a fearful fate.

"What about Erling? He might understand."

"Halvard says no. He says he wants to do great deeds and earn me."

"That's probably the wisest course."

"But what if he gets killed?"

"I think a girl like you isn't likely ever to choose a man who'd die in bed."

"No," she said. "I've thought about it. I think we should all do what the Gospel says, and turn the other cheek and love our enemies, and never fight a battle."

"If you really feel that way, perhaps you should be a nun."

"I'll become a nun if I can't marry Halvard."

"Well, you're not yet fifteen summers old. Perhaps you'll feel differently in time."

"That's what I'm afraid of!" she said. "I want to make my life before I get old and stupid, like the rest of you."

CHAPTER XVII

"Bless me, Father, for I have sinned," said the lad Enda.

"I know it, my son," I sighed. "Whatever possessed you to do such a thing?"

Enda knelt at my feet in the mud of the steading. His hands were tied behind his back, his face was tracked with tears and grime, and the wet snow fell on us. There are no trees in Jaeder high enough to hang a man on, but someone had fixed a beam to the peak of one of the storehouses, and we spoke in its shadow.

"It was a bonny knife, and the man has many knives. I only thought it would be pleasant to carve something with such a knife, and sell it maybe."

"You knew it was death for a slave to steal," I said.

"Father, don't you see—sometimes a man's got to reach for the thing he wants or he'll go mad. And if he can't—well then why not die and be done? What's the use of living this way?"

"I've pled for you with Lord Erling, but he says there's naught he can do."

"I expected nothing more, once they found the knife in my bed," said Enda. "Please hear my confession, Father."

As he recited his little sins for me the crowd grew impatient and took to murmuring. Lord Erling told them to be quiet and gave us our time. Lemming stood nearby, a coil of rope over one shoulder. Hanging was thrall's work, but Erling had had the kindness to hire the big man rather than force one of Enda's friends to do it. If Lemming felt one way or another about the job, he showed no sign.

I shrove the lad and he said to me, "One last thing I ask, Father."

"Anything."

"Pull out the thong about my neck."

I fumbled at his collar and fished up a small wooden crucifix. It wasn't expert work, but it showed promise (dear God, what a word!). It was also unfinished, Christ's feet melding into the uncarved wood at its base.

" 'Twas the thing I was working on," said Enda. "I know it's incomplete, but I'd take it as a favor if you'd wear it when I'm gone. It would be . . . as if a part of me went on in the world."

Blinking back my tears I said I'd be honored to wear his cross. Then I patted his shoulder and turned away as they strung him up. I pushed through the men and women staring up at the last struggle, and took the path down to Sola Bay. The snow, melting as fast as it hit the ground, soaked through my shoes. Still, I thought, I'm not as cold as Enda. I wanted to cry, or punch somebody. I walked along the sandy shore and watched the gray waves, and let the gray sound of them wash over my soul.

"An unpleasant business," said a voice. I turned to see Lord Erling behind me.

" 'An unpleasant business,' " said I. "We'll raise a stone to the lad and carve on it, 'An unpleasant business.' "

"I take no pleasure in hanging thralls," said Erling. "There's no glory in it and it's expensive. But the law's the law. For God's sake, if he'd only been patient he could have earned his freedom. Why in the name of all the saints must thralls always act like thralls? If they're my brothers, as you say, then why don't they behave with honor?"

I rounded on him and yelled in his face. "Honor! Honor is something for a man with a home, with family, with friends! You act with honor because you've a place you must go where they'll drink to you if you're brave and shame you if you're a coward. But the thralls—you drag them from their homes and their land, you pen them up with strangers in a place where all despise them, and you expect them to act with honor? Where was Enda's father, where was his uncle, to teach him honor? How can a man have honor without a clan?"

Erling sighed. "I did not make the world. If God makes some men thralls, what can I do, except treat them with the best justice I can?"

"Justice! Would you hang a free man for stealing a knife?"

"I've never heard of a free man stealing anything. I suppose his own family would kill him, out of shame."

"What if it were a woman?" I asked. "Would you hang a thrall woman for stealing too?"

"No. We'd cut an ear off her."

"And if she did it again you'd take the other ear?"

"Of course. The third time we'd take her nose. After that, she can steal as much as she likes."

"Most amusing, your law," I said, and plopped down on a wet rock.

"I'm not making it up. Actually, the law for a foreign-born thrall who steals is flaying alive. I refuse to do that."

"You're too kind."

"Answer me this then, Father. What could I have done other than what I did? Give me your counsel."

"I don't care, my lord. This morning I don't give a herring's nose about your duties, or your honor, or what you can or cannot do. I heard the confession of a lad not yet twenty, and now he's rotting meat. Pardon me for being judgmental."

Erling reached a hand out and jerked me off the stone, pulling my face up close to his. I'd never felt his strength before. My feet dangled in air.

"You are my priest," he whispered, and his face had gone red. "I found you in a slave pen and set you free. I gave you a life and I gave you honor. You've no right to speak to me that way!"

"String me up then!" I screamed back. "You're so high and mighty and righteous, you've no need of a priest anyway!"

Erling tossed me backwards onto the sand, turned and went home. I sat on an icy rock and watched the sea.

And it was thus I caught the fever that kept me in bed until nearly Christmas.

CHAPTER XVIII

They call Christmas *Jul* in Norway, and it used to be celebrated in mid-January, but Haakon the Good, who failed in so much, at least got most of the Norse to change it to December 25 and the eleven days following.

The thralls ran about, cleaning and washing and airing beds, cooking, fetching and carrying, but they did it with a good will, because Jul was a good time for them as well as the free folk. Ragna rousted me from my bed Christmas Eve and set some of them sweeping my house out. "We'll have to get you a house thrall," she said. "That slut of yours is never here in the daytime, and you keep house like a bear. How long is it since you've had your clothes washed?"

"I don't want a thrall," I said.

"Well, you'll get one anyway. Set him free if you like and pay him wages, but you can't go on living like this."

"I haven't been well."

"You're fine now, and you need a thrall." She gusted out the door, then poked her head back in. "We will have mass tonight, won't we?"

"Yes, of course."

I wasn't keen for Christmas. I was still angry about Enda, whose crucifix now hung about my neck, and the thought of spending the festival among barbarians and far from home did not set my heart singing. It occurred to me, for no particular reason, that I didn't know when Easter would fall the next year. I wondered how I'd find out, and if I really cared.

I poked my head outside and saw Erling walking through the steading with his red-haired cousin Aslak Askelsson, who had come to guest with him for the feast. Aslak had brought news that Jarl Haakon was dead, and everyone was waiting to hear the story.

We got to hear it the next day, after I'd said the high mass and the toasts had been made and we'd all honored the Lord with drunkenness and gluttony. Erling said, "Aslak, tell us this tale of the fall of Jarl Haakon. I liked him when he was sober—did he make a good death?"

Aslak, seated in the guest seat and looking a little shy of the honor and attention paid him, coughed, and Halla brought him a horn of mead, which made him blush. He said, "Sad to say, he was unlucky in his dying. It happened this way—

"Haakon was feasting at Medalhus in Gaulardal, but he'd left his son Erlend with his ships at Viggja. The drink must have addled him, because he sent his thralls to Orm of Leira and demanded Orm send his wife Gudrun to him."

"Orm wouldn't take that well," said Erling.

"Indeed. He sent the war arrow out and soon the whole district was in arms. Especially the smaller bonders, because Haakon had often done the same to them, and they'd no protection. But Orm of Leira is another sort of man altogether. He blocked the roads so Haakon couldn't get back to his ships. Haakon sent his men away to fend as best they could, and to try to get word to Erlend to sail home to Hladir, and he fled across the Gaular River to his leman, Thora of Rimul. He drove his horse into a hole in the ice and left his cloak close by so men would think he'd drowned. Then he went to Thora, and the thrall Kark was with him.

"Meanwhile, as Erlend sailed out of the fjord, he was met by a man named Olaf Trygvesson—"

"Olaf Trygvesson!" cried someone. "Is he in Norway?"

"Aye. He sailed from England this autumn, and met with his kinsmen at Opprostad, and then sailed north with five ships to kill Haakon. He must have uncanny timing-luck. He killed Erlend and took his ships without trouble, then came ashore to find that every man in the district was eager to join him.

"Well, naturally they looked for Haakon at Rimul. The dead horse in the river didn't fool them a bit— Haakon had left too many tracks. They marched up the valley and held a Thing at Rimul, and Olaf stood on a big rock and shouted that any man who killed Jarl Haakon would be richly rewarded. But nobody betrayed him, so they finally went to Hladir, which Olaf seized for his own.

"The next morning up came Kark, and in his hand he carried Jarl Haakon's head."

"I can't believe it," I said. "I knew Kark. He hadn't the kidney for that kind of work."

"It happened this way—" said Aslak, "— at least

this is how Kark told it. Thora had had him, I mean Kark, dig a large hole in the pigsty at Rimul. Then they laid boards over it, and Haakon and Kark went underneath with a lamp, and Thora covered the boards with dirt and ran the pigs over them, and no one could tell their hiding place.

"But when Olaf had come to Rimul, the rock he had stood on to speak was hard by that pigsty. And Haakon and Kark had heard every word. And Haakon had whispered to Kark, 'You're not thinking of betraying me, are you?' and Kark had denied it, and Haakon said, 'We were born on the same day, and I think it likely we will die on the same day. Remember that.'

"And when Olaf left and evening fell, they slept, and towards morning Jarl Haakon cried out in his sleep. Kark tried to wake him but could not, and he was afraid because he didn't know whether some of Olaf's men might still be about, so he took his knife and cut the jarl's throat."

"A bad death for a great man," said old Bergthor.

"And what reward did Olaf give Kark?" I asked.

"The reward he deserved. He had his head cut off and set the two heads side by side on the gallows out at Nidarholm. Every man who goes by throws stones at them."

I got up to go outside, afraid of what I might say.

"Stay, Father," said Erling. "This needs talking of."

"I don't feel well," I said.

"Still. I want your counsel. This matter of Olaf Trygvesson is a tangled one."

"Jarl Haakon is dead. Olaf rules in the Trondelag now. What concern is it of yours?"

"Haakon was lord of most of Norway. Olaf wants no less, I'm sure. That's why he went to Hladir, not to his own inheritance in the Vik. If he's to be another Harald Finehair, every landed man in Norway will have to decide how he stands towards him. Aslak, what do Olmod and the cousins think of all this?"

Aslak said, "Olaf is kin to the Erikssons of Opprostad. There's little likelihood he'll come to us in peace."

"Yet Olaf was friendly enough when we met," said Erling.

"When you met?" asked Steinulf.

"Don't you remember the tall Viking from Russia with the two ships at Tunge? Who do you think that was?"

A murmur coursed through the hall. Everyone wondered to think they had come so close to the great Olaf Trygvesson, and not a blow struck.

"Then he must have sailed south to Opprostad to get support from his kinsmen, then shot north to Haakon," said Steinulf.

"That's what I think," said Erling.

"Yet you made no move to stop him?"

"I didn't know it was he at the time. I thought it possible. Perhaps I failed in my troth to Haakon, but Olaf made no attack, and I don't care to molest fellow Christians and priests on mere doubt."

"And Haakon had about come to the end of his thread," I muttered. Erling stared at me.

"He looked a king from head to foot," said someone. "He wore an embroidered shirt of scarlet, and a rich fur cloak, and his arms were loaded with rings."

"He has the blood of Harald Finehair—I should have known it," said old Bergthor. "So many of them have that height, and those bright eyes."

"Are you saying that because you parted from Olaf in peace we might make terms with him?" asked Aslak.

"I think there might be hope," said Erling. "Or are you fitting out a fleet to go against him?"

"No point in it. He's sticking to the land this winter—taking the road to the Vik to rally his kin there. We'll be boxed between the Tronds in the north and the Vikers in the east, not to mention the Erikssons, before we get our chance at him."

Then they began the game of "What If?" which means so much in war and state, and my mind wandered. I thought of Kark, and I thought of Erling, and it seemed to me there was little to choose between them.

Then Steinbjorg came in and whispered in my ear, "Gunnlaug is come to her time. She's calling for you. She says she knows something's wrong, and the child must be christened."

We went to the house where the woman Gunnlaug lay, with other women about her. No man was there but me; even her husband, one of the bullyboys, feasted in the hall. We heard her cries before we got there, above the patter of the rain, and I could smell her sweat when I got inside.

Someone told her the priest was come, and she cried for my prayers between her screams. Yet today I can see her face, drawn to the skull with pain, the hair pasted to it like seaweed on a rock, her mouth stretched to bare the gums as she cried again and again, and it never seemed to end. I prayed my prayers and prayed them over, and the women made her walk about the room to loosen the child's grip, and still it went on. I looked at Steinbjorg, kneeling at her head or holding her arm, and thought that she would suffer so as well, a few months hence. I wondered how it was for the blessed Virgin, nearly a thousand Christmases before. Could it have been easy to bring the Son of God into the world? Must not her body and all of nature have protested the invasion, shrinking in wonder and fear from the fullness of time?

But this child was nothing like Mary's, when at last she came forth. She was red and shriveled and slimy of course, like all babies, but this one cried strange, bubbly cries, and her mouth was wrong. The women tried to hide her from Gunnlaug, but she croaked, "I know it's ill-formed. Let me see it. I want to hold it." So they wrapped her in a cloth and gave her to her, and she held her and cooed to her, weeping. Then she said, "Father, you must christen my child now."

I said, "I think she'll live. She can be christened in the church."

Gunnlaug looked at me, and her eyes were miles deep, with all the misery of Eve's curse in them. "She will not live, Father. You must christen her now."

There was water there, so I christened her Maria, as her mother wished. I had barely finished when the door burst open and Gunnlaug's husband came in, followed by Soti, a halting and fearful shadow.

"Let me see the child," said the father.

Wordlessly the mother gave her up to one of the women, who passed her to him.

He looked at the face and cursed. Then he turned and carried the child out.

"Where's he going?" I asked.

Soti answered. He stood before the door. "He goes to expose it on a hillside. That is our way with the deformed ones. It keeps the race strong."

"This is an abomination!" I shouted. "Lord Erling will hear of it!"

"It's the law," said Soti, smiling. "A strong law for a strong land, and strong gods."

"It's murder!"

"By no means. That thing is no human. It cannot walk. It cannot talk. It cannot even feed itself. It's a beast like other beasts, and if it's not worth its feed we put it down. It's the decision of the father, or of the owner if the mother's a thrall."

"Get out of my way, Soti."

Soti stepped aside, still smiling.

I'd not known how much of the night had passed in Gunnlaug's labor. When I got to the hall everyone was dozy with drink, and Erling nodded in his high seat.

"Gunnlaug's child is born," I said, shaking him. "She has a harelip. The father took her out to expose her. You've got to send men to stop him."

Erling stared at me with fuddled, sad eyes. "I'm sorry," he said, "but I can do nothing. It's the law here. Soon, perhaps, we can change it, but—"

"Sod you," I whispered. "Sod you and your law and your land."

I rushed out into the rain and wandered paths through the night, listening for a cry, tripping over stones and stone fences, getting mired in icy bogs. I never found the baby.

At last I followed the smell of smoke back to the steading in the dark, a long stumble that left my feet slashed and my shins bloody. In my house Steinbjorg waited. She rushed to strip me of my wet things and said, "Where have you been? Have you gone mad? You could have sunk in a mire, or been taken by wolves, like that poor baby. What's gotten into you?"

I shuddered like a horse's flank. Steinbjorg bustled me into bed and wrapped herself around me, and blankets around both of us. Through chattering teeth I said, "Don't you see? Don't you see what Soti meant?"

"What are you talking about?"

"You're his thrall. When our child is born, he'll find some flaw in it. He'll expose it, unless I do his will."

I stood in bright sunshine in a patch of meadow somewhere in the Sola neighborhood, although I don't know how I knew that, since nothing I saw looked familiar. The ground wasn't very promising: boggy and full of rocks.

I heard a noise behind me and turned, and for a terrifying moment I thought it was the black giant with the axe, but then I saw that it was only the abbot. He held in his hand an iron-shod wooden spade, such as the thralls use to break up the fields in spring. As usual he looked at me as at something a maggot had vomited up.

"This is your patch," he said.

"My patch?"

"Your patch, lumpkin. It's here you must work and raise a crop, to earn your freedom."

"I'm free already!"

"You? As far as I can see, your useless head remains on your shoulders. Or don't you remember, you would not pay the price to enter the land?"

"There's little point in paying such a price," I said. "What good is freedom, or entering the land, or catching the white hind, if I lose my head?"

"A head like yours would be little enough loss, but be that as it may you've made your choice, so nothing remains but to work your patch. Sow the seed, cultivate it, harvest it, and we'll give you credit for the value of the crop." He extended the spade to me.

I said, "Do you mean I may enter the land after all, and pursue the white hind, if I do this?"

"If you buy your freedom. But be warned that freedom is not cheap or easy, and, as you yourself have observed, yours is a pretty poor patch."

"You just watch how fast I can buy myself!" I cried, seizing the spade, and I turned from him and set to work with a will. I manhandled the rocks out, and dug ditches to drain the boggy places, and spaded and planted. Faster than I could ever have imagined the shoots began to sprout.

I watched the shoots with love and fascination. They were not like any plants I'd ever seen. They were pink instead of green, and as they matured I saw that they were not plants at all, but small, perfect children.

Looking on them, I loved them. I felt tender care for each precious, precarious little soul. "How will I harvest them? How will I sell them?" I wondered. "How can I endure to part with the least of them?"

And then I heard a flapping sound behind my head, and spinning round I saw, against the sun, great black wings. Ravens were raining from the sky, coming to snap up my precious babies. They were large as a man, these ravens, with red eyes and golden beaks sharper than shears, and there were hundreds of them. I flailed my arms and swung my spade, trying to drive them away. They came on as if I didn't exist, and began to grasp my little ones in their beaks, and they pulled them out of the earth, threw their heads back and gulped them down. It was done faster than it takes to tell. All my sweet innocents were slaughtered, and the ravens, with one contemptuous look back at me, took to the sky again, blocking the sun out with their shadows, leaving me alone on the desolate ground.

"GOD!" I screamed.

CHAPTER XIX

My fever came back of course, and I missed most of Jul. By little I grew aware of a presence in my house, and when I came to myself I saw an old man sitting on the step of my bed, staring at me. He had thick black eyebrows and a sloped forehead below his cropped white hair, and there was no valley between his forehead and his nose. I recognized him as a thrall named Caedwy, a Briton.

"What are you doing here?" I asked, hoarse.

In reply he stood up, pulled down the skin under his right eye so that I could see the crescent of red flesh beneath, and scratched his crotch with vigor.

"You're mad," I said, turning to the wall. My muscles ached.

"No use to deny it, I can tell one of the Brotherhood when I smell him," I heard him say. "How could you do the deeds you've done without you were one of us? Eh?"

I said, "I don't know what you're talking about."

"The men with the long ears. Long, long ears, like rabbits. They hear everything that's said in all the worlds, and if only we'd feed our horses on wool, they'd live to be a hundred. Iron makes a bonny pillow. When they burned men in wicker cages you

163

could hear the screams fifty miles, and the gods were pleased. The great god shone in those days, and it didn't rain all the time like now."

Dear Lord, I thought. *They've given me a Druid for a thrall, and mad to boot.*

Ragna granted, when she came in to check on me, that the old man was daft, but she said he was too bent for field work and ought to do something for his feed. As we spoke he sat by my fire, picking lice out of a blanket and saying a prayer for each as he flicked it into the flame and heard it pop. I asked why I couldn't have a Christian, and she said it would breed jealousy; the priest's servant would put on airs. "Anyway, you should convert him. That's your job."

When Erling looked in I pulled the blankets over my head and pretended to sleep.

"I'd not have sold you," he said.

At first I couldn't think what he was talking of.

"In Visby," he went on. "At the time I was serious, but when I'd thought it out I knew I'd never sell a Christian priest back to the heathen. If you'd refused I'd have taken you somewhere where there was a church."

I'd known that for some time, but I wouldn't give him the satisfaction of saying so.

Halla came the next day. "Erling is hurt that you won't speak to him," she said, sitting on the edge of the bed with an easiness that troubled me.

"Good," said I.

"You've been like the wrath of God ever since they hanged that thrall."

I held the crucifix up where she could see it. "He made this," I said. "His name was Enda. He was about your age. He was young and rash, and he tried to better himself by stealing from his enemies. If he were Norse they'd call him a Viking and skoal him in the hall."

"So what would you? Should Erling make a law that thralls may steal?"

"He needn't hang them."

"Most men say he's too kind. They wanted the boy whipped to death."

"I'm sure Enda was most grateful as he strangled."

"Are the laws so much gentler in Ireland?"

I rubbed my eyes. "It's the whole way of things, the waste of lives, using people like cattle. Keeping them down because you know that if they get a fair chance they'll have plenty of their own to get back from you. Look at what happened to that bastard Kark."

"He murdered Haakon. You're not condoning murder, surely?"

"Olaf had sworn an oath. He saw no need to keep it to a thrall."

"The oath wasn't meant for Kark. And it wasn't meant for as craven a deed as Kark did. Kark knew that. He betrayed his lord, who'd given him gifts. Even a free man would be despised for that."

"And is Erling different? He let Haakon's enemy sail out of his hands, just because he thought Haakon was doomed and Olaf might make a better friend."

Halla stood up, her face pale. "Do you believe such a thing of Erling?"

"I don't know what I believe of anyone in this country. I thought Erling worthy of my trust. Now I wonder."

"You think like a thrall," she said, and went out.

"Perhaps I do, perhaps I do," I muttered.

Erling came to see me again soon after. He stood for a while a few feet from my bed while I ignored him.

"You're free to go," he said.

"What do you mean?" I asked, surprised into speech.

"When the spring comes and sailing's good, you're free to take the first passing ship bound for Ireland. You've repaid your price and more since you've been here. I'd thought you'd like to stay and see the thing through, but perhaps it's best you go home. If that's what you want."

Don't be generous!, I screamed inside. *I don't want your generosity!*

Aloud I said, "I want to see my child born."

Erling went out.

And finally came Steinbjorg, a shape in the darkness, a warmth and weight against me in bed. I could feel our baby kicking at my ribs.

"I think it was wonderful, the way you tried to save the child," she whispered, putting her arms around my neck.

It was good to be praised. I kissed her cheek.

"And afterward, when you said you were frightened for our child," she said, "that made me very happy."

I muttered something.

"And I thought, 'If he loves the baby, perhaps he loves the mother, too. . . .'"

I said nothing. We lay unspeaking, with no sound but the wind and the muffled surf. I could have lied to her. I'm not sure why I didn't.

"What did Lord Erling say when you told him of the danger?" she asked finally.

"The danger?"

"To our child. Soti's threat."

"I didn't tell him."

"Why not?"

"Is he the father of the child? Is he God? Do I have to run to my master with my every fear and beg him for protection? Can't I guard my own flesh?"

Steinbjorg turned away from me. "You talk just like the thralls."

CHAPTER XX

The next day I rose a couple hours before the morning meal. Steinbjorg had gone, the peat fire burned low, and Caedwy lay on the bench curled up in a blanket, arms wrapped around a cur dog he'd adopted when he came to me. He slept by himself, and needed the animal for warmth. The dog twisted its neck and stared at me as I pulled on breeches and socks under my robe and tied my shoes on.

Caedwy's head turned too, and I could dimly see their four eyes reflecting. "Feeling better, master?"

"Yes. I'm going out."

"Cold morning."

"I'd noticed." I went to my chest, fished out the key I kept on a cord around my neck, and unlocked it.

"Anything you want?"

"No. You needn't get up." I took out a hefty sealskin pouch. Inside was the silver I'd gotten as my share of the Vikings' plunder that day off the point of Jutland, plus the price Erling had paid me for Lemming. I hadn't had a use for it until now.

"I've heard you talking of that boy Enda," said Caedwy.

"What of him?"

"A good boy, that. 'Twas a shame."

"Yes."

"I can see why you're cross. We of the Brotherhood, we who've seen the great mysteries, we know that such laws as hanged poor Enda, they're nothing. We've seen the true law, and men like Lord Erling are blind to it, and will always be."

"For the last time," said I, "I am not of your Brotherhood, and I know nothing of your mysteries, nor wish to."

"That's how I know you're a Master, master. In these times a true Master would never reveal it but to another, and I, the gods help me, have never attained mastery."

I went out saying, "Go back to sleep."

There was an old turf house on Sola, half fallen in from rot, and there Lemming lived by himself. I left tracks in virgin snow as I walked there, and I couldn't see the house at first for the fog. The air was as still as inside a chest.

I stood outside the door and knocked. I feared he might anger at being wakened, but he answered right away and bade me come in.

He had a fire going, and by its glow I saw him sitting on a pile of skins. He didn't look like a man just wakened. He might have been sitting there all night, power at rest, staring into his fire.

I drew the pouch from my bosom and tossed it down in front of him, making a clatter. "I want to hire you," I said.

He stared at the pouch as if he'd never seen one

before, then raised his eyes to me without speaking. One scarred eyebrow rose, and I took it for a question.

"You'd probably do it for nothing," I said. "This is a job you'll enjoy. But I want you to do it for my need, not yours."

He said one word: "Soti."

"I helped stop you killing him once. I repent it now. I thought I was saving my soul, but I sell it today anyway. I've no wish to hang, nor to see you hang. It must look like an accident."

Lemming gazed at me as an animal would. It unnerved me. His look might have meant anything, or no more thought than a skull's.

"It's a pity Jaeder has no cliffs," I said. "Cliffs are wonderful for accidents. They're often deserted, one push and he's over, and who's to say he didn't slip?"

The look did not change.

"I don't know why you hate him so," said I. "I'm sure you've good reason. My reason is that he's threatened my unborn child. I wish I could kill him myself, but I don't think I'm a match for him, even crippled. I'm sure God—my God, that is— understands that. But whatever guilt there is, I take on myself. By paying you I take the guilt. At least that's how I see it—"

I saw I was babbling and stopped my mouth. Why justify myself to this heathen beast? We stared at each other across the fire for a moment.

Then Lemming grinned at me, showing broken teeth.

I went back to my house and found that Caedwy had rearranged my few bits of furniture. My chest, my stool, even the pile of peat turves near the hearth, had all been aligned parallel to each other and at a shallow angle to the walls and benches. A small enough thing, but I didn't like it. I went out to find him and ran him down in the church, where he was doing the same thing to the chest and the altar furnishings, all the time droning some song about an ash grove.

"What are you doing?" I cried.

Caedwy looked at me with Christmas eyes. "The perfect conjunction!" he cried. "East and west, the path of God. We do all in humility, that we may right ourselves with the ways of the heavens. When the stars were sheep, their beards fed the fish. These northerners know not the true path of God, but I can always tell, even in the dark, even in a fog, even a hundred miles under the earth. Why don't men have breasts?"

"Put everything back the way you found it," I said. "Do it now."

"Of course!" said Caedwy. "I see! How wise you are, master!"

Erling greeted me when I went to the morning meal, my first in the hall since Jul, but I answered coolly. He left me to myself then, and spoke to others.

A singular thing happened before we were finished. A strange man rushed into the hall with a spear in his hand and cast it through the body of one of the men at the table across the hearthway. Everyone was up in a moment, and I vaulted our table, leaped over the fire and pushed through the bodies to the stricken man, whose friends had already laid him out on their table. At the same time several of the bullyboys seized the intruder and began knocking him about. I couldn't recall whether I'd seen the wounded man in church or not, and I was asking him if he was a Christian and wanted last rites, but the noise was too great for me to hear his answer. Erling's shout finally brought quiet.

"Silence!" he roared. "Stop hitting that bastard—hold him until we know more. Father Ailill—how is he?"

"Nearly gone," said I. I spoke to the man. "Are you a Christian, lad?"

"No," he said. "I go with Thor. But I need to know—why?"

Erling needed to know the same thing. His face was bright red. He had the attacker brought before the high seat.

"My name is Arnor Baardsson," said the man. "I come from Thornheim farm near Randaberg."

"Randaberg is Kar's home," said Erling, referring to the man bleeding under my hands. "What's your quarrel with him?"

"I was trying to say, my lord, before these men stopped my mouth, that I have slain Kar Thorsteinsson lawfully in daylight, and before witnesses, in vengeance for the death of my brother Bjorgulf."

Kar whispered, "I know nothing of Bjorgulf's death."

"He says he knows nothing of it, my lord," I said to Erling.

"What say you, Arnor?" Erling asked.

"Within the last week feud has broken out between

Thornheim and Randaberg," Arnor answered. "It began with the killing of my cousin Asmund. Since then two more men are dead of my family, and now three of theirs that I know of. I've been a day traveling."

"Kar had no part in any crimes against you."

"He's the greatest warrior of his family. It was more honorable to kill him than some weakling."

"Did you think that it might make you a powerful enemy, to kill one of my bodyguard before my eyes in my own hall?"

"I know you for an honorable lord, Erling Skjalgsson. You will not have a man slain out of hand for a lawful killing."

"Don't chop law with me," Erling almost whispered. "You've killed a man of mine in my own hall, without giving him any chance to defend himself. I can take you out and have you hanged, and never pay a ounce of mansbot."

"My lord, may I speak?" asked Halvard Thorfinsson, who sat on our bench down near the women's end. When I heard his voice I couldn't help glancing at Sigrid, who watched her love with great eyes.

"What has this to do with you, Halvard?" asked Erling.

"Arnor is kin to me. I too knew nothing of this feud, but I beg you to accept self-judgment, and ask you to name what price you'll take for the offense."

"It's unwise for young warriors to make pleas for the enemies of their lords."

"Arnor's no enemy of yours, Lord Erling, unless you'll have it so. His fight is with the Randabergers.

He has acted rashly, but it was a bold deed nonetheless. There will be blood enough shed before this business is over with. You can leave the killing to us."

Erling's face had gone back to its wonted color. "The mansbot for killing a lord is thirty-six *aurar*," he said. "I'll have no less for this offense to me."

"Our kin will pay it."

"I do not like these feuds in my lands, Halvard. They waste men and wealth."

"A man must have vengeance for his kin," said Arnor.

Kar died then. There was blood everywhere.

I looked at Sigrid again. Her eyes shone like blue stars.

They let Arnor go his way, and carried Kar out. I hadn't finished my breakfast, but had no stomach left.

I was just walking out into the steading under a leaden sky when I heard the cry of "Fire!"

Everyone looked for the smoke, and we saw it coming from the direction of the smithy.

I was one of the first there, and only had time to glance at the man who knelt over a charred body outside the door before we were all scooping snow up in our hands and throwing it inside. The smithy had stone walls, and the beams inside were already aflame, so there was little we could do. Men started bringing up buckets of water from the well, but the fire only died when the turf roof fell in and smothered everything.

Then we turned to see Lemming kneeling by Soti's black body, heaping snow on him to cool his burns.

The smith's big chest rose and fell, but he did not move otherwise.

"He must have caught a spark from the forge in his clothes," said someone. "Did you pull him out, Lemming?"

Lemming nodded.

"Will he live?"

Lemming shook his head.

"Soti always kept water nearby to douse himself," somebody said.

"Perhaps he couldn't move fast enough on his bad feet," said the first. "Anyway, he caught fire."

"Strange Lemming would try to save him," said someone else. "He hates Soti."

Lemming widened his eyes.

"When you see a man burning," I put in, "you just act. You don't think whether he's your enemy or not." Lemming turned his eyes on me, and I walked away.

Caedwy awaited me at my house. " 'Tis good, 'tis good!" he cried. "A wicker cage would be better, but we do what we can. You're all black with soot and blood, master, like the men who lived on the moon when the stones fell up. I'll bring water to wash you with."

CHAPTER XXI

They bore Soti to his house in a blanket to die, and his burial was the following day. I watched from a distance. That night when I came in from the hall I found Caedwy sitting beneath the lamp in my house, staring into a small basket he held on his knees.

"Tell him to stop it," said Steinbjorg from the bed. "He makes my skin prickle."

"What are you doing?" I asked.

"Telling our fortunes, master."

"What's that mess in the basket?"

"The guts of a pig. I got them from the kitchen."

"You're divining from pig guts?"

"A horse's or a man's would be better, or a black cat's best of all, but we make do." He blinked his large brown eyes up at me.

I sat down on the bench, weary and not a little drunk. "And what do your guts tell you?" I asked.

"You will live long and see great things," said Caedwy.

"I'd prefer to live long and see little things. Great things have a way of coming out bloody and bitter."

"You'll be offered your heart's desire. But you'll cast it away."

176

"That sounds like me. And what of you?"

"You'll set me free."

"Not if you keep up this soothsaying. It's devil's work, and puts both our souls in danger. Get rid of those guts. I want to go to bed."

"He said I'd die," said Steinbjorg.

I reached over and grabbed the man by his shirt and shook him. "What did you tell her?"

"I didn't say she'd die. I said I see darkness before her and darkness within her."

"If I ever catch you playing this Hell's game again, I'll twist your head off. Do you understand me?"

Caedwy threw the mess to his dog, who attacked it with relish.

"He tells the truth," said a voice at the door. I jerked my head up in fright. My door usually squeaked loudly on its leather hinges when opened. How Ulvig got through it in silence I'll never know.

"What do you want?" I asked.

For a reply she walked to me and slapped me across the face. I leaped up, raised my hand, then stood poised.

"If I were a man, you'd strike me," she said.

"So?"

"You think you're safe now that you've killed my Soti. Think you I don't see your hand behind it? But you've missed the mark by a long span. You'll find that of the two of us, Soti was the gentle one."

She left, leaving the door open to the bitter wind. Caedwy and his cur huddled in a corner, whimpering, and the guttering light made the room sway like the sea.

❖   ❖   ❖

Ragna came to me one day and said, "You must go and speak to Halla."

"What's wrong?"

"She's gone mad. I've tried to talk to her, and so have all the women, and she's raving. It must be a devil."

I put on my cloak and followed her to the hall. As I started up the stairs to the loft, I looked back to see Ragna still standing below.

"Aren't you coming along?" I asked.

She shook her head. "The old gods speak through madness. It's not right I should see their faces. I'm too lately out of their worship."

"She's a fair woman and I'm a priest. It's not right we should be alone in a sleeping chamber."

"Just go to her before she does herself harm. We've taken all the steel from the loft, but the mad can always find ways."

"Call your daughters or a serving woman then."

"They won't come near."

A scream from above decided me. I clattered up to the balcony and in to Halla.

Loft rooms are always smoky, but my first thought as I entered was that the place had caught fire. I couldn't see anything, and my nose and mouth clogged with something that stopped my breath. I staggered out the door and found I was covered in down. Halla had slaughtered a cushion. When I went back in I found her laughing at me in a swirl of drifting feathers.

"It's snowing inside!" she cried. "It's Fimbul Winter, the end of the world!" She wore an everyday overdress and shift, and they were disarranged, besides which she was covered from head to foot in feathers.

"What's the matter with you, lass?" I asked.

"What's the matter with you, Father Ailill?" She shook her long hair in a spray around her head.

"Ah well, we haven't time enough for that, and you're the one making a fuss."

"I'll be good," she said. She sat down on a chest and folded her hands on her knees. She blew a feather off her nose and giggled. "I always do what's expected of me, and I never, never, never make a fuss. When my father says 'You'll go with Lord Erling and be his leman,' I go. When Erling takes a wife, I'll welcome her and not make a squeak, or go home to my father if he sends me. I'm a good girl. Aren't I a good girl, Father?"

"You're a rare girl, my daughter, but I fear you're making a fuss nevertheless."

She looked around at the settling feathers. "It's my cushion. I sewed it with my own hands. Why shouldn't I set it free? I want to see it fly away!" She ran to the door, opened it, and stood trying to shoo the feathers out into the breeze.

I got up and closed the door to keep her off the balcony, and she sighed. "They won't go," she said. "They like it here. They love me, and now they can't understand why I tried to send them away. I'll gather them up and sew them a new cushion if that's what they want. I didn't know. I thought they might like a change."

"Did something happen to trouble you?" I asked.

She knelt at my feet and took my hands. "Do you think me fair, Father?" she asked.

There was a bench behind me and I sat on it, still holding her hands. "I think you're as fair as a summer morning with the sun rising over Lough Erne. The grass is dewy and fat, so a man could live on it, and the flowers open their mouths and praise God with a song of sweet odor, and the birds raise a hymn they learned from Solomon two thousands of years since, and have passed on in secret to their children ever after. And far across the water you can see swans swimming, and the sunrise tints them pink, and the breeze is so mild and gentle it's like the hand of your mother on your forehead when you're a child, and sick, and she fears to lose you." Unfit words for a priest, but they came out of me like the feathers from her cushion, as easy lost and as hopeless to recall, once the fabric was torn.

She pulled away from me. "How am I like a lough?" she asked, shaking her head. "Am I flat as water? Do I make waves when I move? How am I like grass? Am I green?" She began to struggle out of her overdress, then lifted her shift saying, "Where am I green? Tell me where I'm green!" I covered my eyes, sweating with the hunger to look on her.

"Why do you stop your eyes?" Halla asked. "Am I so ugly—flat like the water, green like the grass? Perhaps I have legs like those swans. Perhaps I am a swan. If I could fly away, I'd know better what to do than a lot of stupid feathers—"

I had to open my eyes then, for I could hear her footsteps toward the door, and I feared she might run out on the balcony and leap. I caught her as she worked the latch, and held her naked in my arms. Her skin was very smooth, her bones very small.

"Put your clothes back on, Halla," I said.

"Why?" Her eyes were wide and innocent.

"Because your clothes love you, and it hurts them that you cast them off."

"I wouldn't want to hurt them. I wouldn't want to cast anyone off." I let her go and she got her shift and slipped it on again, unashamed as a child. I couldn't take my eyes off her. Then she put on her overdress and sat on the chest. I sat across from her.

"You look at me with angry eyes, Father," she said.

"I'm not angry, daughter. I just wonder what brought you to this."

"You mustn't wonder about things. When you wonder about things you think about the future, and when you think about the future it makes you sad, but you can't help anything. I'm never going to wonder about anything again."

"The future shouldn't make you sad. God holds you in His hands."

"There's much road to walk between today and Heaven. It's what I'll meet on the road that frightens me. I wish I could fly to Heaven this moment. If I ran out and jumped from the balcony, maybe—"

"You'd probably only break some bones. And if you died you'd be a suicide, and God wouldn't have you."

"I don't think God's fair."

"You're not the first nor the last He'll hear that from."

"You have something on your face."

"What?"

She laughed. "You have something on your face. It looks funny."

"Where?" I rubbed my nose and cheeks.

"Not there."

"Where then?"

She got up and came toward me. She leaned down near my face and peered closely. "Right there," she said, and kissed me quickly on the lips.

I couldn't move. She put her hands on my shoulders and kissed me again. "If I lay with you," she said, "and I had a child, we'd never know if it was yours or Erling's. Wouldn't that be funny?"

I stood up and pulled away. "Don't say such things."

"Don't you like me?"

"I'm a priest!"

"You lie with Steinbjorg."

"Steinbjorg isn't Erling's woman."

She plumped down on the floor. "Yes, it should be Erling's child. I want it to be Erling's child. That's why I went to Ulvig. I'm getting sleepy, Father."

I gaped at her. "You went to Ulvig?"

"I know it's wrong. To go to a witch. But I want to have Erling's child, and she can give you drinks to open the womb."

"Is that what she gave you? A drink to open your womb?"

"Yes."

"And when did you take it?"

"This morning. Before breakfast." Her head was nodding now.

"Don't go to sleep," I said.

"I can't—I can't keep my eyes open."

I took her in my arms and half carried her outside and down the steps to find Ragna. "Ulvig gave her a potion for barrenness," I said. "God knows what was in it. Get your daughters and some of the women and we'll keep her walking in the snow until it wears off."

And that's what we did through the rest of the day, and long into the night. She was sweaty and pale, and she shivered and screamed, but I loved walking her about when my turn came, and I could not forget the sight of her body in the loft, or the curve of her back under my hands.

CHAPTER XXII

Erling was furious with Ulvig and threatened to bring suit at the next Thing, but she told him to wait and see what harm had been done; and, God help us, in time it became plain that Halla was with child. I thought no good could come of such a conception, but the lass was happy; and what could I have done anyway? I made Erling promise to let me christen it in its birth hour though.

"Why did she do it?" he asked me in private.

"I'm not free to answer that," I said.

"Then just tell me if I'm wrong. Does she think I'll marry her if she has my child?"

I said nothing.

"I see. I never knew she took it so much to heart. I must think on this."

The rains came and washed away the snow, and then it snowed again, and then the rains returned. We had thunderstorms in February, which is a pleasureless thing. I took a wild guess on when Lent should begin, and proclaimed the fast.

In mid-March the thralls began carrying manure out of the byres in baskets on their backs to spread on the fields with seaweed. And in April the cranes and wild geese came back, and the heathens made sacrifices in secret places, and the thralls put on wooden clogs and began spading late in April (or early in Cuckoo Month, by the Norse reckoning), and then I had my hands full setting up the freedom plan. Those thralls who had no crafts got plots of land to work, and there was a lot of grumbling and comparing, and I had to knock a few heads together before everybody was happy.

A ship sailed in one day from Hordaland with a summons from Olmod and the Horder lords for Erling to meet them and discuss Olaf Trygvesson. He sailed off in *Fishhawk*, leaving a strong guard (strengthened by conscripted bonders) under Eystein, and plenty of watchmen along the coast. Along with Erling went Halvard Thorfinsson, to be dropped off near his home and join the feud. No one saw Sigrid weep, but she went about with reddened eyes. I said a special mass before they left, but Erling and I did not bid each other goodbye.

The following day one of the thralls came to me and said, "I can't work that plot you set me on."

"What's wrong with it?"

"Nothing wrong with the land. The land's fine. But a man can't go out in the countryside these evenings. The troll'll get him."

"Troll? What troll?"

"Haven't you heard? He's been seen by many after dark. Sometimes skulking around Ulvig's house; sometimes out in the fields or the hills. I can't go out and work that land in the evenings with him around. What use is freedom when you're eaten by a troll? And if it's not the troll, it's the underground-woman."

My ears pricked up. "You've seen an elf-woman?"

"You mustn't use that word. They don't like it. I haven't seen her myself, no. But she's been seen. And there's nothing more dangerous than an underground-woman. I'd rather face a troll than an underground-woman."

"What does she look like?"

"What do you expect? She's beautiful. She's—how do you say—ripe. A man looks at her and hears her voice, and he forgets who he is. The next thing he knows it's forty years later, and he thinks it's been but a night, and he's shaking all over and his hair's white."

I said, "I'll tell you what. You get some sticks and carve yourself a crucifix. Then come to me and I'll bless it, and that should protect you from trolls and . . . undergrounders."

"Will it really, Father?"

"Without a doubt."

It was worth a try. I went to the hall for supper mulling over the fact that someone else had seen my elf-woman. This was good from the standpoint that I might not be mad; it was bad from the standpoint that she might really be around, and would have to be dealt with. I had no illusions regarding my strength in spirit. I believed in God again, but I did not love Him, and if He'd done things through me it was only for want of a proper tool.

And there was a part of me that thought, "It might be worth forty years and white hair to put hands on that creature."

I crossed myself and said the Pater Noster.

The mood in the hall was cheerless, as most of the bodyguard would have liked to have gone with Erling, and the bonders wanted to be home for planting. This was worsened by the knowledge that there would be red meat to eat in Hordaland and most of their homes, while we made do with fish because of Lent. Lent was my fault, and some of them let me know it.

"The trouble with your god, god-man," said Bergthor, "is that he acts like any other king. He comes along and does something that he says is for you, and you're expected to thank him for it and pay him back for it, even though you never asked for it in the first place. I'd just as soon face the Devil myself, man to man, and make a fight of it without any meddling from priests or kings."

"It would be no fair fight," said I. "The powers that oppose us are not so great as God, but you and I are less than fleas in their sight."

"Well, size and strength aren't everything," Bergthor replied. "A man can kill a bear or an aurochs because he's smarter than they."

"Devils are also smarter than we."

"I don't believe it."

"It's true," said another man further down the bench. "I know a thing that happened—it happened to a man I knew—well, I didn't actually know him, but my cousin knew him. He lived up on Kormt Island, and was a fisherman."

"Not a fishing story!" said Bergthor.

"It proves how much shrewder the spirits are than we. This fisherman went out in his boat one day and set his lines, and when he tried to pull one line up, he felt a heavy weight at the end. He thought he'd caught a fine big fish, but when he pulled it up, what did he see but a man's face! He pulled further, and saw he'd caught a merman. Of course he knew that a merman can tell you anything you want to know, so he caught him fast and bound him with the fishing line. 'Now, tell me how I can be sure I'll always make good catches,' he told the merman, but the merman wouldn't answer. So he rowed home as fast as he could and carried the creature, struggling, on shore.

"As he climbed up from the strand his young wife came down from the house to greet him, and she said, 'What have you caught, husband?' and he said, 'I've caught a merman, and I'll force him to tell me how to make good catches, and we'll be wealthy folk,' and his wife kissed him and made much of him. The farmer liked this, and when his dog came up and began jumping about them he kicked the beast so it ran away howling.

"And the merman laughed.

"As they made their way to their house, the husband carrying the merman, he had trouble watching his step because his prisoner struggled so, and he tripped over a tussock of earth and almost lost his grip.

" 'Curse you, you stupid tussock!' he cried. 'I don't know why a thing like you was put there to trip up honest men!'

"And the merman laughed.

"When the fisherman got home, he set the merman in a corner of his house and told him, 'There you'll sit, my good fellow, and neither food nor drink will you get until you answer me every question I wish to ask you.' But the merman said nothing.

"A little later the fisherman's thrall came in, and the fisherman told him he needed him to make him a new pair of boots. 'And do it right this time,' he said. 'The last pair you made had soles much too thin. I don't want these wearing out in a season, like the last pair.'

"And the merman laughed.

"The merman said not a word for a full week. At the end of that time, he said to the fisherman, 'Row me out to the spot where you caught me, set me free, and I'll squat on your oarblade and tell you all you wish to know.'

"The fisherman knew the merman would not lie, so he carried him down to the boat and rowed out to the very spot where he'd caught him, and cut the cords that bound him. The merman leaped out onto the oarblade and squatted there, saying, 'Ask now.'

"The farmer said, 'How can I be always sure to catch all the fish I want?'

"The merman said, 'Use a three-barbed hook, forged from new iron and tempered in blood. Bait one barb with fish, one with pork, and the third with human flesh. Use a fishing line made of a man's gut, and you will always catch all you can row off with.'

" 'Good. Now explain to me. Why did you laugh when I kissed my wife and kicked my dog?'

" 'Because you're a fool. Your dog loves you, and would die for you, while your wife hates you and has a lover, and wishes you were dead.'

" 'And why did you laugh when I cursed the tussock?'

" 'Because you're a fool. There's a Viking treasure buried under that tussock, and it's destined for you. You cursed your own fortune.'

" 'And why did you laugh when I told my thrall I wanted thick soles on my boots?'

" 'Because you're a fool. Those boots will last you the rest of your life.' And with that the merman leaped off the oar and down into the sea, and was seen no more.

"Well, the farmer rowed home as fast as he could, and ran and got a spade, and he dug up that tussock, and there was a heavy chest buried there, just as the merman had said. He carried it home, and his wife said, 'What's this, husband?' and the fisherman said, 'This is our fortune, my dear,' and they broke it open and it was filled with gold and silver. And the fisherman was so happy he forgot all the rest the merman had told him, and he and his wife drank and were merry till early morning.

"And when he had passed out drunk, his wife stole away to her lover's house and she said, 'The old man has found a treasure, and no one knows it but I and you. Let's kill him now, and flee with the money.'

"They crept up to the house, and as they came near the fisherman's dog began to bark, and the lover killed him with his axe. And at the sound of the barking the fisherman awoke, but was too drunk to get out of bed, and the last thing he ever saw was his wife's lover coming towards him with his bloody axe.

"And they buried him in his new boots.

"So you see, it's no use thinking we're smarter than the devils. They always laugh last."

"That's an uncheery story," said Bergthor.

As we sat thinking about it, Ulvig came down the hearthway.

"You are all prisoners," she said. She said it to all of us but her eye was on me.

"What rot is this?" demanded Eystein.

"The kinsmen of Soti have come for revenge. There are more than a hundred of them, and those not stronger than he are greater magicians than he. We have the wardens, we have the balefires, we have the thralls, we have the children, we have the armory."

"Codswallop," said Eystein. "No hundred men could come on Sola unseen."

"Soti's kinsmen can. They can cross new snow without leaving a mark. They can steal upon a rabbit in broad daylight and seize it with their hands. When you think you see them, it's only the shadow of a cloud, or a wolf prowling. When you see them not, then they are surely there."

"Why do you come to us like this," I asked, "instead of just firing the hall?"

"We want only one man's death—yours, god-man. But your death is not enough. You will sacrifice to the old gods first."

"Never," said I.

"We have Steinbjorg. We can cut her child from her belly and offer it."

I reeled. Eystein said to me, "Don't listen to her. We'll fight our way out and kill these heathen."

"Not before the woman and child die," said Ulvig.

"I'll sacrifice," I said.

"It's not worth it—not for a thrall!" said Eystein.

"Before God she's my wife, and the child is my flesh!" I said.

"Let's be clear," said Ulvig. "Let's see that all is understood. Your holy ones who died in Romaborg, they let their wives and children be tortured and killed rather than sacrifice to other gods, did they not?"

"Aye," said I.

"But you will sacrifice to save your woman and child?"

"I will."

"And your god will surely send you to Hel for it?"

"Without a doubt."

She beamed at me. "Good. Very, very good. All you men, and you women too, leave the weapons behind and follow us."

She led the way out into the night. *Enough, God. You've asked of me all I can give. There is an end to endurance.* I said to Ulvig, "Do I have your sworn word you'll spare Steinbjorg and the child, and kill none but me?"

"Unless they threaten us, all may live."

I knew she'd keep her word. I'd have done this for Maeve, given the chance. At least I could do it for Steinbjorg and the babe. Then to Hell with me. What did I matter anyway?

The men who ringed the hall bore torches, and some of them were tall and broad, like Soti, dressed all in furs, and others were small and dark, with odd tasseled caps and shoes whose toes curled up. The big ones carried spears and shields, and the small ones had bows and arrows.

Ulvig led the way, never looking back, sure of her power. We took a path I knew well. It led to the Melhaugs.

We had a full moon for it. We could make out Big and Little Melhaug far off—just humps of earth, grown with heather. The same good earth that feeds us, and will cover us someday, only this earth was not good. Drums were beating, a rhythm like the thumping of a coward's heart.

As we drew near, someone lit a fire near the bigger mound, and I saw what looked like a huge, long-legged insect rise up in its light. I had a brief terror that I'd be fed to this thing like a fly to a spider; then I saw that it was a platform, twenty feet high, and the small men from the north were raising it on six poles and lashing its supports tight. And they had built an altar of stones nearby.

They ranged us, men and women, in a wide circle about the mound and the platform, and Soti's kin stood armed behind us. Ulvig took a place near the fire, and this is what she said:

"This night belongs to Frey, and to Freya his sister. On this night the gods say to us, 'Men, be as we are.' The laws were made by the gods for men to obey, and it is good that we should submit to them; but the laws do not apply to the gods. The gods are in the earth, and the earth is cruel, miring men in bogs, breaking them in rockslides, bringing forth poisonous plants. The gods are in the air, and the air is cruel, bearing sicknesses, sending hails and snows and lightnings. The gods are in the water, and the water is cruel, withholding its fish when men starve, and drowning them far from home. The gods may lie, as Tyr lied to Fenris. The gods may murder in secret, as indeed they do each day. The gods may couple, parent with child and brother with sister, as Frey and Freya do.

"The gods will be with us tonight. What does it mean when the gods are with us?"

Soti's kin cried out together, "ALL IS PERMITTED!"

I shuddered. Bergthor, beside me, said, "I'd heard of it, but I'd never seen it. This wasn't our custom here, even under Skjalg. In the old days yes, but it'd gone out of use before my father was born."

"What are you talking about?"

"The great summer sacrifice."

The little men from the north piped on pipes in time with the drums, and Ulvig began a dance around the fire, slowly at first, then faster and faster. She wore a heavy black robe with fur trim I'd never seen on her before, and soon her face glowed with sweat and her eyes glowed with joy. There was a kettle cooking over the fire, and one of the little men brought her a dipper of whatever was in it, and when she'd had it she cast off her headcloth and let her long red hair fly free, and it spun out a rain that looked like blood in the firelight.

And then a man came from somewhere, and I'd have sworn it was Soti if Soti weren't dead, but I couldn't see his face as he wore a woolen mask, and on his head was a ridiculous bronze helmet with horns, and he too wore black, and they danced together in the moonlight, and the dance was shameful.

And the little men piped and drummed, and they sang a song in a strange tongue, and danced in place with small steps.

And one of them brought the dipper to me, and I saw and smelled that it was some kind of meat stew, and I thought of Erling's martyred priest as I drank it.

Then Ulvig staggered to the platform, and she began to climb, unsteady as if drunk. When she had gone up a few feet, she stopped and cried, "I see all the Northland! Everywhere the gods walk unseen, and they mark who keep the sacrifices, and who have set them aside for the White Christ. And they send pestilence and bad seasons and unpeace to their enemies!"

She climbed a little further and cried, "I see all the world! The gods are everywhere—called by other names, but remembered, and honored, and fed. I say to you, men of Jaeder, the great world is not Christian as you think! Our gods are mighty, and they remember their friends!"

And she climbed yet again, and came at last to the top, and she stood on the swaying platform and spread her arms in the moonlight and shouted, "I see the heavens and the nine worlds! I see Asgard, where faithful warriors go when they die, and there they battle by day, and at night their wounds are healed, and they feast on pork and drink sweet mead, and listen to brave songs, and lie with the fairest virgins! But the followers of the White Christ go down to Hel, and there the trencher is called hunger and the knife Famine, and they lie down at night on a bed called Sickness."

And the little men piped and drummed, and sang their song, and there was a company of folk dancing in the firelight, men and women.

Ulvig cried, "Bring now the god's gifts!" And there were brought a ram, and a boar, and a hound, and a stallion, and last of all Freydis Sotisdatter, wrapped in a white bearskin and carried on a pallet, seeming half asleep. They laid the child on the altar.

And the beasts began to roar and bay and rear and kick, so that those who led them had to hold tight to the ropes. And then I saw what had panicked them, for dancing with the dancers was my elf-woman.

"As was done with me, and with my mother, so it will be with my daughter!" cried Ulvig. "She is twelve summers old, and she will be made one with Freya by coupling with a thrall, and a ram, and a boar, and a hound, and a stallion, and so she will be mother and wife to all things in the earth! Then the thrall, and the ram, and the boar, and the hound, and the stallion will be sacrificed! Bring the thrall!"

Then came the elf-woman, smooth as water, to take my hand and lead me forward.

And as she came to me, soft and silken and rosy and filling my nostrils with a scent like flowers and rain and moldy wheat, I thought, *What could be more right? The horse is happy because he's a horse, and does not try to be an angel, and he runs and he eats and rolls in the grass and he fornicates with any mare who'll have him. He is not good or evil— he's just a horse. But a man chokes his head with a thousand puzzles of right and wrong, and for all his trouble he never feels right. Except for these*

heathens—they're happy, like beasts. They don't
wage war on the world they live in. Why have I
wasted all these years wrestling myself? I could be
happy right now, this moment . . .

And God help me, I went willingly. I'd forgotten
right and wrong like a tale heard years since, and a
dull one. I think not one man of Erling's knew shame
at that moment, or would have done otherwise.

I've never been so ready. I was ready as any beast
who smells the female in heat. The hand of the elf-
woman felt hot on my arm. I almost ran to the altar
where Freydis lay, fumbling to pull my robe up.
My own sacrifice meant nothing to me if only I could
plant my sacred seed.

And then Halla was before me, and I swear I didn't
recognize her at first as she screamed in my face,
"NO! THIS IS EVIL!" and struck me.

And I blinked, and suddenly I knew her, and I
remembered who I was, and I looked at Freydis
and saw a little girl with tears on her cheeks. And I
shouted, "NO!"

The elf-woman clutched at Halla, and Halla
slapped her face. The elf-woman swung her arm,
and Halla flew ten feet backward, landing against
a man of the bodyguard and bowling him over.

Then the music faltered, and everyone looked
up, and we saw the platform sway, and under was
Lemming, lifting one of its legs, every sinew
straining, and we watched in silence as the whole
structure toppled, and Ulvig fell with it, screaming,
to land in a heap that did not move.

And I turned and tore an axe from the hand of
one of Soti's kinsmen, too stunned to resist me, and

I brained him with it. And Lemming killed another with his bare hands, and then Erling's men came to their senses and followed our lead. Then there was bloody work, and many dead on both sides, but the heart was out of our enemies, and we slew every last one we found. If any of the little men got away we could not know.

But before it was over I found Halla lying in the grass, and I held her in my arms and asked her if she was all right, and she wept and said, "Father, I think I'm losing the baby."

I sat crouched in the furrows of my patch, weeping over my lost children. As my sobs died, stifled in mere exhaustion, I looked up and saw the abbot there again, leaning on his stick.

"Gone are they, all your pretties?" he asked. "You've found the work harder than you expected? Your strong arm and your clever brain aren't quite up to the work?"

"No man could save my crop," I sobbed. "The ravens are too many, and too strong; and the crop so precious . . . I can't bear to plant another."

"Are you ready to pay the toll then?"

"My head? What good would that do, you blood-thirsty bastard?"

"And is it thus you speak to your betters who mean naught but your welfare?" His face twisted in anger and he raised his stick to strike me. I awaited the blow unmoving; I was past caring. The moment hung suspended like a water drop at an icicle's tip, but the smiting never came. At last I looked up to see him standing above me, stick hanging from his hand, face turned to the sky. He seemed to listen to words I could not hear. At last he shook his head, crossed himself, and lowered his gaze to me.

"Very well then," he said. "My advice to you, and it is the advice of a man both old and wise, is to dig."

"Wait a moment," said I. "What's happened now? Who spoke to you? Did they tell you not to beat me?"

"You ask too many questions."

" 'Twas Himself, wasn't it? He took my side! He took my side and you've not the guts to tell me!" It was as if a small, pale light had been struck in my heart. Much as I'd pitied myself through the years, and deeply as I'd felt my grievances, I'd never before been able to believe that God might truly side with me even once.

"What of it?" the abbot cried. "A blind hog finds an acorn now and again, and even such as you can't be wrong all the time. It doesn't change the fact that I'm your superior, and your digging remains to be done!"

He was right of course. A just God would not punish me more than I deserved, but my deserving was plenty enough. "Dig, you say?" I asked.

"Dig. Take your spade and dig. There is a treasure hidden in the field. Dig and find."

I stood and picked up the spade. "Where shall I dig?" I asked.

"Where you stand will do as well as anywhere."

I set my foot to the spade, dug it in and levered up a bladeful of stony earth, then another. "How deep do I dig?" I asked.

"As deep as necessary."

I dug and dug, until I had dug myself down waist-deep. "I'm not finding anything," I complained.

"Then I suppose you must not have dug far enough."

I dug and dug until my head was below ground, and yet I found nothing. I asked no more questions, but kept digging. With each spadeful I had farther to pitch the dirt over my head and out of the hole; often the clods and stones came back down on me. But I dug on. My hands grew blistered, my arms and legs cramped and aching, but on I dug.

I looked up at last, forced by weariness to rest myself. The sky was a small blue eye looking back at me, the abbot's head its pupil.

"Find anything?" he asked.

"Nothing," I panted.

"Then carry on."

Stifling a curse I stamped the spade once more into the earth, put all my weight on it, and with a sudden shudder and uprush of air the ground beneath me gave way, and I fell for the time it takes to pray three Pater Nosters (and believe me, I prayed them) before I came down with a splash into water.

I plunged deep and came up again floundering, gasping for air. I swam for shore, dragged myself onto sand, and looked about me.

It was Jaeder again; I stood on the sands of Sola Bay. I was puzzled for a moment, but one never troubles much over such things in a dream. The light might have been stronger than a real Jaeder day, the colors somewhat brighter; otherwise the only difference from the land I knew was the presence of one huge fir tree on Sola's high ground. "I'll go see this marvel," I said, and took the path to the farm.

I stopped outside the steading to stare. The farmstead was deserted. No warrior, free man or woman or thrall was there, no pig, no horse, no hound. In the center of the steading the fir tree grew, its boughs filling the yard.

"There's a hawk's nest at the top of the tree," said a voice behind me, and I turned to see the abbot.

"Is there indeed?"

"In the nest is an egg of gold. Inside the egg is a hawk who can protect your crop from the ravens. But you must find the hardest thing in the world to break the egg, else the hawk can never come forth."

"It's a very tall tree," I observed, cocking my eye at the top.

"Better get started then."

So I pushed my way in among the fir boughs, rough and resinous and cool in the shade, and set my foot on one of the lowest limbs, and began to make my way up, scaling as if on a ladder. It was easy climbing, but it never seemed to come to an end. Climbing inside the tree, as it were, behind the sun-loving needles, I couldn't well make out how far I'd come. Hours—even days—might have passed; the light never seemed to change. Only very gradually did the limbs grow smaller and shorter, and a moment came when my head emerged into the sunlight. The day seemed no further advanced than when I'd started. So either I hadn't climbed near as long as I'd thought, or I'd climbed a full day. Or two or more.

I turned my gaze upward, and now I could see the nest above me, still a long way up, where the tree seemed dangerously narrow and whippy. But I climbed on, and the further I climbed the further the crown bowed out under me, so that we were bent almost flush with the horizon when at last I reached the hawk's nest.

And there, just hanging under the nest's brim, was my golden egg. I took it in my hand with a shout, and as I shouted I lost my grip and fell toward the earth.

I fell in a strange calm. *If I'm to break the egg,* I thought to myself, *I might as well fall on top of it; perhaps one of the stones on the ground will do the job.*

And then I struck the ground, face down. I felt nothing, but knew my body had been shattered. I heard the abbot's voice above me. "A bad fall," he said. "Very poorly done." I felt his hand on my shoulder as he turned me over.

"The egg," I croaked when I could see his face. "Did it break?"

For an answer he held the thing up, shining and unmarred.

"You've got to heed the instructions," he said. "Only the hardest thing in the world may break this egg."

"What's harder than this cruel northern land?"

"Your heart, of course." And he reached his hand into my crushed chest and drew forth my living heart. Only it didn't look like a heart, it was only a rounded gray stone, like thousands you could find along the sea strand.

He took my stony heart and struck the egg with it, and the shell shattered like a sunburst, and a beautiful white hawk with red wings shot forth and soared into the bright bosom of the sky.

CHAPTER XXIII

The morning after Erling's return he came to me in the church and I said to him, "My lord, I must confess to you."

"I have no power to absolve you," he said.

"Still I must confess. I've judged you harshly, and I've no right to judge. You've heard what I did the night of the sacrifice?"

"I pray God I'm never tested as you were."

"I failed at every point."

"You did not do the thing at last."

"I ate horsemeat. Your martyr priest died rather than do that. But I can forgive that in myself, because I wanted to save my woman and child. I'm not a hero. But when I think that I was on the point of raping a twelve-year-old maid—I, who bled for my sister! I could dwindle to a mayfly, and fly away to Eastland and be eaten by an elephant, and the elephant be eaten by a hundred men, and all those men and all their descendants would die of my shame.

"I know what you'll say—there was magic at work, and the elf-woman, and the music and dancing, and the moon, and whatever they put in that stew. But they couldn't have called me if I hadn't known their tongue. I've seen—it's as if a man looked at his reflection in a pool, and saw a troll's face there."

Erling went to the altar and straightened a candle. "I know too little of God's teachings," he said, "but isn't this what they call repentance?"

I could not answer. No, it wasn't repentance, or not full repentance. I still hadn't told him I was no priest. I'd thought I might at first, but my courage failed.

"Lay a penance on yourself," he said. "Suffer and be done with it. I can't have my priest going about moaning over his sins. What I liked in you from the first was your spirit, and you'll not get far in Norway without it."

"How can I stand before the church when everyone saw me at the sacrifice?"

"Those with any sense will be as ashamed of themselves as you are. Those who blame you I'll mark, because I've noted that most men condemn loudest those sins they themselves haven't mastered. Perhaps that's why God is so merciful. Having no sins of His own, He finds nothing unforgiveable."

I shook my head. "That poor child. They brought a stallion! She'd have been killed, surely?"

"Most times they are, or so I've heard. But the ones who live are accounted mighty souls."

When I'd heard his confession and absolved him, Erling said, "Come with me to Lemming's house. He has a story, and I'll get it from him if I have to hold his feet to a fire, like Soti."

The big man was sleeping when we walked into his hovel, and he jerked up and nearly struck Erling before he saw who had shaken him.

Erling and I sat on the other bench as he stretched and scratched, wordless as a bear.

"I'll have your story," said Erling, "and I'll have it now. There are limits to our patience. You can't act as you have without explaining yourself."

Lemming leaned back against the wall and stared at us from shadowed eyes.

"What do we know?" said Erling. "We know you served Soti for years, and that you came to Sola with him from the north. You hated Soti—hated him as a man hates death. And you showed no special love for anyone else. Yet you lit the balefire at the risk of your life. Why? It seems to me there must have been someone at Sola for whom you did care."

Lemming stared and said nothing.

"Then came the great summer sacrifice, and again you put your life at risk. For whom? For Father Ailill? Not likely. But who else was in danger? If the sacrifice went on, none but he would have died."

Lemming's mouth twisted, and the cords of his neck stood out.

"But there was one in danger of another kind. The child, Freydis."

Lemming looked away.

"Ulvig said, I'm told, that the ceremony was performed on her when she was the same age. So she would have coupled with a thrall. And I ask myself, was that thrall Lemming? Is Lemming the father of Freydis?"

The big man stood of a sudden and spread his arms and bellowed. Then he collapsed, like a burst bladder, into a pile of flesh and bone unaccountably small, and lay sobbing.

"He can't be her father," said I. "The father would have been sacrificed, unless the custom was different then."

"Who was Freydis' father, Lemming?" asked Erling.

The voice came up from the sobbing heap as from a grave. "My brother," he said.

Erling rose and put his hand on the man. "You are her only decent kin," he said. "You shall raise the child. You shall have Soti's house, and work his forge—you know the work—and have his property. Only this I demand—the child shall be christened, and brought to church each week. You need not be a Christian if you want it not, but Freydis has seen too much devilment."

Lemming made a lunge and caught Erling by the hand. "I'll die for you," he croaked.

We found Halla in the same women's house where Gunnlaug had given birth, propped up on cushions in a box bed. Erling walked to her, bent in and kissed her.

"I've brought Father Ailill," he said. "Will you marry me, Halla?"

Halla looked pale. "Now?" she asked.

"If you like. Or we can wait and do it properly, with feasting and music and rich gifts all around. I'll marry you any way you wish, if only you'll be my wife."

"It's very sudden."

"From God's point of view it's too long coming."

"But why?"

"Because I heard the tale of what you did the

night of the sacrifice. And it came to me, like a blind man walking into a wall, that I'd never seen you as you are. I'd looked on you as a toy and a playmate, but you're a fine woman, equal to any in the land. If I marry any other, I'll rue it the rest of my life. Will you marry me, Halla?"

Halla passed a hand over her forehead. "I need time to think," she said. "Forgive me—since losing . . . since what happened I've thought new thoughts. I'm honored, and I love you very much, but will you let me go to my father's house awhile, and think and pray?"

Erling looked disappointed but said, "Anything you wish. I make you a promise, Halla. While you live, and while you are free, I will wed no other woman." He took her hand in his.

She drew the hand against her cheek. "Don't promise that," she said, her eyes shining.

"It's done, and I never break my word. Now eat, and rest, and go to your father when you will, and come back to me ready to be mistress of Sola."

"Not quite the outcome I'd looked for," said Erling when we were outside.

"I'm glad nonetheless," said I. "I've prayed for this."

"Yes, you saw Halla's worth from the start. You stung me, Father, I'll not deny it, when you questioned my word. I feel no shame in the matter of Olaf Trygvesson and Jarl Haakon, but my heart puckered as I thought of Halla. Father Ethelbald once told me that a man and woman who lie together become one flesh, and I saw of a sudden how much Halla had become a part of me. Then I came home and heard what she'd done, and I knew what I must do.

"Tell me, Father, what's it like when a man finds that the woman he's played with as a toy is a human soul to whom he owes the same honor and fair dealing he gives a fellow warrior?"

"Ah well, I'd say it's like finding yourself working and fighting among the grown men one day, and it comes to you that you're one of them, though it seems yesterday you were only a boy."

"Yes. As always, you have the words. In fact it may not be like becoming a man—it may be the thing itself. Perhaps I've never been a man till now."

"What does your mother think?"

"She doesn't know yet. She'll be none too pleased, but she likes Halla for all that and will get used to the idea. I hope I can say as much for my kinsmen in Hordaland."

"Do they disapprove of Halla?"

"No, but they greatly approve of Astrid Trygvesdatter. That was one of the matters we discussed up north. They want to wed me to Astrid to make peace with the Sigurdssons and Olaf Trygvesson."

"But Astrid's the lass you've dreamed of for years!"

"I heard a priest preach on a text once that said, *'When I became a man I put off childish ways.'* Astrid was a dream. Halla is a real woman, and my wife before God."

That left but one thing for me. I walked to my own house, where I knew I'd find Steinbjorg. I'd tell her we were safe—Soti and Ulvig were dead, Lemming had Soti's property and would surely sell her to me. I'd tell her I was not a priest, and that when a true priest came to Sola I'd confess to him, give up my office, do the penance he laid on me, and marry her. She wasn't Halla, but she was more than I deserved.

The moment I stepped over the threshold I knew something was horribly wrong. Blood has a smell. As my eyes made peace with the dimness, I could see the body by the hearth, and there was blood everywhere—gallons of blood—a sea of blood—

"I made the sacrifice, master."

There was Caedwy in the corner by the bed, hiding like a naughty child, eyes wide, still holding the bloody sickle, his clothing soaked in gore. I gaped at him.

"They stopped the sacrifice," he said. "But the sacrifice had to be made. I knew that's what you wanted. That's what the troll said too. We'll make a big basket and burn her properly—"

I ran at him and knocked the blade from his hand, cutting my own to the bone. I took him by the shirt and dragged him out into the sunlight and shouted, "A rope! Somebody get me a rope now!"

A thrall brought the rope, and I knotted it around Caedwy's scrawny neck, and I dragged him to the storehouse where they'd hanged Enda and flung the rope over the beam, and I hoisted him with my own hands, and held tight until his kicking ended and his breeches filled, and a while longer, while his cur dog leaped about me and barked.

Then I let him drop, and I went back to my house and took the horrid thing that would have been my wife in my arms, and I whispered secrets to it until it grew cold.

CHAPTER XXIV

He came to me in the darkness, a moving shadow, a whisper of stirring in the air, somewhere between waking and sleep.

"Yet another plant plucked up," the abbot said, in a voice uncommon soft for him.

"Two plants. The dearest of them all," said I.

There was silence for a space, and I spoke again to him, at once angered that he'd come and fearful he might have gone. "Are you to be a Job's comforter to me then, explaining how these innocents had to die for my deserving?"

His answer came slowly; so slowly that for a time I thought I was alone indeed.

"I'm sent to beg your forgiveness," he whispered at last.

It was my turn to be silent.

"It seems I've been overhard on you," he went on. I tried to imagine the expression on his unseen face, but couldn't fit one to the features. "The opinion at the . . . the Highest Level is . . . Och! You've got to understand."

"Understand what?"

"You've got to understand about Heaven. Heaven isn't what we thought. Or rather it isn't what I thought."

211

"So you're in Heaven now? Well out of Purgatory already?"

"I'm outside of Time. The question has no meaning."

"And what's Heaven like?"

"That's what I'm trying to tell. There's no words in Irish or Latin. 'Tis a shocking place, Heaven. There's things here—things encouraged, that'd never be allowed below. I can't say what; I can't even hint it, because it would put thoughts in your fleshly mind that would be like to get you damned. But here it's permitted—here all is permitted. '*Love God and do what you will*,' said Augustine, but you can't really do that below because your nature's diseased. It's like Adam and Eve. It was good for them to be naked, but it wasn't good after the Fall. We're not exactly naked here, but . . . it takes some getting used to.

"I spent my whole life mastering the rules. I thought it would please God, and it did. But early on I lost sight of the weightier matters of the Law.

"You though—with your recklessness and wanton ways—I find that God . . . God likes you better than He likes me. He loves me no less than you or anyone, but some . . . many . . . He likes better, and you're one of them.

"When He put on a body and walked among us, He wasn't like me. He was like you. I studied the gospels my whole life, yet I missed that plain fact, near enough to my face to singe my eyebrows. He went to weddings and parties, and played with children and spoke to loose women. Men like me He showed the back of His hand."

Can a blessed spirit sob? I could swear I heard him sob then, but the sound was so soft it might have been the roof settling.

"It's the risk He loves!" cried the abbot. "It's the mad, devil-take-the-hindmost rascality of the saints who throw away their gold or their shirts or their very lives and value it all at a feather for love of Him. God help me, in my whole life I never did one incautious act, and now I repent my respectability; I repent it in sackcloth and ashes."

Long silence then. The world had stopped; the night might linger forever if I gave it no push with a word. I outwaited him; humbled him by forcing him to ask the question once more.

"I've come to beg forgiveness," he said. "Will you give me it?"

"With all my heart," said I. "Just as soon as God gives me my woman and child back."

My memory of the weeks and months that followed is smoky. That we celebrated Easter I know, but whether it was done well or poorly I cannot tell. I baptized and buried, heard confessions and pronounced banns, and did the work of a priest generally. As before, the priest Ailill and the man Ailill were two separate souls, only the man Ailill had died.

Even anger can be pressed to death. I knew the cause of Steinbjorg's murder, and our child's—the judgment of God on my sacrilege in feigning his priesthood—but I was too weary to rail at Him for it. "You are mightier than all the world and slyer than a Scot," I said to Him in a rare moment of plain speaking. "There's no use arguing with someone who kills the innocent to make a point." Then I asked forgiveness and did quick penance, and thought no more such dangerous thoughts.

A man came with a ship to buy grain one summer day, and in the hall that night he declared himself to be, not a merchant, but an agent of Svein Forkbeard, King of Denmark.

"Svein will make you a jarl, Erling Skjalgsson," the man said. "He has heard your name and your deeds, and it's men such as you he seeks for retainers in his Norse domain. Denmark is a richer land than Norway, a civilized and Christian kingdom, and to steer your lands under Svein is far to be preferred over serving whatever sea king thinks he can hold a few woodlots in Norway for a month or two."

Bergthor said, "Does Svein think to send the Jomsvikings to conquer us again?"

Everyone laughed, and the agent reddened. Someone explained to me that Bergthor was harking back to an attack from Denmark years before, which had turned out badly.

Erling smiled, turning the gold ring the agent had brought from Svein in his hands, and said, "It's good to know the king of Denmark invites me if I need him, but all in all I prefer a Norwegian lord."

"Do you think you're likely to make peace with Olaf Trygvesson, whose uncle you slew?" asked the agent, and after that things were unfriendly, and the man went on to the next district unsatisfied.

I was giving the host to Ragna one day at mass when I noticed, as one suddenly notices a cobweb that's been flourishing in a house corner for days, that the woman had grown thin, and the skin hung loose and pale on her jaw and neck. I went to her in the women's house later and asked her if she was unwell. She smiled at me from her seat and said, "No, I've only been fasting much lately."

"Is there some matter I should have in my prayers?" I asked.

"No. I mourn my old sins, and the days of heathendom. My husband was a heathen and so was I, Father, and I loved him much; but now I see that our lives were wicked, and he burns in Hell, and I am only saved, if saved I will be, by God's mercy. When I walk about this farm, I sometimes think how I miss Thorolf, and then I tell myself it's wicked to miss so evil a sinner, so I do penance. And sometimes I think how great have been my sins, and how short a time I have to atone for them, and I do penance that my stay in Purgatory may be the less. So with one thing and another, I've been eating little. And truth to tell, I find I want food less than I did. I suppose that lightens the value of my fasts, so I must fast even more."

"You shouldn't abuse your body so as to break your health," I told her. "The body must serve us as a horse serves his master, but only a fool would starve his horse."

She smiled a small smile. "I think what time I have left will not be shortened much by penances. I have thought that when I've seen my son married, and a new mistress in place at Sola, I will find a convent in England or Germany, and take the veil."

I said that would be an honorable undertaking.

"The great thing is to get Erling wed to Astrid

Trygvesdatter," she said. "When I see that done I can bid the world farewell with a good heart. And in Heaven I can tell my ancestors I have left the family higher in the world than I found it. Only my ancestors won't be in Heaven, will they? Ah, me."

One morning in June I was awakened by somebody beating on my door. I stepped out into a blue and shining morning, and the bullyboy who'd roused me said there was a stranger in the steading, and that Erling wanted me. As my head cleared, I realized a voice was shouting, and shouting in Irish.

I hurried to the gate, where a crowd had gathered around a tonsured man in a tattered monk's robe, accompanied by a huge wolfhound which snarled at Erling's hounds. The man stood with his arms stretched out and his face turned to heaven, crying, "Now, Lord, let thy servant depart in peace; I have finished the course, I have kept the faith; let the arrows of the heathen pierce me through; let their spears transfix my bowels and their axes hack my corpse, still in my flesh I shall see God. Though I walk through the valley of the shadow of death, Thou art with me; I shall not be afraid for the terror by night, nor for the arrow that flieth by day; from the end of the earth I cry to Thee, when my heart is overwhelmed; lead me to the rock that is higher than I; for Thou hast been a shelter for me, and a strong tower from the enemy. . . ."

He had to take a breath some time, and when he did I put in, "I'm sorry, brother, but if you're seeking martyrdom you'll have to look elsewhere.

We have a few heathens left here, but we keep them on a leash."

He opened his eyes and stared me in the face, and had I not known better I'd have thought from his look of joy that we were long-lost kin. He was a long, ginger-haired fellow with a crooked nose, thin to the point of unhealth, and his chin and tonsure needed shaving. "Praise to the Beloved, a Christian priest!" he cried, and he leaped on me and grappled me to his breast, giving me ample proof that along with food and a shave he needed a bath (it didn't occur to me until later that I'd dwelt in heathen lands so long that I'd come to despise the honest stink of a holy man). His rangy hound leaped about our knees in brainless sympathy, and Erling's hounds put their ears back and growled at the sight.

Erling stepped nearer and said, "Now that we've eased your confusion, brother, may I offer you the hospitality of my house? I am Erling Skjalgsson, lord of Sola. The fellow whose back you're trying to break is Father Ailill, my priest. Breakfast is nearly ready, and I beg you to join us and tell us how you came so far by yourself."

"Fishermen found him wrecked on the reef this morning and brought him here," Erling told me when I'd gotten loose and we were all headed for the hall. "He was sitting on the rocks, singing, they said, with the dog howling at his side. When my men took charge of him he assumed they were going to kill him."

"A natural assumption, if you're from Ireland," said I. "He must be a White Martyr."

"A White Martyr?"

"White Martyrdom is when you go off by yourself, far from your homeland, to live or die by God's providence. It's not so common anymore, but in times past many a monk set sail in his curragh and was never heard from again. Somehow this one got carried here."

Once we were seated and I'd blessed the food, and our guest had refused the washing bowl, I began to question him, and there was whispering as the Irish speakers translated for their friends.

"My name is Moling," he told me, "and I am a man of Armagh, a wicked transgressor before God, guilty of sins of the flesh and sins of the spirit." He spoke cheerfully though, as if the memory of his sins troubled him not at all. He ate a bite of the food set before him and passed the rest bit by bit to the dog who sat with his muzzle on his knee.

"It's not horsemeat," I said, recalling my own sins.

"What? Oh, of course not." Moling's eyes had gone dreamy, and he snapped back with a smile. "I had no such unworthy thought. I've no wish to insult the hospitality of Christian brothers in an alien land. It only seems I've less need of food than I did, since I've been spending much time with God, and my friend Conn here, God bless him—" he patted the hound "—he's a purely carnal being, as God intended him to be, and better able to appreciate these things. So I enjoy spiritual food, and Conn enjoys fleshly food, and we praise God according to our kinds."

"What led you to take up the White Martyrdom?"

Moling smiled. "I killed my father and mother," he said. "I killed my wife and children, and I raped my neighbor's daughter, and I robbed the church and I betrayed my king, and I took the homes of the poor and drove them weeping into the road. I broke fasts and labored on Sundays and lied to my confessor and slandered the Blessed Virgin and spit on the crucifix, and stole the sacramental wine and got drunk on it. I moved my neighbors' boundary stones, and accused them falsely and perjured myself at their trials. I lent money at interest. I burned down houses, and stole cattle, and took slaves, and—"

"You kept busy," said I.

"I? Oh yes, it's rather a lot for one life, isn't it? And I'm not as old as I look. But then perhaps it wasn't me at all. Perhaps it was some other fellow. Or perhaps I only dreamed of doing them, and so sinned in my heart. What does it matter?"

"It must matter somehow, else why are you wandering the earth to earn forgiveness?"

He stared at me. "To earn forgiveness?" he asked. "You can't earn forgiveness. Surely you know that."

"Then why this penance?"

"For the Beloved, of course. When a man as wicked as I has all his sins forgiven and debts paid, he must love the One who forgave. And love wishes to be with the Beloved. If I could suffer a thousand thousand White Martyrdoms, and a thousand thousand Red Martyrdoms, they wouldn't begin to repay what He spent on me. But as I let go everything that separated us, I am drawn closer and closer to Him, and my joy is sometimes such that I think that this world, where I seem to range as a starving stranger, is Paradise itself, and I wander in blessed groves and eat the apples of Heaven and

hear the music of angels. Did you hear them this
morning? They sang the strangest song to me as I
sat on the reef. 'Maeve lives,' they sang. It was
beautiful, but I don't know what it means. I know
a couple lasses named Maeve, but why shouldn't
they be alive?"

I reached out and took him by both shoulders.
"What else did they sing?"

"Nothing. Only 'Maeve lives.' Is this Maeve
someone to you?"

I let him go. "My sister," I said. "Taken by Vikings.
But what use is it to tell me she lives without saying
how it is with her?"

Moling laid a hand on my arm. "In the end, we
none of us ever know how it is with another, even
our dearest. We must leave each of them in God's
hands soon or late."

"I don't mind leaving her in God's hands. It's the
hands of some greasy Viking master I can't bear to
think of."

"There are many kinds of White Martyrdom, my
brother. Embrace it as a bride, and find your true
love."

"Let's speak no more of this," I said.

Moling spent the day playing with children and
watching Lemming in the rebuilt forge until supper,
which he fed again to his hound. Then he passed
the night in a byre, refusing absolutely to sleep in
a house, and after I had said mass the next morning
he made ready to set off north overland. We told
him it was a long, dangerous journey, sometimes
roadless, pitted with mires and unfriendly men, and
the Boknafjord only the first of many waters he'd

have to cross. These things only made him more eager. "I've heard tales of heathen Lapps in the far north," he said. "I must go and preach to them."

"Wait a bit," I said to him, and I ran to Erling, who was in the horse pen, gentling a colt.

"Let me go north to Tungeness with Moling," I said.

"I don't see what help that would be," said Erling. "You don't know the way any better than he."

"I want to speak with him. There are things I can talk over only with him."

"What sort of things?"

"Irish things. Churchmen's things."

"I could send one of the men with you, I suppose. I'd hate to have you end up sunk in a bog."

"Send no one. I must be alone with Moling."

Erling searched my face, then called a thrall. "Get some food together for Father Ailill—sausages and cheese, dried fish—traveling fare."

CHAPTER XXV

The land way north was not an easy one, as Norwegians prefer to go by water if they're traveling any distance, and we had water on both sides. The paths varied, being now wide and easy, now narrow and stony, now low and muddy; sometimes they forked without any hint as to where they'd lead, sometimes they'd disappear altogether in a bog or a grassy waste, and you'd have to go carefully around, or push your way through with the sun as your guide. Sometimes we'd stop at farmsteads for directions, and the farmers and their wives looked at us as if at walkers-again, often slamming their doors shut in our faces. Moling didn't seem to mind anything. He swung his staff and paced along at a remarkable speed, leaving me puffing to keep up. He sang most of the time, songs I hadn't heard for long and long. His hound traveled twice the distance we did, racing ahead, doubling back to see why we came so slowly, then racing ahead again.

It took to raining in the afternoon and I began to look about for friendly shelter, but Moling paid it no mind. We slogged along, waterlogged, cold, and mired with mud to our knees, and it occurred to me that Moling, not understanding the light nights, would go on like this until autumn. I finally said, "We have to find shelter for the night! It doesn't get dark until close on midnight this time of year."

Moling looked at me as if I'd found the answer to the problem of Free Will.

"Is that so?" he asked. "Where shall we look?"

"Well there's a farmhouse up there. We can only ask."

The farmer was heathen, and paled at the sight of our robes, but he respected the name of Erling Skjalgsson, which I dropped with a thump, and grudgingly let us have a place in his byre, empty this time of year. We found straw to spread our cloaks on and opened our scrips, he for his hound and I for the beast within.

"Remarkable, these long summer nights in Norway," Moling said as he fed the dog and scratched its belly. "Are the winter nights short in proportion?"

"Aye. The winters here are like a foretaste of Hell."

"I've spent a lot of nights in the open, watching the moon and the stars. I've come to a conclusion about them."

"And what's that?"

"I think it can't be true that the sun travels around the earth. It must be the other way around."

I nearly choked on my cheese. I'd had no idea how far gone the man was. "That's the maddest thing I ever heard," I said, and I said it to his face. I mean, there are limits. I'd had enough of this kind of nonsense from Caedwy.

"No, think about it. How could the earth be the center of the universe? This is a fallen place, a cursed place. The sun, on the other hand, is glorious and gives us life. The sun is a symbol of the Beloved. The earth must be the sun's dog, running about it as Conn does with me."

"Look," said I. "The earth is down, and it's flat. The sun is up, and it's round. The sun flies. The earth just sits there."

"I've heard that the Greeks believed the earth to be round like a ball."

"It makes no difference. If the earth moved, we'd all fall off it."

"I suppose that's true. It's a pity. It would be much better theology for the earth to go around the sun."

"I hate to spit in your beer, brother, but real things seldom make good theology."

"Ah well, it's no matter. In any case the sun will rise in the morning whatever we think. Now tell me, Father Ailill, what is it you wanted to talk with me about?"

"How did you know I wanted to talk with you?"

"Am I wrong about this too?"

I closed my scrip. "No, you're not wrong. I need to confess to you."

"I'm not a priest."

"If I wait for a priest I may wait forever," said I. "First thing, I'm not a priest myself . . ." and I went on and confided to this madman all my secrets and my whole history at Sola, all I'd wanted to tell my Steinbjorg. For all I knew he'd babble it to the world. When I was done I sat silent.

"I cannot shrive you," he said.

"WHY?" I shouted, and the farmer and his family must have been wakened.

"Because there's no place in your heart for my

forgiveness to rest. See here, the Beloved is like a loving father who comes to his child each day and says, 'I have a gift for you,' and offers him some treasure, but the child is holding on to the gift he was given yesterday, and so cannot take the new gift. You must let go yesterday's gift, my brother Ailill."

I shuddered. "I cannot," I said. "My hands are iron. They will not open."

"Then they must be heated in the forge, and hammered open. The Beloved will do it, for He loves you."

"I'm sick of His love. I'm crushed and crippled under the lead weight of God's love."

There was no answer. I looked and saw that Moling was sleeping, easily as a child, with his dog curled up against his belly.

We went on the next day in much the same way. Again I had trouble keeping up and got no chance to talk. But now I doubted whether there was much use in talk. Moling was like the adults I'd watched as a child, secure in their growth, knowing everything and sufficient for all, whose world I could neither understand nor enter.

There was rain and then fog, and as the fog burned off we heard a sound of shouting and clanging some distance off, but in the direction we were headed.

"There's a battle!" said Moling, and the ring in his voice made me wonder if he hadn't been a warrior once.

"What about it?" I asked.

"Let's go see!" He hitched his skirts up in his belt and set off like a greyhound, catching his dog up, and the two of them raced ahead of me, growing smaller and disappearing over the crest of a low ridge.

When I finally drew up to them we were halfway down the other side, and in the dale below two gangs of men were having it out with swords and axes. There were about twenty in one group, and only six in the other.

"Bad odds," said Moling.

"What can we do?" I sighed.

"We have our staffs. We could fall on the larger group from behind, and the Lord might give us victory!"

"Or they might brain us with their axes."

"Yes," said Moling, and from his eyes I realized that being brained with an axe didn't seem to him an awful thing at all.

And suddenly I thought, *What the Heaven? Let's die here today, saving lives, and go home to the Beloved.*

So I shouted, "Columcille!" and Moling shouted something or other, and we fell on the fighting men like a thunderbolt.

And I swear to God, the moment those men started getting thumped from behind, and turned to see two roaring Irishmen with bare legs and flying staffs, they screamed and fled, nor looked back while we could see them.

Three from the other side still stood. They let their weapons sink, and one of them sat down, and another said, "Are you Valkyries?"

I wish Moling had understood the question. It would have given him a laugh.

I said, "No, we're not Valkyries, we are men and

servants of the White Christ. I am Father Ailill, priest to Erling Skjalgsson, and this is Brother Moling, a holy man of Ireland."

"If you're Erling's priest you're well met," said the man. "We have one of his men here, a Christian, and he's dying."

And I looked down and there lay Halvard Thorfinsson, with blood soaking the belly of his shirt.

"Oh Lord," I said. "Have pity on little Sigrid."

I stepped toward him but Moling was ahead of me. He took Halvard's head in his lap, and gave him water to drink from the skin he carried, stroking the pale hair of the young warrior.

Halvard said, "I want to confess, Father."

I heard his confession and shrove him, silently praying God, as I always did, to accept the faith of the dying in place of my ordination.

"There's much pain," said Halvard when we were done.

"You're a brave lad," I said. "You'll do as well as any."

"It's strange to die this way, and me a Christian. If I were heathen yet, I'd know that Odin would welcome me to Valhalla. What welcome has Christ for a warrior, Father?"

I had no quick answer, and Moling must have seen my trouble, because he asked what the boy had said. I told him.

"Tell him I've had a dream about Heaven," said Moling. "The teachers tell us that the Beloved lives outside Time itself. He goes back and forth in it when He wills. And when we go to be with Him, we too will be outside Time.

"It seemed to me in my dream that at the last day the Beloved called together all the great warriors who had been brave and merciful, and who had trusted in His mercy, and He mustered them into a mighty army, and He said to them, 'Go forth for Me now, My bonny fighters, and range through Time, and wherever there is cruelty and wickedness that makes the weak to suffer, and the faithful to doubt My goodness, wherever the children are slain or violated, wherever the women are raped or beaten, wherever the old are threatened and robbed, then take your shining swords and fight that cruelty and wickedness, and protect My poor and weak ones, and do not lay down your weapons or take your rest until all such evil is crushed and defeated, and the right stands victorious in every place and every time. We will not empty Hell even with this, for men love Hell, but I made a sweet song at the beginning, My sons, and though men have sung it foul we will make it sweet again forever.' "

I said these words to Halvard in Norse, and he died smiling.

I hired a boatman to take Moling across the Boknafjord to Aarvik the next day, and we said our goodbyes, and I got a ride back to Sola in a fisherman's boat.

And then I had to tell Sigrid about Halvard.

I stood in my patch among my children, working with a hoe to keep the weeds from them. A bird shadow swam the earth at my feet, but I looked up without fear, for I knew it was my white-and-red hawk, and although the ravens might fly by in the distance they knew better than to venture closer.

"Doing well now, are you?" asked a voice, and I knew it for the abbot, for who else spoke to me in these dreams? "Getting along fine, no problems?"

I worked on in silence.

"Are you ready to forgive me?" he asked.

"Still on that?" I asked. "You harp on it as if my forgiveness were worth the wealth of Dagda."

"What do you know of worth?" he cried. "If you knew the value of one word of forgiveness, you'd be all day coining indulgences like the king of Ulster at his mint! To have such wealth at your fingertips and never to touch it ... if you could see things from my side of the river, you'd think yourself a pauper living on a mountain of gold, and all unknowing."

"I'm just being holy, as my Heavenly Father is holy. He doles His forgiveness out in jealous dribs and drabs. Why should I be prodigal with mine?"

"All saints and blessed angels! Did I teach you so badly? Think you really God is a hammer-tongued old *fir darrig* such as I was? Think you all the praises and thanksgivings of scripture are but flattery to a tyrant?"

"I know how God has used me. I know nothing more."

"You know nothing at all! You've never seen, and you will not look, and you haven't the sense to—" Then he fell silent, as if a hand had stopped his mouth. I plied my hoe until he spoke again.

"Would you hear a jest from Heaven?" he said. "A thing to make you laugh? I've learned I was never meant to be an abbot, nor even a monk. I was born to be a married man and a father. There was a girl I grew up with, whom I used to dream about, and I always thought those dreams a torment from the Devil. As it turns out, 'twas she God had intended for my wife. And my cramped nature came from being a man out of place in the world, trying to make shoes with a cooper's tools, so to speak.

"You, on the other hand—you'll laugh when you hear this—you were born to be a priest. Isn't that rich?"

I didn't laugh, not at all.

"You've overlooked one thing, you know," he said at last. I didn't want to listen. I wanted to toil here among my children, looking at their bright faces, hearing them laugh, watching them grow. I would never sell them. I would keep them forever, and if I never earned my freedom, so be it.

"What you fail to consider is that your whole prosperity depends on the white-and-red hawk. But no hawk is forever."

I whirled to face him. "What are you getting at?"

"Behold," he said, and with a long finger indicated the sky.

I turned unwilling eyes upward, and I saw that another bird was approaching from the west, a great white eagle, larger than the hawk.

"Does he come as an enemy?" I whispered.

"Watch."

The two great birds circled each other for a minute, then the white-and-red hawk stooped before the eagle, and flew his circle lower than before, while the white eagle circled above.

"They watch together!" I cried. "Instead of one

guardian, I now have two! You're a poor prophet, Father."

"Yet watch."

Then came a great flock of ravens, all the ravens in the world, so many they blocked the sun out like a thunderhead, and they attacked the eagle and the hawk. And great was the battle then: the noble birds fought like hurricanes and thunderbolts; one after another the ravens fell in blood like rain, and yet there were so many of them that still they came on, and the hawk and eagle were wearied. And as they fought, the battle moved off, drifting eastward before a westerly wind, until all the birds were gone from sight.

"So fine, so brave; can they both be lost?" I cried.

My answer was to see the white-and-red hawk return alone. He took up his watching post above my patch, and the white eagle was seen no more.

"Thank God this one was spared me at least," I said.

"Yet watch."

Now came a red eagle, greater even than the white one. This time the hawk did not greet the larger bird with obeisance—he flew in his face with rage and flashing claws, and great was their battle, so that the blood fell down in my eyes. But at last the red eagle struck the hawk down, and he fell like a hailstone to land among my children and lie unmoving, his eyes gone lightless.

I knelt and wept for the white-and-red hawk, for whom I had suffered much, and who had repaid me well.

"Now see who wards your patch," said the abbot.

I looked up and saw that the red eagle had grown to even greater size, and was circling as the other noble birds had done. But all the birds of the earth, eagles and hawks, ravens and crows, even bluebirds and gulls, gathered together against the red eagle. He fought valiantly, but I thought they were too many for him.

I lowered my eyes. I no longer cared.

"Erling is the white-and-red hawk, isn't he?" I asked.

"You worked that out all by yourself? Perhaps there's hope for you yet."

"Why should he fall before that bloody red eagle? What do I need with the red eagle? I was well suited with things as they were."

"Perhaps God has purposes beyond what suits you. Perhaps there are more patches in Norway than yours alone, and just as dear to Him."

I looked at the sky. All the birds were gone. "They must have slain the red eagle," said I. "Who will guard my patch against the ravens now?"

"There are no more ravens. They will never come again, or not for a very long time. But there are other dangers."

And suddenly he was the Black Axe-man again, towering over me with his weapon swinging. I turned and ran from him, and as I ran I crushed my children underfoot.

CHAPTER XXVI

"There it is, the Gula Thingstead," said Bergthor, pointing. I'd come to the ship's rail for other reasons than the view, but I raised my throbbing head and saw a sloping, south-facing meadow with mountains at its back above the narrow sound where we rowed. Sogn and Hordaland are unlike Jaeder—tree-covered in their lower parts and rugged in all their parts, and it was no wonder that holding Jaeder's field country meant much to those who lived here.

We'd endured another winter, and it was now the spring of the Year of Our Lord 997, and time for the great regional Thing. We were having a mercifully dry week.

We disembarked at the jetty, and our ships anchored in the harbor. We climbed to the meadow and to Erling's family booth, a foundation dug out of the earth with low walls of piled turves. It needed only the striped woolen awning roof we'd brought to make a comfortable temporary house. As the thralls raised the tent, Erling stood beside me outside and stretched his arms wide, as if summoning the steep green mountain slopes and the bright Gulafjord, thick with ships, as witnesses in a lawsuit. "Is Norway not a fair land, Father?" he asked.

"As Lucifer was fairest of the sons of the morning," I answered. "It's the heart that counts, and it's a wicked, heathen heart this land has." My gaze turned eastward toward the temple, a tall, steep-roofed stave building with dragon heads at the roof peaks.

"Perhaps that will change soon. And we'll help change it by our work here. Look—do you see that company?" He pointed to a line of folk climbing the hill below us and to the east, not one of the larger groups.

"Yes," I said. "What of it?"

"That's Asmund Fridleifsson's household. Asmund is father to Halla. I think—yes, Halla's there!"

"Perhaps they want to accept your marriage proposal."

"I hope you're right. But they could have done that without sailing all the way to Sogn."

I offered to go and inquire, but Erling said to let it be for now.

That evening the Horder lords met in Olmod's booth. Erling asked me to come along.

Olmod sat propped up by cushions and wrapped in blankets in the high seat, the light from the hearth fire shining on his spotted skull. His voice had worn thin, and we strained to hear him.

"The issue stands thus," he piped. "Olaf Trygvesson is lord of the Trondelag, the Uppland districts, the Vik, and Agder. Now word has it he's sailed to Rogaland, and the Rogalanders, urged by the Erikssons, too are submitting to him, being baptized, and acclaiming him king. Our bonders have already invited him here so as to hear what he offers. We can expect him any day. He promises friendship and great gifts to those who bow to him, but he's bloody-handed with those who resist.

"So the question is this, kinsmen—shall we gather our forces as the western lords did in Harald Finehair's day, and meet this Olaf Trygvesson in battle? We might hope to have better luck than they did, who had their lands seized, to the profit of my father Horda-Kari and my older brothers among others."

"We need to know what the Sognings and Fjorders have to say to that," said someone.

"And they're waiting to hear what we say," said Olmod. "It's come to this—that of all the kins of the Gulathing-law, our word bears the most weight. That's a good thing, but it won't last if we say nothing, and what we do say had better be wise."

"It seems to me we'd be wise to follow Horda-Kari's example," said Erling. "He and his sons threw in with the king and made their fortunes thereby. I've met this Olaf Trygvesson, and I'll stake my head he's born to rule."

"It's no surprise you'd lean to Olaf," said another man. "You're a Christian, as he is. Harald Finehair never forced any man to change his faith. Make Olaf king and we end our way of life. We'll be like the southerners, and as weak as they."

"Weak as Brian Boru?" I asked. "Weak as Alfred of England?"

Erling put a hand on my arm and said, "My priest speaks out of turn, but he has a point. The southern lands are rich, and they grow rich by work, not just stealing the wealth of others."

"This is Norway!" said the man. "We haven't any

broad fields like England, unless our names are Erling Skjalgsson, and even your fields aren't as fine as theirs, Erling. We haven't their long summers, or their mines of metal. Their god gave them these riches for profit, and our gods gave us strength that we might share the profit!"

"Going a-viking isn't what it once was," said someone else. "In the old days Horda-Kari could take a few ships and catch the English asleep. Nowadays it's harder to surprise them. You've got to join some great army and march up and down the country and beat them down until they pay you Danegeld. As long as that half-wit Ethelred sits on the throne we'll make do there, but he'll die someday, and suppose his heir is another Alfred? And it's the same in France. Even in Ireland and Scotland they've taken to standing together against us."

"If Olaf Trygvesson and his god come to rule, we can say goodbye to harrying forever. Christians teach that all men are on a level—that an Irishman has the same worth as a Norseman, if you can believe it!"

"Still they say Olaf fed the ravens well in England," said someone else. "They say there hasn't been a warrior like him since Haakon the Good. Haakon was a Christian too. Maybe there's something in it."

The man who'd spoken of broad fields said, "Norway is great because we're wolves in a world of sheep! If we turn sheep as well, we won't even be among sheep. We'll be the poorest, skinniest sheep of all. We'll starve on our frosty mountainsides, and the world will pay us no heed, even to pity us."

"It's well to speak of what should be," said Olmod,

"but let us consider what is. Can we, do you think, with the combined force of Hordaland, Sogn and the Fjords, defeat Olaf Trygvesson with the men of Trondheim, the Uppland, the Vik, Agder and Rogaland behind him?"

"Have we come to this?" asked Broad Fields. "Do we judge now based on whether we may succeed or not? If to submit is to lose our honor—and I say it is—then let us die, each man, rather than submit. Remember Horda-Kari! Would he have asked such a question?"

"He did," said Olmod.

A hush fell over the company.

Olmod said, "My father and brothers had no wish to be Harald Finehair's men. Why bow to a king when you can be rulers free and clear over your own lands, however small? But they saw how many lords had bowed, and how many were left to oppose the king, and they asked themselves, 'Would it be such a shame to be Harald's men? Do the lords of the southern lands blush to lay their hands on the king's sword pommel and pledge troth? And would we not be better off with one king and one law for all the land?' And they turned their backs on their neighbors and sailed to Harald and offered him service. This I had from their own mouths."

There was quiet for a while.

"How do we approach Olaf?" someone asked.

"There is one among us who is known to Olaf Trygvesson by face and reputation, and who is a Christian as well," said Olmod. "I have proposed before that we bid for Astrid Trygvesdatter's hand for Erling Skjalgsson."

"Will he wed his sister to a mere hersir?"

"Let him be made a jarl."

"Shall Skjalg's son be advanced above the rest of us?"

"Who else among us will Olaf make a jarl? Do you think he'll promote a worshiper of the old gods? And do we want to live in Olaf's Norway without a jarl from our kindred to stand before the king? Suppose Olaf promotes some kinsman of his own over us?"

"Won't the other families have candidates too?" someone asked.

"Most of them owe us favors. And they buy grain from Erling."

"There is one hitch," said Erling.

"What?" asked Olmod.

"I've sworn to wed Halla Asmundsdatter, and as a Christian I may have but one wife."

Olmod settled deeper in his robes. "We would never ask you to break your word, Erling. We all know your word is sacred, as it should be. But there are other counters on the board, and they may be more changeable than your honor."

I broke away from Erling as soon as the meeting was done and ran through the encampment, asking the way to Asmund Fridleifsson's booth. A word to a thrall brought Halla out to speak to me, and I suggested we walk to a more private place. Privacy was difficult to find, but we finally found a spot on the strand. The sun still glowed in the west, and a hundred ships' prows, stripped of their figureheads so as not to offend the land spirits, gleamed in its light.

"You may be in danger," I said.

Halla took my hand and I shivered from crown to footsole at her touch. "What do you mean?" she whispered.

"Erling's kin want to wed him to Astrid Trygvesdatter—"

"I know. They've sent men to speak with my father."

"Don't be afraid for that—Erling refuses to break his word to you. But Olmod hints that there are other ways. And it comes to my mind that your death would be a happy chance for them."

"Surely they wouldn't go so far?"

"They feel this wedding is their best hope of favor with Olaf. They're jockeying to keep their power. A woman's death more or less would be little to them."

"Erling would never consent to their will if they killed me."

"It could look like an accident. Or sickness, if they worked by poison. I'm not saying it'll happen thus— no doubt they'll start by leaning on your father. How strong is your father?"

"His strength is no matter, Father." She looked at her feet and then back up at me. "Father, I think you care for me."

I was grateful for the dim light. I hoped she didn't see me redden. "Of course I care for you, my daughter."

"I don't mean that, Father. A woman knows when a man wants her, and I've seen it in your eyes. I mean no shame to you—you've ever been the decentest of friends. And now I tell you with no shame on my part that I'll be your leman—if you still wish it."

The earth bucked beneath my shoes. I had to clutch at something to steady myself, and Halla was the only thing to hand. I put my hand on her neck, and ran my thumb across her cheek.

"Erling cares for you," I said. "He'd never forgive me."

"He must marry Astrid, Father. Olmod's men spoke to my father and me, and we're agreed. How could I live with Erling, knowing he'd be a jarl but for me?"

"You're worth a jarldom, daughter. Never disbelieve that."

"It's for the land, too. The bonders, like my father, who need a lord in the king's favor. There are always lords, Father—we don't often get the chance to have a part in making them, and to advance a good . . . a good man." Here her voice caught.

"All my life," she said, "men have decided for me. This decision is mine alone to make. Why should Erling be the only one who gets to be a hero?"

I might have kissed her then, but a shadow suddenly approached and took the shape of Erling Skjalgsson.

"Go back to the booth, Father," said Erling. "I want to speak to my betrothed."

I left them embracing by the water. "Well, Ailill, old son," I said to myself, "you've just fulfilled that bastard Caedwy's prophecy. You were offered your heart's desire, and you cast it away."

❖   ❖   ❖

I was stooping to enter the booth when a sound caught me up short. I'd know that voice if I were deaf—I'd know it if I were dead and in Hell. The elf-woman.

I hurried around the corner of the booth and saw her in the twilight, talking to Sigrid, touching her hair.

"Begone, devil!" I cried, and, to my horror she ran laughing, holding Sigrid by the hand. Sigrid laughed too as she ran, and they flitted lightly through the encampment. I shouted "Stop! Kidnapper!" but the people we passed only stared at me as if I were mad, pursuing a quarry that was not there.

They led me up the mountainside, they nimble as shorebirds, I puffing and hulking my way, falling further and further behind at each step. They neared a gray wall of rock that rose sheer above us, and I labored to pump my legs faster, for I guessed what was there.

As they drew closer the elf-woman cried a word out, and a great door, tall enough for a giant, opened silently to them. Once they were through it began to shut itself. I strained my heart near breaking to reach it before it closed, and threw myself through the crack at the last moment, feeling the brush of the stone on my heels. I lay panting on my face and looked about me.

It clutches my heart to this day to remember what I saw there. Tir Nan Og, the land of youth, must have the look of the country I saw inside the mountain. The sky was fair and blue, with a sun of its own that gave light and warmth but would never burn you. The hills and meadows were green as

Ireland (oh, sweet memory!), all soft grass and moss
with never a prickly or noxious weed. The breeze
was gentle, bearing soft melodies just outside clear
hearing. Rivers ran through the dales, so clear you
only knew there was water in them because the
bright things that swam there were fish and not birds.
And here and there parties of fair folk in bright
raiment danced and played on instruments, laughing
and careless and ate dainty food from silver platters.

Yet there was a strangeness to the place as well.
I once saw a book in the monastery on a subject
called Geometry. It had drawings of things that
weren't objects, but only pure shapes—cones and
cubes and what do you call those round things? It
seemed to me that whenever I turned my attention
away from any particular thing in the land inside
the mountain, it resolved itself, at the corner of my
eye, to one of those pure shapes. But when I fixed
attention on it again, it returned to the form of a
tree or a flower or a butterfly, or what you will.

I do not know how long I wandered in that
beguiling place, seeking the elf-woman and the girl.
At last I found them, lounging in a meadow under
a blue and yellow awning, not hiding from me at
all, and why should they? I was in the other world
now, the door shut behind me.

"Welcome, Ailill," said the elf-woman. "Sit beside
us while I call for refreshments."

"I'll not drink anything in this land, or eat anything
either."

"Speak not so quickly of that you understand not.
Think you you barely made it through the door? It
would have closed you out, or crushed you, had I

commanded it to. I let you in so you'd see where Sigrid had gone. All this fair land is hers to dwell in; rich clothing and sweet foods will be hers. Are you so in love with your world that you'd force her out of all this to return there?"

I turned to the girl. "Is this what you want, lass? Never to see your mother or sister or brother again? To cut yourself off from the Lord and His salvation?"

Sigrid smiled at me as a child would, her head tilted. Her blue eyes were empty as a crone's womb. "It's lovely here," she said, "There's music and dancing, and good food, and soft garments to wear, and the winter never comes, and no one ever falls in love. . . ."

"You can't take a christened soul," I said to the elf-woman.

"But she can stay with me if she wills, and she does will."

What could I say? What could I offer in God's world that would match this place? I racked my brains for an argument and found none.

"What of you, Ailill?" the elf-woman asked. "You've naught to hold you at Sola. If you renounce your faith you may remain with us here. We can become . . . close friends."

There was that smell again I'd smelled in the old gods' shrine. Something tingled at my groin, unruly as another man's dog.

Never had I been so alone. I had no ally—not God (did He hear prayers from this place?), not even myself. I wanted to stay. I wanted this fair creature. Had I ever wanted anything—Halla, Maeve, my freedom, my child, God Himself— as much?

Desperately I clasped my hands, trying to pray, and pressed them against my chest. And there beneath my hands I felt Enda's cross that hung about my neck. Its touch was like a bucketful of cold water in my face.

I lifted it and looked on it. Wonderful work it was, for an unskilled hand—you could read the pain and patience on the Lord's face, almost feel the agony of screaming nerve and outraged muscle. Down at the foot where the carving ended unfinished, it was as if Enda had left his name behind—his and the names of all those who lay down the promise of tomorrow for the dream of eternity—and the name had been taken up into the Beloved's own passion.

And in that moment all my seeing changed. This was not a wide, fair land—it was a great, knobbly cave at the roots of the mountains, lit only by a few fissures in the rock, and the air was cold and damp, and there were bats about, and those who danced were starveling, hollow-eyed mad children in rags who jerked or rocked to tunes inside their heads. And the food they ate was dirt and leaves and rocks and bat dung.

"It's a seeming, every bit of it!" I cried. "A lie, a fraud and a madness! Not a thing here is real!"

"Real!" the elf-woman cried. "What use is reality? What good has reality been to you? Your real world is cruel and bitter; it swallows all your dreams, then it swallows you! Do you think these children here would go out into that world again, even if you could make them see as you see? Lay the wooden Jew aside and join us again! In this world no one ever suffers as its maker did—there are no meaningless sacrifices like his!"

"Meaningless?" I looked on the lovely thing in my hand. Curious how an image of such suffering can be the most beautiful thing in the world. "It's the risk," I said. "This thing is beautiful because it was made in danger. All real beauty is risky. All love is risk. Sigrid said it—'Here no one falls in love.'

"I see Christ in this carving, not just because it's a man on a cross, but because the One who chose the cross is present whenever men and women give their lives for something greater than themselves. At the cross God entered our danger and our failure, and at His rising they rose as well. I wouldn't trade this cross for all your country!"

"But we can give you that too!" said the elf-woman. "You want to feel danger? We can make you feel danger such as you've never imagined! You'll feel a hundred times alive when you've done!"

"A seeming is not enough! Not for the sons of Adam. It's the truth of the risk—the threat of real loss—that makes the beauty! The risk God Himself took when He made things that could say no to Him! If Enda's danger had been only a seeming, the beauty would be only a seeming too. But Enda carved his name into the bedrock of the cosmos, into the place where the cross is planted. And there it will remain when the world is ground to dust."

"Great talk!" shouted the elf-woman. "But who is equal to it? That's God's failure! He asks too much. The followers of the old gods sacrifice their food, their beasts, their goods and even their children rather than make the sacrifice He demands. Even you won't pay that toll!"

"Perhaps I will," said I. "But even if I cannot, I'll not settle for your safe world."

"I'd not walk blindly into the danger you've chosen, not for all of Heaven," said she.

"I know. Therefore you are damned."

She was silent a moment. "You say the sons of Adam need the truth. I say the sons of Adam— and Christians in particular—cannot bear the truth. I'll make you a wager on it."

"I've no reason to play games with you."

"I'll give you a reason. I'll let the girl return with you to the outside. But I can always call her back, now she's tasted the life we offer. Win the wager and I'll let her alone."

I frowned. "You leave me no choice."

"This is the wager. Erling Skjalgsson will soon be offered the hand of Astrid Trygvesdatter. To wed her he must break his vow to Halla. I'll wager he breaks his word. Will you wager on his Christian troth?"

"If you can foretell the future, what's the use in wagering?"

"I see you have your doubts about Erling's word. Fear not, I do not know the future. I only speak aloud what I sense in men's hearts."

"Erling is the truest of men. He'll not break his word to Halla."

"Then it's a wager?"

"It's a wager."

"And not a word of this to Erling!"

"No. Not a word."

"Done!" And Sigrid and I stood in the dark outside the mountain.

❖   ❖   ❖

"Here is how Olaf Trygvesson bore himself in the Vik," said Arinbjorn Thorsteinsson, a hersir of Sogn. "He went about the country and called Things, and there he cowed the people with his armed men and demanded that all be water-sprinkled in the name of his god. And any man who spoke against it was killed on the spot, or tortured, or had a hand struck off, or his eyes gouged out." The assembly of bonders and lords murmured over these unlawful carryings-on. We all stood in the rain, facing the great boulder on which Arinbjorn stood to address us. Near him the judges sat on their benches, with Olmod the Old, who was lawspeaker, chief among them, and around them the Peace Rope had been strung.

Askel Olmodsson spoke for his father. He was no great speaker, but everyone listened carefully because they knew his words came from Olmod. Beside him his son Aslak stood, much grown and filled out since I'd seen him last, taller than his father now. "Everyone knows Olaf picked up outlandish customs in Russia. We can't help that just now. The question is whether we can meet his fleet in battle and defeat him. If not, we must do our best to make him welcome and hope to remind him what conduct befits a Norse king."

"The sons of Erik Bloodaxe were Christians like Olaf," said a bonder. "While they reigned the winters were hard, the summers were dry, and the herring never came."

"And Charlemagne of France was a Christian," said Erling. "So was Athelstane of England, who fostered Haakon the Good. I haven't heard that their lands suffered bad seasons because of it."

"France and England are not Norway," said the man.

"And which land has most reason to regret that?" asked Erling.

"They say Olaf is as great a warrior as Haakon," said another bonder. "They say he can juggle three knives, and cast a spear as well with his right or left hand, and run outside his ship on the oars. He's been lucky in all his battles, and won much booty. Do the gods give such gifts to a man who displeases them?"

"No one denies that Olaf is a great warrior, and well fitted to lead an army," said Arinbjorn from the rock. "But if we submit to him he'll demand that we cast off our old faith, as he has everywhere else. He's not content to worship his own way and leave us alone. He says every man must pray as he prays, or suffer for it. This is the point. Will we submit to that?"

Olmod whispered to Askel, who said, "Do we have a choice? Have we the ships? Have we the men? Have we the luck? The lords who defied Harald Finehair and got away sailed west, to the Shetlands and Orkney, to Ireland and Scotland, to Iceland. I haven't heard that there are untilled fields in those lands awaiting new settlers today. Erik Thorvaldsson has found land west of Iceland, but the word is that's filling too. Where will we go if we cannot live in Norway, under the king? Flee where you will, you'll find the kings Christian."

No one spoke for a time.

"What do you propose then, Olmod?" asked Arinbjorn at last.

"Let us hear what Olaf has to say. Let us talk to him. We will say to him, 'Olaf Trygvesson, we respect you, but we do not fear you. Show yourself our enemy, and we will fight you and cost you ships and men. Be our friend, and we will serve you and take your god.' Other regions have met this man with defiance and poured blood out for nothing. Let's ask him what he'll do for us if we give him what he wants."

A bonder cried, "I like that! I don't mind being sprinkled if there's some profit in it."

The crowd seemed to agree, and Arinbjorn was calling for quiet when a man in a blue cloak came striding through the crowd to the Peace Rope. He turned and faced the crowd and said, "Hear me! I come from Olaf Trygvesson. He has received the call of the Gulathing bonders to meet with them. His answer is that before he speaks to the bonders he will speak with the lords. He will come with one ship tomorrow morning. He says he wants to greet you all, and will show you how generous he can be to his friends, and how hard he can be with his enemies."

CHAPTER XXVII

They had a handsome ship, painted red and gilded, with a sail patterned in red and gold diamonds. They disembarked at the jetty and climbed the hill, a double line of fair folk dressed in the brightest hues and richest fabrics to be had from the eastern trade. They looked like summer birds, or butterflies, and the sun shone for their convenience. I'm sure I wasn't the only one who suddenly felt himself a mud-daubed, homespun-covered, louse-ridden yokel squatting in the world's remotest nook . . . which will have been the intention.

First of all came the bishop and all six priests, in vestments so pure and lovely you'd think they'd sprung from the earth on flower stalks that morning. Then came twelve tall, handsome men whose high heads and easy bearing marked them more clearly than the pommel calluses on the heels of their right hands as warriors, undefeated and in their prime, young enough to think their prime would last forever.

Then came Olaf, a face and blazing blue eyes I recognized, not so tall as Lemming but easily as tall as Erling. What is it that sets kings apart from other men? Even in the Estonian slave market he must have had that look about him. The slavemasters must have beaten him often. At his side walked two golden-haired young women, very tall, very lovely.

"There," said Erling, beside me, "is Astrid Trygves-datter. The taller one."

I felt cold as I thought of Sigrid. "She's very fair, but not as fair as Halla," said I.

"How can you compare the sea and the sky?" asked Erling. "Does the best wine taste better than a loaf of fresh bread? Each is fine in its own way."

"How stands it with you and Halla?" I asked pointedly.

"She's being stubborn, but let's not talk of it now." His eyes followed the women.

Then came the Erikssons from Opprostad, Sigurd and Jostein and Thorkel, and about fifty more warriors, all lovely to look on, and none of them anyone you'd want to tangle with having nothing more than the right on your side.

Olaf and his party trooped to the law rock. Olaf climbed to its top alone and said, "I greet you, lords of the Gulathing. I am Olaf Trygvesson, by God's grace king of Norway."

Olmod stood, supported by Askel, and said, "We bid you welcome, Olaf Trygvesson. Your fame comes before you. We have long awaited the chance to see your face."

"I rejoice to be here," said Olaf, "to see your honest Norse faces and hear your plain Norse speech. Many years I spent in strange lands, in king's halls and on muddy battlegrounds, but whether I slept on scarlet silk or a cloak thrown on the ground with my brynje on my back, I always dreamed of home, and the light nights, and the glaciers, and the fjords, and eating lingonberries and flatbread, and watching towheaded children play in the heather. There are those who call me an enemy of Norway, but that I can never be. No man loves his mother more than he who has lost her, and Norway is my mother, whom I have found again as I found the woman who bore me, against all hope."

I hadn't heard before that Olaf's mother had been rescued too. I knew a moment of envy, hot as an abscessed tooth.

"I say it again—no man could love Norway more than I do. But because I love her, it pains me to see the sad state she stands in today. There is no high king, and where there is no king the law is weak and divided. Men fear to travel by land, and they fear to travel by sea, for the landway and the seaway are infested with thieves, and so trade is leashed, and everyone made poorer. And lords fall upon each other like wolves to steal each other's property, and there is no one above them to knock sense into their heads. And foreign lords like Svein of Denmark look at this land and lick their lips, saying, 'She has no king; her lords are divided; she is ripe for the picking.'

"But saddest of all is this—on every hill and in every grove I see the temples of devils, the old gods who are no gods, who have eyes but see not, and hands but feel not, and feet but walk not. I want to weep when I think of my own people bowing down to blocks of wood and slabs of rock and offering to them the beasts of their flocks and the fruits of the soil, and yes, sometimes even their fellow men. I weep for the folly of this worship of senseless things, but even more I weep when I think of the hatred and cruelty of the devils who lie behind those images, who have bought the souls of my people for little price.

"It is my dream—it is my purpose—to see Norway brought out of its darkness of ignorance and foul custom, and into the pure light of the Christian faith, to stand beside England and France and other lands the true God has blessed in the brotherhood of Christendom. I offer my love and my shield of defense to all who will be baptized and accept me as king. To those who cling to the old ways I promise only steel, and hemp, and fire. That is the word of Olaf Trygvesson."

Olmod Karisson stood up again among the judges and whispered to Askel, who spoke for him, "Your words, Olaf Trygvesson, are both hard and fair, as a sword is hard and fair. We know that this is your way when you come to any district, and we lords have given much thought to how we should answer you. We are proud men in the west—the first ships to take the Viking road to England came from here. An ancestor of mine sacked Lindisfarne, and brought back such treasure as had never been seen in Norway. It follows that if a man comes to us demanding to be made king, and telling us to break our laws and change our ways just because he has a force behind him, well, we know something of force ourselves. On the other hand, if a man comes to us offering himself as king, and promises to advance our interests and promote our kinsmen, well then such a man we will welcome, and we will swear to him undying loyalty. Forgive me, I am an old man, and my ears are not as sharp as they were. What sort of speech did you make us, Olaf Trygvesson? Was it a threat or an offer?"

Olaf said, "The answer to that lies with you. Will you accept the baptism of Christ, or cling to the worship of devils?"

The lords began to whisper to each other, and Arinbjorn the Sogning hersir stood up and said, "As for me and my family, we have decided to give up the old gods and worship the White Christ. Indeed, we have turned our temple, which you see yonder, into a temple of Christ, and placed an image of him inside, such as you Christians worship. It is a very holy image, my lord, for if you watch it carefully, it can be seen to move."

"We do not worship images," said Olaf, "but it would be outside reason to expect you to understand that so soon. We would see this temple of yours, and this image, so that my bishop may judge whether what you say is true, and if so, whether it is of God or the Devil."

I was surprised by Arinbjorn's sudden conversion, and it struck me as odd that I'd heard nothing of this image before. I said as much to Erling, and he whispered that we must watch Arinbjorn closely.

When Olaf came down, Olmod called Erling to them and presented him. Olaf said, "We've met before, Erling Skjalgsson, and I know you are a Christian. I'm pleased to meet a civilized man in this place."

Olmod said, "We think Erling the most hopeful young man in Norway."

Erling introduced me to the king and I mumbled

something polite. The bishop and priests were close by and I preferred not to make an impression. Kings don't mind if you mumble. They don't care about anything you have to say anyway.

We trooped up to the temple, and the king's twelve bullyboys went in first. Then followed the king and his priests and Arinbjorn, then Olmod (leaning on Askel), Erling and me.

As my eyes adjusted to the dimness, lit only by the hearth fire, I could see a strange crucifix planted in front of the gods' dais. It seemed to be life-sized and very lifelike, but why was Christ wearing a tattered robe, and why—dear God!—why had a dog's head been fixed at the top of the upright?

Then I forgot the image, for there was a sudden shout and struggle, and I saw Erling grappling with Arinbjorn, each with an arm around the other's body, right arms raised high. In Arinbjorn's hand a knife gleamed, and Erling's hand gripped his wrist.

The king's bodyguard leaped upon them and had them separated in a moment. "Thor lives!" shouted Arinbjorn. "The gods have cursed you, Olaf Trygvesson! You'll die far from home, forsaken by your Christ!"

"Shall we hang him?" asked one of the guard.

"No," said Olaf, looking around him. "He comes of a high family. Let him be outlawed." There was a sigh from the onlookers, and outside we could hear those who had seen telling those who hadn't.

"I swear none but Arinbjorn knew of this," said Olmod.

"Erling Skjalgsson," said Olaf, "it seems I owe you my life. You've a good eye and a quick hand. What reward can I offer you?"

"Let's speak of that in counsel with my kinsmen," said Erling.

"So be it," said Olaf. "Now, what of this crucifix?"

I looked at it and said, "That's no crucifix, my lord, that's a living man. Where's that knife? Cut him down!"

The guard who'd taken the knife ran forward with me and leaped on the dais to slice the ropes that held the wretch on the cross. Many hands lowered him to the floor, and I said, "I know this man," and knelt beside him. It was my friend Moling. "Get him water," said someone, and footsteps ran off.

Moling breathed in shuddering gasps; he was pale as parchment and weighed no more than a baby, and his skin felt cold. "Brother Ailill," he croaked. "Can't see your face. Know your voice. It seems I've turned my White Martyrdom to Red after all." Then he fell to coughing.

"How long have you been hanging there?" I asked.

"Can't tell. Dark in here, even when I could see. But there's light in my—in my heart."

"Will you be cheerful even now, madman? You can't tell me this is God's good will."

A cup of water was pushed at me, and I put it against Moling's lips. We spilled most of it, but I think a little got down his throat, because he spoke more easily.

"It's the difference between us and them, brother," he whispered. "They sacrifice and carve their runes and chant their spells to bribe their gods to give them what they want. We pray and fast and subdue our flesh so that the Beloved might give us . . ." And Moling died in my arms.

"Here dies a saint," said Olaf Trygvesson.

CHAPTER XXVIII

"I've a shameful thing to confess, Father," said Erling to me. It was the morning after Olaf's meeting with the lords, and Moling's death. Erling had called me away to talk under four eyes, and we'd climbed the hillside and sat on a large rock overlooking the thingstead. "Last night I dreamed of Astrid Trygvesdatter."

"Show me the man who can put a bridle on his dreams, and I'll show you a man who needs not God's mercy," said I.

"She's very fair," said Erling. "Have you seen her, walking with Olaf? She's as graceful as a hawk on the wind. And when she smiles—"

"Don't torment yourself, my lord. You're not the first man to want a woman he can't have."

"But I can have her, Father. All I need do is break my word to Halla. Halla would understand. My kin would cheer me, since it wasn't a proper betrothal after all. My mother would be so glad her hair would go gold again. And it would be good for the land, so everyone tells me."

"But you won't break your word," said I with a dry mouth.

"No."

I sighed. "Halla's worth it, my lord," I said.

"Aye."

We fell silent for a while. It troubled me that Erling didn't agree with all the fervor I'd have used.

"Astrid Trygvesdatter's not perfect," I said. "Her upper lip is too short. And she has a proud look. Any husband who wants to rule his home will have to wrestle her for it, I'll wager."

"Any horseman knows that a beast with spirit is best for the true rider."

"I'm a peasant, my lord, with peasant tastes. I can't see things through a lord's eyes. But it's a sin against yourself to dwell on her like this. If you've made your choice, be done with it. Don't put your hand to the plow and keep looking back."

"I know that," said Erling. "And that's what I mean to do. But I had to talk to someone about it. The priests are right, you know. A man should lie with one woman in his life, and she his wife. Otherwise it ends in unfair deeds."

We went back down to the booths, and I thought in my heart, *You take Astrid, and I'll take Halla, and the whole world will be a happy place.* Then I thought of Sigrid and asked forgiveness and laid a penance on myself.

We went to Olaf's booth, where the Horder lords were gathering. Olaf's priests stood outside. I winked at one of them and he looked away quickly. I had found with pleasure that, far from being eager to question me, they were snubbing me altogether, as English priests are wont to do with the Irish. Even in the heart of heathendom they wouldn't lower themselves to talk shop with a man of my tonsure.

I hadn't had a chance to test Bishop Sigurd, but I assumed he'd be worse than the priests.

We all went inside and sat on the benches. Olaf had the high seat, and Olmod sat across from him in his blankets.

"I have two matters to discuss with you," said Olaf. "One is a lesser thing, though great in itself, and that is my debt to Erling Skjalgsson for the warding of my body. The second is what terms we shall make in exchange for the baptism of all the men of the Gulathing-law. You men of the west are lucky to have a leader as wise as Olmod Karisson. Wherever I've gone in the land, no lords until now have had the wit to meet me in this businesslike way."

"These two matters you speak of are one in our view," said Olmod. "We have taken counsel, and we have but one wish as to what you shall do for Erling, and for us. We wish you to wed Astrid Trygvesdatter to Erling Skjalgsson, so that we may ever be certain of a place near the king's heart."

"You ask a great thing," said Olaf, scratching his beard. "Kings' daughters and kings' sisters are born for high matches, profitable marriages to kings and the greatest lords."

"We have no objection to Erling's advancement," said Olmod with a smile.

"I need to warn Erling, too, that Astrid will make a formidable wife. If she lacks any virtues, they are that sweetness and biddability which are a woman's greatest charms."

"I must speak," said Erling. "There is no woman alive I'd rather wed than Astrid, and no man I'd be prouder to have for a brother-in-law than you, King

Olaf. But I've given my promise to another woman, and I mean to keep my word as a lord and a Christian."

"Well then, there's no point to this," said Olaf.

"Let us set it aside a moment," said Olmod. "Arrangements are being made which may change Erling's mind. In any case, you'll want to set the matter before your sister."

"I would not give Astrid's hand without her consent," said Olaf. "I'm not sure I could if I tried. But it seems we've gone as far as we can in this business for today."

"There is one other thing," said a man. We turned to see that Sigurd Eriksson had stood. "My brothers and I have endured much shame over the years through Thorolf Skjalg's holding of our odal lands. Now we're told we may have to look on Erling Skjalgsson as a kinsman. If this is to be, we must settle once and for all who holds what land in Jaeder, and who shall be lord there."

One of the Horders said, "Will we never hear the end of this Jaeder business?"

"An end to it is exactly what I ask," said Sigurd.

"Do you think I'm going to turn my property over to you?" asked Erling.

"I think you will if the king commands it."

"And would the king command such a thing?" asked Erling, turning to Olaf.

"The king will do what's best for the peace of the land," said Olaf. "Any lord who opposes him will know he has an enemy."

"It would ill become you, O King," said Jostein Eriksson, rising, "to set aside the rights of your near

kinsmen for the profit of the sons of Horda-Kari.
Don't you see how sly they are? We haven't taken
a step since we got here that hasn't been foreseen
by Olmod Karisson. He says he knew nothing of
Arinbjorn's plan to kill you, but we've only his word
on that. If we don't watch ourselves, they'll steal
the ships from under our feet as we sail away and
leave us swimming in the fjord, wondering how it
was done."

"If you've some charge of false dealing to make,
let's hear it," said a Horder.

"None of your kin has ever dealt fairly. Your women
trade off nursing babies so you'll all learn to suck
what's not your own!"

Then the two of them were at each other's throats,
and in a moment Olaf was down among them, taking
each by the scruff of the neck and shaking them
like puppies. The tales of his strength were no lies.

"Now sit down and keep your mouths shut," he
said when they were quiet, "or I'll sew you in a sack
together and dump you in the fjord. This is not how
civilized men act in the presence of the king. Do
you understand me?"

The two men bowed their heads and mumbled
apologies.

"All right. Don't let it happen again."

He went back to his seat and said, "Thorkel
Eriksson. You're a halfway bright man. Set your case
before me. Why is Erling's advancement an offense
to you?"

Thorkel stood and said, "It's all right for Sigurd.
He has Opprostad, and he's hersir. But Jostein and
I, as younger sons, must make do with lesser

inheritances. Ogmund and Skjalg took some of our best farms. If we held them, we'd be great men as our ancestors were great. While Erling holds them we are that much the less, and the poorer, and we feel the shame of it. It galls us."

The king frowned. "So your complaint is that your lands are too little, and you have to look on Erling Skjalgsson's prosperity."

"We are uncles to the king, my lord. We should not be smallholders in the land."

Olaf nodded. "There's truth in that. Yet I can hardly give Astrid's hand to Erling, if that's what God intends, and then take estates from him. Be silent for awhile, everyone, while I think."

And Olaf set his chin on his knuckles and thought for several minutes while we watched him, quiet as well-behaved children.

At last he sat up and said, "Let me make a proposal. In my business in the Vik, I was forced to outlaw several lords and take their estates. Suppose I were to give the finest of those estates to you brothers, Jostein and Thorkel? The Vik is better land even than Jaeder, and its lords have long been the richest in Norway. Would you be willing to be lords in the Vik, and live far from Erling Skjalgsson?"

Jostein and Thorkel said "Aye" without hesitation. They'd been in the Vik with Olaf and seen the property there.

"Then so be it," said Olaf. "Erling and Sigurd will divide overlordship in the west. I think the two of you can get along without cutting each other's throats, can't you?"

"May I speak, my lord?" asked Sigurd.

"Of course."

"I want to rule no lands but my own. It is my wish to stay at the king's side always."

Olaf leaned back in his seat. "How great a lord does that leave you, Erling Skjalgsson?" he asked.

"I am your man, my lord," said Erling. "How great do you want your man to be?"

We broke up the meeting soon after that. As the others were going out, Erling went over to Olmod. I nosed over to hear what he'd say.

"If any harm comes to Halla Asmundsdatter," he told the old man softly, "I swear I'll go abroad and become a monk."

Olmod said, "What ugly thoughts you have, kinsman."

Murder defiles a holy place, even among the Norse, and after the meeting everyone agreed that it was time to carry out the king's will. A company of men went to the temple and brought out the images of Thor, Odin and Frey, and the smaller images. They broke off all the gold and silver and piled the wood together, and Olaf himself set a torch to the pile. A wailing from the crowd went up with the smoke, bonders and their wives seeing their faith torn from them by the king's word.

"It's a sad sight, in a way," said a voice beside me. I looked and gave a start, for it was Bishop Sigurd. He was young for a bishop, though his hair was iron gray. He had a pleasantly homely face with a long chin and the eyes of a sick man, at once sunken and puffy.

"I'm surprised to hear you say so, my lord," said

I, with caution as I knelt. He bade me rise.

"On Sunday we'll dunk all these people in the fjord and call them Christians, but in their hearts Jesus will be just another god they've heard of, less interesting, perhaps, than Thor. And any who refuse we'll torture or kill, although there shouldn't be much trouble of that kind here, as the people generally follow their lords. Still it's not very Christlike, is it?"

"We tried torture at Sola once," I said. "It did us more harm than it did the man we pained."

"I know well what you mean. My hair was brown when I came to Norway."

"Then why, my lord?"

The bishop stared at the fire.

"Come away with me to a place alone," he said, and I led him up to the rock where Erling and I had sat earlier. The bishop seated himself and said, "Do you know what the sin against the Holy Spirit is?"

"I know it's unpardonable. I've never understood what it means."

"The theologians wrangle over it. I have my own idea. In the Gospel, Christ speaks of it after His enemies have seen Him work miracles, and they've said He does these things by the power of Satan. I think what the Lord means by the sin against the Holy Spirit is a state of mind like theirs, in which a man looks at good and calls it evil, or looks at evil and calls it good.

"I must confess to you, my son—I couldn't say it to my own priests—that sometimes I fear I've committed that sin. Much as I study the scriptures, I find in them no word permitting me to force men to be baptized through violence. The screaming! The smells! I dream of them at night. And a voice says to me—'God would give you hearing ears, to listen to the voice of His Spirit, but day by day you make your ears deaf to the cries of men, and one day they will be deaf even to Him. And then you will have committed the unpardonable sin.' And you cannot shrive me of this sin—not you or any priest— because I cannot turn from it."

"Why not?"

"You're Irish, aren't you—Ailill's your name, am I right?"

"Aye."

"In Ireland, did you ever see a Viking raid?"

"Oh aye. That I did. Up close."

"The Norse tell jolly tales about their gods, and I enjoy hearing those tales. But those same gods teach them that might is right, and that Norsemen are people and foreigners are beasts, and that as Norsemen they have a right to catch and herd and brand and slaughter and sell foreigners as livestock. Only Christ can teach them differently. Ethelred of England said to me when I was commissioned, 'Do your work well in Norway and you'll be more protection to my people than ten thousand warriors.' God knows we men of Christendom are brutal enough with each other. But when we slay our brothers we at least know them for our brothers. In time we may learn to act like brothers. But men who worship Thor will never learn that in a thousand years. Every image I burn, every heathen I baptize, may mean one house unburned, one man unkilled, one child not enslaved."

His words brought back memories of Maeve, and my imposture, and the death of Steinbjorg; and thinking of Steinbjorg made me think of Halla. If she were free of Erling, and Erling free of his vow, and I were free of my lie—

"My lord," I said, "I've not made a confession in more than two years. I've grave sins to be quit of." I knelt as I spoke, and I told all, and I remained kneeling for some minutes after I'd finished, wondering if the bishop had fallen into a trance.

"How very strange are God's ways," he said at last.

"I wonder each day that He slays me not with fire from Heaven."

"I didn't mean that. Oh, you've sinned, and you'll have to do heavy penance. But I was thinking of how the Lord plucked the unlikeliest man in the world out of Ireland and brought him here to do His work. That's so like Him. He never uses a sword when he can do the job with the jawbone of an ass."

"Ass is a fitting word," said I, "but I can hardly say I've done God's work."

"What do you call it then? If I'd gone to Sola I'd not have lasted a week. I'd have been martyred like Erling's first priest. It's fine to have martyrs, but somebody's got to be alive to say the masses."

"My masses weren't effectual! And when I think of the babes I've christened, all still heathen, and the couples I've wed, living in ignorant sin—"

"A layman may christen if there's no priest to hand and the need is great. And marriage is a complicated issue. . . .

"From what you told me, you seem to have been

ordained by the greatest bishop of all in a vision.
I'm inclined to accept that vision. Ordination by
vision is irregular, but what's not irregular in Norway?
I've burned men's flesh in the name of Christ—
who am I to carp at your ordination?"

"You wish me to live in my sin?"

"No—if your conscience is troubled, we can't have
that. Bow your head."

And he placed his hands on me and absolved me,
then said the last words I'd expected to hear—the
words of ordination.

"There. You are now a priest ordained by a bishop.
And as your bishop I declare all your priestly acts
efficacious retroactively. I'm not sure I can do that,
but I'll chance it. If this is sin, I take it on myself.
That way I can also claim some merit in your victories.
Because when you look at it straight on, Ailill my
son, you've been a very successful missionary. So
stand and take up your cross again. And for heaven's
sake, come with me now and get a proper tonsure."

"I'm not sure I even believe in God," I said,
numbly. I'd had dreams of wedding Halla, and
instead I found myself condemned to priesthood.

"Believe in God? You who've seen the walking
dead and Odin and the elf-woman, who've done a
miracle? Do you think the healing of Erling was
by your own power? If you don't believe in God, I
don't know who does."

"All right, I believe in Him," I cried. "But I hate
Him! I'm as heathen as the worst of the Norse. God
is my enemy. He let them kill my family and enslave
my sister. He let my leman be killed, and my unborn
child!"

"Does that make Him your enemy? Does God give pleasant lives to his friends, and pain to his enemies? I haven't seen that to be true."

"I hate Him, my lord. I hate God. If that's not the unforgivable sin, what is?"

"You miss the point. You've seen evil, and you called it evil. That's not the unpardonable sin. You're mistaken in thinking all this makes God your enemy, but that's an error, not apostasy.

"Think of this, my son. God's love is a light. It shines brightly on His children in this dark world. What happens to a man who stands in the light in view of his enemies?"

"He becomes a target, I suppose."

"That's what you and I are. Do you know the story of Job? God's love, shining bright on Job, made him an easy mark for the enemy. Granting that we have an enemy, it's natural we'll be attacked. Or don't you believe in devils?"

"Oh, aye. I believe in devils. I believe in God too. But I don't love Him."

"Do any of us love Him worth the use of the word? He loves us—that's the point. Even the best of us raise our pitiful love to Him as a child raises some dead thing he's found in the field and brought home to his father, and the father pretends it doesn't stink and says thank you because he loves his child. When your friend Moling died, what was it he said? 'We fast and pray and whatnot that the Beloved would give us—' You know what he meant, don't you?"

"Aye," I said. "I know what he meant." It was the end of the game—God had cleared the board.

Just then we heard a woman's scream down in

the camp, followed by a stream of loud and furious name-calling.

"What's that?" I wondered.

"It sounds like Astrid Trygvesdatter," said Bishop Sigurd. "I would imagine she's just been told that Erling refused her hand."

CHAPTER XXIX

Erling and I sat outside our booth with the others, eating our evening meal. I had to run my hand over my head from time to time, feeling my strange new tonsure. "The tonsure of St. Peter," the English call it. Our Irish tonsure they sneeringly call "the tonsure of Simon Magus." As if we weren't serving God in our tonsures while their fathers were kissing mares and licking sacrificial bowls.

"Have you talked to Sigrid, Father?" Erling asked me.

I peered at him. "Why do you ask?"

"She seems so strange these days. I find her wandering about among the tents, singing to herself. She doesn't hear when she's spoken to. I brought her to the Thing in hopes I could make her a good marriage, get her mind off that boy who was killed. But it seems she's distracted with grief. Perhaps I should keep her away from steel—"

"No," said I. "Keep her always near steel."

Erling's voice lowered. "The underground folk?"

"I can say no more."

"Sigrid is my sister. I must know."

"Trust me in this, as we all trust you. I've said all I can. Tell me how it goes with Halla and Astrid."

Erling looked at the ground and said, "All is well. Astrid utterly refuses to wed me. She says she wouldn't marry a mere hersir in the first place, and certainly not one who has the cheek to refuse a king's daughter's hand." He was putting a good face on it, but it hurt him.

"What of the settlement with Olaf?"

"I can be a jarl without marrying Astrid. Olmod and his plotters will be disappointed, since they say there's nothing like a marriage to make a peace. But when you think of it, how many peaceful marriages have you seen?"

"So you'll wed Halla?"

"Aye. I'll have a fine wife. A fine wife."

I said, "Here comes Sigurd Eriksson. I wonder what he wants."

Sigurd was alone, and when he stopped and stared at the man on the bench across from us, the man got up and walked away. Sigurd sat in his place. "A sweet evening," he said.

"Aye," said Erling. "Sogn is a fine place for beauty."

"Not as good as Jaeder for grain though."

"Not nearly."

Sigurd said, "The king has told us we must live at peace, Erling Skjalgsson. So we're at peace—by law. But there's never a real peace until men make it in their hearts. Can we make true peace now, at last?"

Erling said, "I've never wished trouble with you, Sigurd, nor any of your family. I didn't wish the death of Aki—he left me no choice. I'm sorry you feel cheated by the deeds of my fathers, but it's too late to change that without uprooting my life and wrecking my fortune. Nevertheless, I offer you self-judgment. What penalty should I pay you, that the bloodshed may cease and bad feeling be buried?"

Sigurd leaned his elbows on his knees and stared at the ground awhile. "We're Christians now," he said, "but this Christianity is hard to master. The priests say a Christian must love his enemies, and turn the other cheek to a man who strikes him in the face. How can a man do these things and keep his honor? As far as I can see, no one's worked that out. They talk about it, but no one practices it, not even the priests themselves.

"Still, I say to myself—when a feud has gone on for generations, and there's nothing to be gained, and my family is now better off than yours thanks to Olaf's bounty—what's the use in carrying it on? Yet my kin will not accept peace, I think, unless you pay some price."

"Name the price."

"You'll be a great man in Norway. Everyone knows this. You have property; you have the king's friendship. In these things you are my equal. I don't begrudge it. I think my kin would begrudge it, though, if you were raised above us as a jarl. When the king offers you a jarldom, refuse it."

"That's a high price."

"Your reason need be no secret. Say it's to please us. My kin will be satisfied then."

"I've turned down the sister of the king. Now you bid me turn down his jarldom. I might as well slap Olaf's face and see if he'll turn the other cheek."

"I'll speak for you with him when the time comes. He listens to me."

"I gave you self-judgment, and I must abide by your wishes. But it's a hard thing you ask."

"You gain my friendship with this, Erling. I am no worthless friend."

Sigurd went away, and Erling said, "A man's word should be a cable of steel. But he mustn't be surprised if that cable hangs him one day."

The next morning a messenger came asking Erling to come to the king's tent. We went together, with Erling's bullyboys following.

Olaf stood before his booth, wearing a red linen shirt. He had a horn of ale in his hand, and as we came near he said something that made all the men standing around laugh.

"Erling Skjalgsson!" he cried when he saw us. "It's good to see you this fine morning! I've something to ask of you!"

"Anything I can give in honor is yours," said Erling, going to him.

"As my men and I drank together last night, someone got to talking of your adventures. He said that when it comes to strength and skill with weapons you are my only equal in Norway, perhaps in the world."

"I've never made such a claim," said Erling.

"That's not the point, you see. The point is that some men have bet on me, and some have bet on you, and it's up to us to decide the thing for them."

"I'd rather not compete with my king."

"Well, your king commands it." Olaf's eyes were red—I guessed he'd drunk his breakfast. "And he commands that you not hold back to let him beat you, as if you would. We will run, we will cast spears and we will wrestle. And if I'm not winded and bleeding when we're done, I'll lay a heavy fine on you."

The king's bullyboys cleared a course across the Thingstead and set a spear in the ground at each end. The idea was to run down the course and back, rounding the further spear before returning to the near one.

Someone brought a horn of ale for Erling, and as he drank it I said, "I mislike this. A king's pride is touchier than a mortified wound. He'll not punish you for obeying, I expect, but you might lose your favor."

"Has it ever occured to you, Father Ailill, that I can be beaten?" asked Erling, wiping his mouth with his sleeve. "Anyway, I've no choice. Perhaps it's God's will I be a small man in Norway."

"Just be careful."

The footrace, run carrying an axe and a shield, was quickly done, and Erling won it easily. Speed was one of his gifts, and although he and Olaf were nearly of a height, he was built along the lines of a stag, while Olaf was more of a bull. He reached the goal several strides ahead of Olaf, and wasn't even breathing hard.

"Ale for the victor!" cried Olaf, and a horn was brought to Erling. "Drink it dry!" the king commanded. Erling had already had more than his morning measure, but he did as he was told.

A reindeer skin with a bull's-eye on it was next stretched between two spears a distance away, and Erling and Olaf took turns casting three spears each. Olaf's first cast was a little off, while Erling's was clean on the mark. The king ordered a drink for each of them before they cast again. This time both struck the mark. Again the king called for drinks, and the third time both missed by a finger's breadth.

"Now with the left hand!" shouted Olaf. They both missed the first cast, but Olaf was closer. Olaf called for ale. Both missed the second, but Erling was even further off. On the third, Olaf's spear just touched the mark, and Erling was a hand's breadth off.

So the spear throwing was called a draw, and the king called for more ale.

In that moment I understood Olaf Trygvesson, although I dared not say a word to Erling. Olaf was addicted to ale. Like all men so enslaved, he actually grew steadier in the morning when he'd gotten a few measures in his belly, while Erling's senses were dulling.

"Now we wrestle!" cried Olaf. "I warn you again, Erling Skjalgsson, don't hold back a finger! I'll know it if you do!" He pulled off his shirt and crouched, and Erling took his own shirt off, handed it to me, and made ready to meet him.

I gasped when I saw Olaf's back. I'd guessed that he must have been a headstrong slave, and his skin bore witness to it. I'd seen thralls who'd been beaten savagely and often, but I've never, before or since, seen a back as scarred as Olaf's on a man who yet walked. Every color known writhed in its knots and furrows, with white and brown most common. He had to suffer constant pain from the ruined nerves. No wonder he drank so.

The two men approached one another and took the Norse wrestling stance, which involves standing breast to breast, each man looking over the other's right shoulder, his right hand on his opponent's trouser waist, the left grasping a bunch of his trouser leg. They circled, swinging their legs to try to trip the other, for the first few minutes, never looking down (which is bad form). Olaf attempted a tricky hip maneuver, but Erling twisted free. Erling then tried to lift Olaf and drop him off balance, but Olaf avoided that. Then they circled some more, breathing heavily.

Erling tried a cross-hook with his right leg against Olaf's, but Olaf countered with a lift and a knee maneuver. Erling stumbled and nearly fell, but managed to keep his feet. I didn't think he looked well, and he swayed a bit.

"Come on, come on, you'll have to do better than that!" said Olaf. "You want to be a great lord, you'd better learn to fight! You want to scorn kings' sisters, you'd better learn to fight like a troll!"

"I never scorned your sister," said Erling, panting. "I only keep my word, as I mean to keep it to you. Besides, I'm not good enough for Astrid. Ask her."

Olaf kicked out with his heel to hook and trip Erling. Erling stood firm and they grappled a moment, until he got an outside legstroke on the king, which the king struggled out of with a leap and a jig. Then they circled some more, moving slowly now.

"Astrid's changed her mind," said Olaf. "Last night I took her favorite hawk, plucked its feathers out, and sent it to her. She took the hint. She says she'll marry as I will. What's the use being a king if I can't make a jarl of whomever I like?"

"About that jarldom, there's something I should say—" said Erling, but Olaf got a hip under him just then and lifted him high, then threw him to the ground. Erling lay winded a moment, his mouth open, and as he did so Olaf threw himself down and got his legs around Erling's neck (which was not strictly within the rules).

"So what about my sister?" cried Olaf. "Will you marry her, or shall I break your neck?"

Erling croaked, "I cannot break my word to Halla Asmundsdatter."

Olaf said, "Askel, speak your piece!"

Askel Olmodsson stepped out of the crowd and, like a child reciting before his elders, said, "I have offered betrothal for my son Aslak to Halla Asmundsdatter, and her father has agreed to it."

Erling said, "What?" and Olaf took his legs away. Erling sat up, rubbing his neck. "Halla would never agree."

"She has agreed," said Askel. "It's a high match for a bonder's daughter."

"Aslak's just a boy."

"He's nearly a man now—taller than I am. And Halla is little older."

Erling fell backwards on the grass and lay with his arms stretched out a moment. "This is Olmod's doing," he said.

"It's the head of the family's business to arrange marriages."

When he sat up Erling looked like a man loosed

from a chain, and his face shone like his honor.

"I'll be very happy to wed your sister, my lord," he said.

Somewhere up in the mountains a scream rose and died. No one seemed to mark it but me.

CHAPTER XXX

I found Halla walking with her distaff near her
father's booth. I asked, "Is this what you're settling
for then? This stripling? Do you think you can ever
care for him as you do for Erling?"

Halla smiled at me, sweet as the Mother of the
Lord. "It's different for women than for men, Father.
We like to love, but what we need most is to be
loved. Erling will never love me as he loves Astrid,
but I think Aslak will. And I think I can make a
man of him. Perhaps not an Erling, but a good man
still."

"Erling has chosen the lesser woman."

"Don't undervalue Astrid. She's no fairy story
princess living her life in a garden. She lost her
parents young, and she's known exile and poverty
and danger."

I shook my head. "The truth is—I'd hoped that
I could . . . see you about Sola each day, as I used
to. If I were free—but I'm a priest now for life,
and I'd not have you as less than a true wife—"

"You weren't meant for marriage, Father. You have
the love of God, the best love of all."

I only looked at the ground.

Halla said, "I remember once when I was a girl,

there was a family of cottagers living near us, and they never really made enough of the ground to feed them. In the end they went away, but one Jul before that my mother took pity on them and took me with her to carry a basket of fresh barley bread to their cottage.

"The woman thanked us, and one of the children grabbed a piece of bread the moment he smelled it. He took a bite, then spit it out. He said, 'It's bad!'

"You see, they'd done what many of the poor do. They mixed ground moss into their flour to stretch it. There's no good in the moss for food, except to fill your stomach awhile. But those children had never known anything but moss bread. When they tasted real bread, they thought there was something wrong with it.

"A woman's love, even the best woman's, is only moss bread, Father. When you get used to real flour you'll like it, and it'll feed you as moss never can."

"Is that how you really feel? I would God I had that peace."

"I'm not made of stone. It hurts to say goodbye to love. But I have faith. I learned it from you, even if you didn't understand the lesson."

"He'd better be worthy of what you've done for him," I said. "If he isn't, I swear I'll break his neck."

Tears ran down her cheeks then. I wanted to hold and comfort her, but there were people about.

"I was Erling Skjalgsson's woman once," she said. "They can't take that from me."

"You're Father Ailill's woman, too," said I. "And that you'll always be, for whatever it's worth to you."

CHAPTER XXXI

The Gulathing broke up at last. Aside from acclaiming Olaf king, they made one change in the law that amused me. From that time on, when the land was attacked, thralls were compelled to take up arms.

When I bid the bishop farewell I spoke to him in private. I said, "My Lord, would you be offended to receive the counsel of a man poor in wisdom but rich in scars and bruises?"

He gave me smiling permission to proceed.

"Lay down the iron and steel," I said. "Do the Lord's work the Lord's way. Don't build His house on sand."

I left him with tears in his eyes and no words in his mouth.

Once we returned and gave Ragna the news she'd hoped for, that Erling would marry the king's sister, she began taking her food again and there was no more talk of convents. Like an old king called out to use his life's skills in one last battle to defend his realm, she threw herself into the task of preparing food and drink, finery and bedding for the largest wedding ever seen in Jaeder. "I'm too old for this; I should be sitting close to the fire and knitting mittens," she told me, but she loved it all. I laughed secretly at first, until one evening in the hall I got to talking to Steinulf and learned that he was Ragna's brother. I don't know why I'd never learned this before—it made sense. The maternal uncle always keeps a wing over his nephew in Norway as in Ireland, and who better to lead your bodyguard than the man who, next to your father, made a warrior of you?

"It's a wonder Ragna has a life at all," he told me. "She was the oldest of us children, and our father's only daughter. Our father was a strange man. You could probably say he was mad, though a son shouldn't speak so. When our mother died, he was still young enough to take another wife, but he didn't even take a leman. He just turned all his love on Ragna. I don't mean he did anything improper to her. I never saw any sign of that. But he thought of her as his wife reborn—in fact he changed her name to Ragna because it was Mother's. In the old religion, we believed that if you gave a child the name of a dead relation, the dead one would live again in the child. And he did a very queer thing to make sure she would never leave him alone. An evil thing, when you look at it straight on. He told her she was ugly.

"Now you and I know that even today she's not a bad looking woman. She wasn't as beautiful as Astrid Trygvesdatter or Halla Asmundsdatter, but she was a handsome girl who could have brought a rich dowry to a husband as well. But Father didn't want her to marry. So every day, almost whenever he saw her, he'd say something like, 'You're a good girl, Ragna. It's a pity you're ugly as a troll, because otherwise you'd make someone a fine wife.' I should have tried to tell her otherwise, I suppose, but when did you ever see a younger brother build up a sister? I'm afraid I joined in the game.

"Then came Thorolf Skjalg. Aside from his squint he was a handsome young man, and rich, and from the day he came to buy horses from our father and saw Ragna, he swore he'd have her. He sent kinsmen to Father and made suit, offering a generous bride-price, and Father refused, saying Thorolf must be a squinter indeed if he thought Ragna fair. Thorolf sent his kinsmen back, naming a richer price, and still Father refused. When he made his third offer, it was so high—high enough for a king's daughter—that our uncles came and threatened to thump Father if he said no. So Ragna was married at last. The day of her wedding she told me, 'I looked at my reflection in a bowl of water this morning and asked myself, "Is this an ugly woman? This woman who has brought the highest bride-price ever known in our family? No, no one pays such a price for an ugly woman." ' And from that day she walked with her head high, and she was fairer to look on than I'd thought she ever could be."

"It must have hurt her to lose Thorolf," I said.

"You've no idea. It's a wonder she didn't try to rope Erling to her in Father's manner. She's lost four children over the years, between illness and adventures. It must have been agony to her every time she watched Erling sail off in *Fishhawk*, her treasure floating on a wood chip out where the great serpents play."

"Little wonder this wedding means so much to her."

"Erling is all her hope."

The wedding was set for a day near Midsummer, in June by the Christian calendar, and I'd made sure to check the notches on the stick calendar I'd kept against Bishop Sigurd's so that we'd have no confusion.

If you love ships you'd have loved our neighborhood the day before the wedding. They anchored them in Hafrsfjord so that you'd swear it was a winter forest from all the masts; they even anchored some latecomers up in Risa Bay and drove them overland in wagons to Sola. When they arrived Thursday the guests found a freshly painted hall and garlands of summer flowers everywhere. Pipers and harpists played loudly if not elegantly, and everyone danced. There was food and ale for all, and masses morning and evening. My church had been whitewashed within, and there were golden candlesticks and beeswax tapers, gifts from the bishop.

Olaf and his following, a couple hundred people, made a handsome procession from the jetty to the hall, even more gorgeous than they'd looked at the Gulathing. I'd like to tell you how the bride looked but she'd been veiled against bad luck. Olaf headed the company, looking like a man who had come through blood and steel to take what he wanted from the world, who knew he was living in a saga and was proud of it. I heard someone whisper as he passed, "A king—yes, that's a king." The Erikssons were there too, and Olaf's bent mother, and Aslak Askelsson, looking proud of his new wife, the grave and graceful Halla.

When he got to the steading, Olaf unstrapped his rich swordbelt and handed the weapon to Erling. "I declare the wedding-peace," he said, and then all his company gave up their arms to thralls, who carried them off for storage. Erling and Olaf embraced, and everyone went inside, the men in the great hall, the women in a couple of the other buildings, to begin the business of feasting.

There was food in plenty—porridge and wheaten bread and four kinds of fish and pork and ham and beef, and angelica stalks in honey for a sweet, and there were oceans of ale and mead. The more fighting there is at a wedding, the luckier for the bride and groom, they say. They also say it's a shameful thing to go home from a wedding sober. Not to mention unlikely.

"Organization!" cried Olaf Trygvesson from the high seat, a horn in his hand, barely heard above the arguing and calls for ale. "Organization is what I mean to bring to Norway. Think of the length of the country—from the green fields of the Vik to the icy headlands of the North, where mists shroud the end of the world. A man from the Vik can barely understand the speech of a Halogalander, if at all. And do they think of themselves as Norwegians? Never, unless they're talking to some Englishman who's ignorant enough to call them Danes. They think of themselves as Vikers or Halogalanders. If we're to be a real nation, like England, we must have one king, one faith, one law.

"The land will be divided into regions. Over each region I'll place a jarl, who'll be my representative and collect my taxes, of which he'll keep a part.

Under him will be hersirs, keeping watch on the districts and ship levies."

"And the tithes," said the bishop. "Churches must be built, and monasteries and convents."

"Of course," said the king. "I'm going to build a town up on the Nid River, in the Trondelag, and in that town there'll be a cathedral. I'll build it there because the Tronds are the strongest heathens in the land, thanks to Jarl Haakon. They've acclaimed me king, but they've not been christened yet. They won't like it, but it will be done."

"The cathedral or the christening?" asked Erling.

"Both. The Tronders are as good as Christian already. I'll save them if I have to kill them all to do it."

I saw Olmod the Old smiling and nodding in his seat. This new religion was turning out much to his liking.

"What about going a-viking?" someone asked. "Are we to raid no more, now that the English and the Irish are our brothers?"

Olaf took a long pull from the horn. "There's little I can say about what men do when they sail out of the land. If they try it here I'll hang them by their own guts, but I can't be expected to ward Ethelred's land as well as my own. I'd prefer that men find honest livings, but I fear it'll take time to wean Norsemen from raiding."

"The king was a great Viking himself in England," said someone else, and then he launched into one of those endless, riddle-packed songs. While he sang, two men challenged each other to climb up into the rafters and race about on them. Both fell, being tipsy, and had to be carried out. Then Olaf grabbed the eating knives of two neighbors and juggled them and his own, to a storm of cheers and table thumping.

"Every king must be a juggler," he said when he sat down again. "He must juggle three things—his own struggle against sin, his struggle against lawlessness in the land, and his struggle against the enemies of the land."

"Yes," said the bishop, "but all these enemies are twofold—there is sin born in the heart and sin born in Hell. There is earthly lawlessness and spiritual lawlessness, such as heathendom and heresy. And there is the foreign king, only a man like you and me, and the king of Hell, whom none of us can fight in our own strength. That is why the church must guide the king's counsels."

"Yes, the power of the old gods is not broken yet," said old Bergthor. "Even here at Sola, where we've had a church for years, there's still a troll who lives in the wastes and comes to steal chickens or lambs sometimes. He's been seen haunting the outpastures and you can hear him howling nights."

"A troll?" asked Olaf. "That would be something to see. I wonder how you'd hunt a troll."

"If the truth were known, it's probably just a wolf," said Erling.

"No wolf ever sounded like that," said Bergthor. "I've heard plenty of wolves in my time."

Then a marvel occurred. I can only describe it by saying that the colors in the hall changed. Everything that was bright—the weaving in Halla's tapestry of David and Goliath, the red and yellow paint on the high seat pillars, the reds and blues and greens of the guests' shirts—all grew brighter, as if in sunlight, while all the dull things—the unpainted wood, the sooty rafters, my robe—seemed to darken almost to invisibility, as if at dusk.

And there was the elf-woman, in a gown of green, her eyes as large as a cow's but more fair, her golden hair drifting over her slender shoulders. Not a man breathed.

She glided to the high seat and stood before Olaf. "I have a plea to set before the king," she said. Her voice was like the call of a bird—an evening bird, sweet and unseen.

"Are you of God or the Devil?" he countered. I won't say he looked frightened, but he was pale.

"Does everything have to be one or the other?" she asked. "Do you ask this question of the horse you ride or the dog you hunt with? I am not of your race—your Christ did nothing for me."

"What are you?"

"Your neighbor. Are you not commanded to do well to your neighbor? I bring a plea."

"Have her seized and burned," said the bishop. "This creature is evil. All spirits that will not name Christ as Lord are of the Devil."

"Am I a spirit?" asked the elf-woman. "Do I not have a body? Look—" and she took a piece of bread from the king's table and ate it.

"This proves nothing," said the bishop. "Spirits can deceive our eyes."

"Will the king hear my plea?"

"What is your plea?" asked Olaf. His eyes had not left her.

"Some time ago a neighbor of mine began to annoy

me. He was ever trying to get me into his bed, but
he was old and ugly and I did not want him. So I
flayed a calf from neck to tail, and left its skin
dragging behind it, and I fed it strong herbs mixed
with dead men's blood until it grew mightier than
a sea gale, and I sent it to haunt my neighbor.
Whenever my neighbor left his house, the bull would
run to him, invisible, and throw him with its horns.
And whenever he went to bed my bull would lie
upon him and smother him. Soon my neighbor died.

"But now the bull has turned upon me, and it
follows me wherever I go, and I have all I can do
to master it. So I beg you, give me some of your
holy water, that I may pour it on the bull and kill it
at last."

"You've earned the fitting reward for your witchery,"
said the bishop. "Before the king can consider your
plea, you must answer me a riddle."

"We never refuse a riddle."

"The body. The human body. Is it good or evil?"

The elf-woman smiled, spread her arms, and
swayed gently before us, and there were sighs from
every side. "The body," she said, "is good—very,
very good."

"Wrong," said the bishop. "The body breeds pains,
and illness, and weakness leading to temptation, and
it grows old and dies and rots, and makes mockery
of our hopes. Guess again."

"I suppose you'd say the body is evil," she sneered.

"Wrong again. Our blessed Lord came in a body,
and it was a true man's body in every way. Since
there was no evil in Him, the body cannot be evil."

"Then there is no answer!"

"There is an answer, but you cannot know it."

"I speak to the king. What is the king's word?"

"I want to lie with you," said the king. The words fell heavy as a man from a masthead. I smelled that mare smell again, as I had in the heathen shrine.

"Renounce Christ. Worship Thor and Odin," said the elf-woman. I wanted to speak, but my mouth was dry as a shinbone a hundred years in the sun.

"I will renounce Christ," said Olaf.

The elf-woman smiled. It was glorious to see (How odd, now I think of it, that I remember her smile. I was sitting on Erling's bench, behind her).

"TO HELL WITH YOU, THING OF EVIL!"

It was the bishop who cried out, and with one motion he snapped the chain of the crucifix from about his neck and sent it flying at the elf-woman.

This is what we saw then. Every man who was there will tell you the same:

The elf woman began to sink down, to shrink in size before our eyes, and her whole body flattened as she sank, from the crown of the head downward, until she was two flat pink disks, the smaller atop the larger.

And then the two disks began to rise again, and there was a white, rounded mass pushing up beneath them, poking up and up from the earth. It rose before our eyes, a hill of white, soft and quaking, towering ever up.

"A breast!" someone cried. "A woman's breast, as big as a house!"

The woman followed the breast, clambering out of the earth, bracing hands the size of ships to pull herself up, elbowing the benches out of her way. And at last she stood free and towered naked above us, and shattered the roof as her head broke it through.

She was a hugely fat woman, as white as milk, with jutting globes of breasts and wide expanse of quaggy hips, and her hair was a mass of black ringlets falling past her shoulders, and her eyes were round as moons and much the same size, and thick, black blood poured with men's dismembered limbs from her gaping mouth.

She screamed, and she was gone, and the hall was as it had been.

The bishop reached out to Olaf, who sat unmoving in his seat. "Bring ale!" he shouted, and a horn was passed, and the bishop poured it down the king's throat.

Olaf coughed and spewed the ale out, then sat for some time with his hands braced on the table, looking down and shuddering.

"I have sinned," he said at last. "Erling, my host, forgive me. I must go to the church and speak with my bishop. The rest of you, carry on with the feast, and pardon me."

These were uncommonly humble words from Olaf, and no one spoke as he made his way out, the bishop holding his elbow, and for many minutes we only sat and stared at each other, wondering.

At last Bergthor said, "This bodes ill, but whether for the king or the wedding I cannot say."

"No," said Erling. "It bodes well. No man attacks another unless he either fears him or knows he has something of value. When the enemy lays on most fiercely, then we know we are dangerous to him, and treasured by God."

"What I can't understand," said someone, "is, if our God is so much more powerful than the old gods, why do all the wonders seem to come from their side?"

A voice said, "Because a marvel is like a sword." Strangely, the voice was my own. "Or like torture. There is no answer to it. The Beloved prefers to woo."

Where did those words come from? I've no idea to this day—I know I'd never thought them. But I pondered them all night, in my bed, until I slept.

I sat on my patch of earth, alone. My children had matured at last, and once mature they had run away from me, with barely a goodbye, and never returned.

I saw a shadow and looked up to see the abbot in his Black Axeman guise.

"Do you forgive me?" he asked.

"Of course," said I.

"Have you done and seen all here that you need to do and see? Are you ready to pay the toll and cross the river?"

"I don't know what I've done and I don't know what I've seen," I said. "I've learned that God pitches camp in the place of pain and danger. Does that mean that evil is good, and God depends on the Devil? Is there no joy without sorrow; no right without wrong? I seem to remember that was heresy."

"And so it is. It's not the evil we need, nor the pain. But we need the risk. The risk we cannot do without. It was God's risk to make the world, and to give Man a choice. All love is risk, and salvation the most dangerous thing of all."

"A man will do anything rather than die. The Lord isn't opposed to that. He's made self-slaughter a sin. Yet the road leads finally to a place where He says, 'Hold still while I kill you.' "

"It's the Death He wants to kill, son. It's your Death you've been clinging to from the day you first popped from the womb and shut your eyes and screamed against the light. Lay the thing down at last."

"It's no easy task. Even Death wants to go on living."

"I didn't call it easy. It's nothing at all He wants from you; but sometimes nothing at all is the hardest thing to give."

"I'm not a hero. I'm not the kind who laughs while they cut his heart out. He says He sees the sparrow fall; but it seems to me He cares only about eagles."

"Aye, it's a thing for heroes, to lay down your right to your safety. Great and small; free and slave; we're all made heroes in the end, or we go to Hell."

"I haven't that to give Him."

"It's not a thing to give. It's a thing to receive. Bow your head now."

I bowed my head. I barely felt the slice of the steel.

The next thing I knew there was golden light, and I was riding again, and the white hind was my steed and we flew over the fair green land, barely touching the ground, steadily approaching a far-off, white-robed figure. Even at infinite distance I knew the face—of all faces in the world most beautiful, most Beloved.

CHAPTER XXXII

On Saturday morning we pulled our throbbing heads out of our beds, or whatever place we'd collapsed in, at Sola or Somme, got some ale inside us to dull the pain, and donned our best togs for the wedding. The day did its duty by bringing out its Sunday weather. The only ill omen I saw was Lemming, watching us motionless as a carrion bird from the roof peak where Enda's gallows was. Erling and his bullyboys and I, singing, trooped down to Somme, where we found Astrid waiting in her veil and bride's crown, and Olaf placed her hand in Erling's.

"With this my sister's hand I make you a jarl, Erling Skjalgsson," said Olaf, "and I make you my man to guard and husband the land of Norway from the mouth of the Sognefjord south to Lindesness."

Everyone gasped, for this was fully half the west coast south of the Trondelag. North of the Trondelag was hardly considered, except for hunting and fishing.

"I thank you with all my heart, and pledge to you my loyalty to the death," said Erling, kneeling. "But I cannot accept the jarldom."

Everyone stood stock-still. Olaf's face went pale

and he clenched his fists. "You despise the honor I offer?"

"Never," said Erling. "I decline with sorrow only. I have promised this as a peace offering to your uncles, the Erikssons."

Olaf turned to Sigurd. "What means this?"

"It is as he says," said Sigurd. "If he remains a hersir he throws no shadow on our house, and it is his mansbot for the death of Aki."

"You made this arrangement behind my back?"

"It was the will of the family."

"So what will I do for a jarl? Shall my sister be wed to a mere hersir?"

"I would have no objection," said Erling, still kneeling, "to being made the highest of that title in the land."

"And so much for my well-planned organization! Well, it seems I've no power in this. Be a hersir then, Erling, and wed my sister and steer all the land I named. It seems the king's will counts for little enough when the lords put their heads together."

"Say not so," said Erling.

And the king bade Erling rise, and the procession moved back to Sola and to the church, where the Bishop waited outside for us. The vows would be made there, and we would all go inside for the wedding mass after.

Halla moved to my side as we made our way along the road, looking splendid in flower garlands and an overdress of green Chinese silk.

"You've changed, Father," she said when we'd greeted one another. "Forgive me for saying so, but you used to walk like a thrall, and you never met my eyes when we talked. Now you hold yourself like a jarl, and look me fair in the face. Do you love weddings so much?"

"I'll tell you about it later, daughter," I promised.

We were gathered in the yard before the church and Bishop Sigurd was just saying, "Dearly beloved," when a pile of leaves and dirt I hadn't noticed by the church door stirred of a sudden and rose to become a great, ragged, leathery thing in the shape of a man. With a roar it reached out a long arm and grabbed Astrid, slung her over its shoulder, and ran. It had an uneven, shambling gait, but it was not slow.

The thing had happened so fast, and was so unthinkable, that none of us, even Erling, had time to react. The man-thing was heading towards the gate, Astrid screaming, and although some of the men further back had the presence of mind to pursue, they hadn't the speed to catch the pair.

The creature was well ahead of them going out the gate, and then we could see, sprinting across the home-field and going fast enough to cut off its escape, a man with a sword.

The man was Lemming, and the sword, unless I was much mistaken, was Smith's-Bane, the blade of Thorolf Skjalg, which no one had seen since the night Erling laid the walker-again.

Lemming leaped the wall into the lane and stood full in the thing's path, sword in both hands and cocked over his shoulder.

The thing drew up sharply, looked forward at Lemming and back at the crowd of us coming at it. After a second it turned and came back our way. It was more afraid of Lemming than five hundred men, almost as if it had been—

"Soti!" someone shouted. "Soti's walker-again!"

"No!" I said. "Walking in the daylight? It can't be—"

And then the thing was among us, throwing men left and right, pushing through the crush of us, one free arm dealing thunder and broken bones left and right.

If we'd had our weapons we'd have been able to hurt it, but we were bare-handed all, and though we crowded round we were afraid to strike it even with our hands because of Astrid. At last it stood in a cleared space in our midst, roaring and baring its ragged teeth, one broad arm around the woman's throat, the threat in its single eye plain.

Then it spoke. "Erling Skjalgsson!" it cried hoarsely, and it was Soti's voice.

"Give me my bride," said Erling, pushing near. "Give me my bride and be gone from here."

"Give me my wife!" said Soti. His eye was large and yellow in his blackened face. "Give my wife back to me!"

"Your wife is dead, and justly so."

"Your bride will die, and justly so!" He flexed his arm, and Astrid cried out.

Then Lemming pushed his way through the press, and stood facing Soti with Smith's-Bane raised.

"I'll kill her!" cried Soti.

Lemming laughed.

"Spare her," said Erling, "and I'll give you anything you ask!"

"Revenge!" roared Soti.

"Take my life then," said Erling.

"Come!" said Soti, beckoning with his free hand.

"Let her go first."

"No!"

"How can I trust you?"

Soti rumbled a laugh.

"Very well," said Erling. "Lemming, put down the sword."

Lemming shook his head.

"Lemming, as you love Freydis, I ask it."

Lemming bared his teeth, but laid the sword on the ground.

Erling walked to Soti, and Soti put a big hand around Erling's neck. Soti smiled broadly, a terrible, lipless smile like a skull's, and as he did so Olaf Trygvesson, who had worked his way behind him, swung a huge fist at his temple.

The blow rang like a whip crack. It would have dropped another man, but Soti only reeled a moment, and in that moment Erling seized Astrid and swung her out of harm's way. A hundred hands reached to Soti, but he swept them aside with a roar and pushed his way through the crowd toward the hall. When he got there he swung himself up onto the roof slope, ignoring clutching hands, and began to climb the turf up to the peak.

Erling pushed through and grasped the eaves to follow, but a hand on his shoulder stopped him. He turned and saw Lemming, whose cave-eyes spoke for him. Erling stepped aside, and Lemming began to climb, the sword Smith's-Bane in his belt.

Soti was on the roof peak now, shouting, *"Thor!*

They say you are dead, but while I live you cannot die! Your hammer killed me not; their torment killed me not; their fire killed me not; I have borne the shock of all the world's weight against me, and still I live, and so I know that you live also! Curse my enemies for me! Let Erling Skjalgsson die as I do, alone, one against many, and let him die at the hands of Christians and kinsmen! Let Olaf Trygvesson die far from home, young, betrayed, his work unfinished, his life unlived, and leave him no son to wear his crown! And Ailill the priest—let him never find the one who is lost to him! Grant me this, great Thor!"

Then Lemming was up in reach of him, and Soti kicked at him, and Lemming caught his foot, and twisted it, and Soti nearly fell and had to jump backwards. Lemming gave a hop and landed on the peak. He drew Smith's-Bane and they stood facing each other high above us, dark as shadows against the bright sky.

Lemming took a step, and Soti stepped back.

"And you, my thrall, who works my forge now and dandles my daughter on your knee, what curse shall I lay on you? I curse you with years of wolf-living in the wilderness!"

Lemming stepped forward, and again Soti moved back.

"I curse you with the hatred and fear of your fellow men. You shall become a thing like me—a shadow in the night, a bogey to frighten the children. And when you come forth to stand with men again, you will die in hopeless battle, and you will be a traitor to your lord, standing in the shield wall of those who slew him. A fitting death for a thrall, who has no honor. They call you a free man, but I call you a thrall. Thrall born, thrall living, thrall in death. Not a man, even less than I am a man."

Lemming stepped forward again, and again Soti shrank from him. The crowd of us pushed back towards the rear of the hall, to watch their progress.

Soti looked down on us, and he spat. "I curse you all!" he cried. "And I curse all of Norway! This religion you have taken as a gift from the southern lands will be a sickness in you that saps your strength and withers you! You will see the priests grow fat while you grow thin, and as you work to feed them you'll have smaller and smaller strength to go forth and do deeds as your fathers did. And in the end you'll be little men, unaccounted in the world and feared by none!"

Lemming crowded him, and Soti backed up. He was getting near the gable end.

"I would not see the Norway you will build! The Norway you will build is not fit for a man with ribs and a backbone! Heroes will find no place to dwell there—they'll flit from bog to woodland, pursued by all, and hunted down in the end, and their blood will be lost, and all who remain will be thrall stock, with bowed backs and big feet, who'll kiss the backsides of the priests and say thank you when they're smacked in their ugly faces. You've chosen, Norway, and good luck to your choice, but spare me the sight of it!"

And with a shout of *"THOR!"* he ran along the roof ridge and sprang into space, spreading his arms like a hawk's wings.

And he flew.

I swear on my mother's bones—I was there and I saw it. Instead of arcing earthward, Soti arced skyward, and as long as his cry to his god lasted, he soared like an eagle, into the sun.

Then his voice died, and he dropped like a stone. We felt the jar of his landing in our footsoles.

He lay where he fell, black blood pooling about him, and we gathered around. Olaf Trygvesson stepped near to him and said, "Was this a living man, or a walker-again?"

No one could say for sure. "Bring me that sword!" Olaf cried.

Lemming was there suddenly, and he gave Smith's-Bane to Olaf.

With a blow, Olaf struck the head off Soti, and laid it at his thigh.

"Every man go and get a stone from the fields," said Olaf. "Heap them on him where he lies until he's covered by a cairn that won't be moved till Judgment Day."

And it was done.

As the men moved out to obey, a wailing was heard from the crowd. For one moment I thought Ulvig must have come back also. But when I turned I saw Bishop Sigurd, in his gorgeous vestments, mouth open and tears streaming down his cheeks.

Chapter XXXIII

The vows were spoken, and the mass said, and we went into the hall to feast, and when the night came on, not really a night in midsummer, we escorted the couple to the loft, tucked them into bed together, and went down to the hall again to drink and sing and tell dirty stories.

And I grew weary of it at last, for despite the joy of the day and a fair measure of ale and mead, the death of Soti had left a mark on my heart, like the black stain he'd once told me the lightning left on his skull. We were killing the old, wicked Norway—no question of that. But what of the new Norway? The king was a drunkard. The bishop, I was certain, was going mad.

So I wandered out and took the path down to the sea, and as I drew near I wondered to hear a roaring, as if from an angry bull. Approaching with care, I saw a man in a cloak picking up great, rounded stones from the beach and, with spins of his whole body, casting them far out into the waves. It was Erling Skjalgsson.

"My lord!" I said, startled. What was I to say? *I didn't expect to find you here?* An understatement.

Erling stopped and turned to me, a stone in his

arms. He panted, and his eyes were as deep and dark as Lemming's. "Just the man I need," he said.

"I'm at your service, my lord."

"I've a bit of a problem in my marriage." He whirled twice and the stone soared out to sea, landing with a great plunk and throwing up a blossom of saltwater. Erling remained standing in a crouch, watching the waves, which leaped at his feet like dogs.

"I've heard men say they're sometimes nervous on the first night—"

"Not that. I'm ready enough. I've never been more ready. But Astrid won't have me."

"Won't have you?"

"She says I may take her by force, but not otherwise. I can't do that."

"No, of course not."

"She says I'm a bonder in a bog, and not fit for a princess. She says refusing the jarldom was a slap in her face. She says if I want her I must either rape her or earn her love."

"Alas, I feared she'd be willful."

"You were right in that."

"Of course she's had a difficult day. Being carried off by a troll, so to speak, isn't what a girl looks for at her wedding."

"Yes, roast Soti. What think you of his curses?"

"It says in the Proverbs, 'As the bird by wandering, as the swallow by flying, so the curse causeless shall not come.' "

"He was a seer though. Perhaps he told me my death indeed."

"What of it? A young man in a narrow place,

fighting deadly odds, that's a saga death, you said. What other death would you ask?"

"It's a thing a man shouldn't know, especially on his wedding day."

"And you don't know it. Soti mixed lie and truth so that you can be sure of nothing. And we'll each of us die, one way or another. No Christian dies alone though. Remember your martyr priest."

Erling stood straighter and pulled his cloak tighter about him. "Thank you, Father. You're right. Someone walked on my grave, but I can endure it."

"What will you do about Astrid?"

"I'll make her love me, Father. If it takes me years, I'll make her love me. I am Erling Skjalgsson, and that's my word."

AFTERWORD:
A NOTE TO THE READER.

If you read historical novels with any historical sense, you know that most authors cheat a little. To get your sympathy, they put social and political opinions into their heroes' mouths which would have gotten them run out of town at best, and burned at the stake at worst, if they'd spoken them in the real worlds they lived in.

Erling Skjalgsson's "self-help" program for his thralls looks suspiciously like this sort of thing. "He wants us to like this slaveholder," you may think, "so he throws in a spot of social consciousness to soften the picture."

To anyone harboring this understandable suspicion, I offer the following extract from the *Heimskringla*, the saga of the kings of Norway, written by the Icelander Snorri Sturlusson (1178–1241):

> "Erling . . . set his thralls to daywork and gave them time afterwards, and allowed every man to work for himself at dusk or in the night. He gave them acres to sow corn thereon for themselves and produce crops for gain. He set a price and ransom on every one of them, and many freed

themselves the first year or the second; all who were thrifty enough had freed themselves in three years. With this money Erling bought himself other thralls. Some of his free men he turned to herring fishing and some to other trades. Some cleared woods and built themselves farms there, and to all of them he gave a good start in one way or another."

Some modern historians point to this passage as evidence that this was standard practice among Viking Age nobles. I'm not a professional historian, but I make so bold as to doubt that. I'm sure the legal opportunity was always there, but to encourage it strikes me as inconsistent with the Viking temperament. In any case, Snorri thought it unusual enough to make a special note of it.

Of course the fact that I didn't cheat on this point doesn't mean I avoided cheating in other places. . . .

A number of the characters in this book come from history, by way of Snorri. Erling and his father, and Olmod the Old and Askel and his son Aslak were real. Jarl Haakon, Kark and Olaf Trygvesson, of course, lived also, as did Bishop Sigurd and Olaf's sister Astrid. Olaf's kinsmen, the Erikssons of Opprostad, are also documented, except that Aki Eriksson seems to have escaped the record. Historians believe that Erik Bjodaskalle, their father, lived at Opprostad in Jaeder, but Snorri insists that his sons had their estates in the eastern part of Norway. I have ventured to resolve the inconsistency (rather neatly, I think).

There is an ancient stone cross in a museum in

Stavanger, Norway, with an inscription that says it
was raised in memory of Erling Skjalgsson by his
priest. We have the first two letters of the priest's
name: AL. From those two letters (and trusting to
the variability of spelling in the Dark Ages) I have
raised up the Irishman Ailill.

Regarding the dangerous issue of spelling: due
to the complicated nature of the Old Norse language,
there are about as many ways to spell Viking names
as there are authors. I have adopted an exacting
and rigorous policy of spelling each name however
I bloody well pleased. Linguists inform me that Olaf
should end with a "v," and Erik should be spelled
"Eirik." I've tried, but I just can't.

I've chosen to refer to the indigenous minority
people of northern Scandinavia as "Lapps" in this
book. I'm well aware that this name is offensive to
them, and that they prefer to be called "Sami." I
have not accommodated them for two reasons: a)
Most Americans have never heard of the word Sami,
so that I'd have had to add a footnote; and b) Erling
and his contemporaries would have called them
"Finns" which is equally offensive and confusing
to boot. My apologies to the Sami, who are fine
people and possibly among my ancestors.

Special thanks are due to Jim Baen for his construc-
tive and insightful suggestions on the manuscript.
Thanks to Richard Lane for reading it, and for his
comments. Also to my father Jordan Walker and my
relatives Oddvar and Hjørdis Rygg; Dagfinnn Kallevik,
Unni and Louisa; Thorleif and Gerd Andreassen;
Andreas and Gjertrud Andreassen; Einar Andreassen;
Kjell and Torbjørg Andreassen; Olaf and Ingeborg

Rygg, Ragnhild Rygg and Kjell-Egil Hovlund, who (among others too numerous to mention) were longsuffering with, and helpful to, me as I pursued a man a thousand years dead across the landscape of Norway.

—Lars Walker
Malabar, Florida

Paksenarrion, a simple sheepfarmer's daughter, yearns for a life of adventure and glory, such as the heroes in songs and story. At age seventeen she runs away from home to join a mercenary company, and begins her epic life . . .

ELIZABETH MOON

THE DEED OF PAKSENARRION

"This is the first work of high heroic fantasy I've seen, that has taken the work of Tolkien, assimilated it totally and deeply and absolutely, and produced something altogether new and yet incontestably based on the master. . . . This is the real thing. Worldbuilding in the grand tradition, background thought out to the last detail, by someone who knows absolutely whereof she speaks. . . . Her military knowledge is impressive, her picture of life in a mercenary company most convincing."—**Judith Tarr**

About the author: Elizabeth Moon joined the U.S. Marine Corps in 1968 and completed both Officers Candidate School and Basic School, reaching the rank of 1st Lieutenant during active duty. Her background in military training and discipline imbue The Deed of Paksenarrion *with a gritty realism that is all too rare in most current fantasy.*

"I thoroughly enjoyed *Deed of Paksenarrion*. A most engrossing highly readable work."
—**Anne McCaffrey**

"For once the promises are borne out. *Sheepfarmer's Daughter* is an advance in realism. . . . I can only say that I eagerly await whatever Elizabeth Moon chooses to write next."
—Taras Wolansky, *Lan's Lantern*

*　　　　*　　　　*　　　　*　　　　*

Volume One: Sheepfarmer's Daughter—Paks is trained as a mercenary, blooded, and introduced to the life of a soldier . . . and to the followers of Gird, the soldier's god.

Volume Two: Divided Allegiance—Paks leaves the Duke's company to follow the path of Gird alone—and on her lonely quests encounters the other sentient races of her world.

Volume Three: Oath of Gold—Paks the warrior must learn to live with Paks the human. She undertakes a holy quest for a lost elven prince that brings the gods' wrath down on her and tests her very limits.

*　　　　*　　　　*　　　　*

These books are available at your local bookstore, or you can fill out the coupon and return it to Baen Books, at the address below.

To Read About Great Characters Having Incredible Adventures You Should Try ☞ ☞ ☞

BAEN